A Dangerous Debut

Ladies of Mayfair

~ Book Five ~

WENDY MAY ANDREWS

ঔ৩

Sparrow Ink

www.sparrowdeck.com

ISBN - 978-1-7750069-2-3

Cover Design by German Creative

www.wendymayandrews.com

Dedication

For my entire family, even the ones who don't read my books.

Mum and Dad, you are the best cheering section any girl could ask for.

Andrew, the love of my life, you are the best!

And for all my readers.

Thank you for your continued support and encouragement.

Acknowledgements

Thank you to my Beta readers:

Marlene, Suzanne, Monique, and Alfred.

Your input was invaluable.

My editor, Julie Sherwood was an expert,

all remaining errors are my own fault.

And thanks for my gorgeous cover go to German Creative.

Chapter One

"What am I going to do now?" Daisy kept her wail silent as she struggled not to panic.

The door was locked, and there was no sign of movement inside. The early morning sounds of carriages, carts, and people going about their business behind her on the busy street could not penetrate the dark sense of dread she was struggling to control. Daisy was staring morosely at the locked shop door when a voice behind her shoulder nearly made her jump out of her skin. She was surprised she hadn't noticed his approach reflected in the gleaming glass of Miss Holstein's shop window, since she had been staring at it so intensely.

"Is aught amiss, ma'am?" the cultured voice slurred, stirring Daisy's amusement, despite the terrifying dilemma she faced.

When she turned to answer, her usually glib tongue stuck to the roof of her mouth. The wellborn man's handsome face stole her breath. His golden brown hair was dishevelled, as though he had been running his hands through the waves repeatedly throughout the long night. His light gray eyes were fringed with long dark lashes. If he were not so ruggedly handsome, they would have looked feminine. But his strong physique declared him an outdoorsman of some note, and no one would ever confuse him with a woman. She realized her confused blinking probably made her look like a simpleton, but she could barely marshal her thoughts into order, they were so scattered.

Seeing the concern forming in his eyes despite the air of ennui about him that declared he rarely cared about anything, Daisy pulled herself together enough to remember his question.

"Thank you, my lord, I shall be perfectly fine." Daisy realized her tone sounded repressive and prim, but she couldn't help herself.

"You do not seem perfectly fine." The handsome gentleman's observation sounded vague. The emphasis on "seem" implying that even though he was bosky, it was apparent even to him that all was not right with Daisy.

Daisy was now beginning to find his presence irritating and could easily see past his remarkable good looks. With her tongue no longer stuck to the roof of her mouth, she was able to make use of it. "I truly am not in need of any help from *you*, my lord," she began, not bothering to mask her disdain. "You may carry on with your own business without concerning yourself about mine."

Daisy's sunny disposition usually prevented her from being snide, but she felt her nose wrinkling as she observed the young man before her. His clothes declared he was a member of the Corinthian set, verging toward being a dandy. It was obvious he was a wealthy nobleman, perhaps even an aristocrat. That thought made her lip curl just a little with feelings of scorn. The air of authority with which he held himself, despite the fact he had drunk too much the night before, declared his position loudly without his uttering a word.

Her resentment began to rise despite her knowledge that it was irrational. She really ought not to be so judgemental. Under normal circumstances, she tried to be an open minded individual, but truly, *aristocratic "gentlemen" are all the same*, she thought with an audible sniff, just as her father had always told her.

ꕥ

Jasper James Seaton, fifth Viscount of Hawthorn, heir to the Marquis of Abernathy, pulled his muddled thoughts together. *Who does this ridiculous young woman think she is?* he asked himself rather absently as he wondered why he was allowing it to bother him.

He wasn't sure what had so captured his attention about the waif-like young woman. While her attire bespoke her straightened circumstances, she had an air about her that drew him. She held herself with a sense of self-possession. The young ladies he was accustomed to would be throwing themselves at his feet were he to show them any attention, while this young woman was making every attempt to dismiss him. Perhaps that was what intrigued him the most.

Jasper cursed the last couple of glasses of his friend's excellent port as he tried to keep his attention focused. He could normally drink like a fish, but he was feeling the effects this morning. He squinted at the girl before him. She was pretty enough, with her wide, perfectly spaced blue eyes and the burnished gold curls peeking out of her bonnet, but he was used to the attentions of the very diamonds of Society, so he rather doubted that it was her looks that had snagged his attention. He gave up trying to figure it out and just put it down to intuition.

All he wanted to do was help the girl, but if she didn't want his help he really ought not to force it upon her. Despite that resolve, he could not resist trying one last time.

"Now see here, miss, as a gentleman I really cannot leave you on your own in obvious distress."

ꕥ

Daisy could hear from his voice that the handsome lord was sobering up. There was nothing he could possibly do to help her, but she was not above the temptation to lay her troubles on someone else's shoulders for a moment. She struggled against the temptation. There was no one to help her but herself. Certainly there was nothing this drink-addled young nobleman could do. She smiled her appreciation at the gentleman but was about to deny him once more.

Her intentions must have been clearly written upon her face because his lordship interrupted her before she had a chance to speak.

"Pardon my manners, miss, I can clearly see that you were staring quite intently at the sign on the door of Miss Holstein's Employment Services. Since it would appear that Miss Holstein is not available to offer her services today, perhaps I might be able to help you, or rather, we might be able to come to some sort of agreement that could be of assistance to each other."

Daisy's sharp gaze came to rest searchingly upon the gentleman's face. Her indignant suspicions must have been etched upon her features for the nobleman quickly added, "Perhaps you would accompany me around the corner to Gunter's, and we could discuss our options over one of his ices."

It was impossible to imagine anyone making inappropriate advances in such an environment, at least in Daisy's limited experience, so she relaxed ever so slightly upon hearing these words. She suspected that had been his intention. It must have been obvious that her determination was wavering, as he persisted in his wheedling.

"If you do not wish to help me with my dilemma, after you have eaten your ice you can always return here and wait for Miss Holstein. It is unlikely that accompanying me for a few minutes will set you back any in your efforts."

Daisy could not deny the truth of his words. The employment office looked well and truly closed for the day. *And one of Gunter's famous ices would be so comforting right now,* she could not help thinking. Before she realized their intention, her traitorous lips had formed into a smile of acceptance. She tried to frown her face into compliance, but the gentleman had already assumed her acquiescence and was offering his elbow. Daisy managed one more objection before she would accompany him.

"But, my lord, I do not even know you," she protested even as she took his offered arm. Seeing the look upon his face, Daisy giggled and offered an apology. "I am so sorry, my lord. Have I just offered you an unspeakable insult by not knowing who you are?"

Daisy wondered if it was the first time in his adult life that a young woman had not known who he was. It did not look as though he would ever admit as much. He simply ignored her question. "I pray you will forgive my poor manners, miss, I am Lord Jasper Seaton, Viscount of Hawthorn, at your service." He executed a remarkably steady bow and elegant leg before raising an inquisitive eyebrow at her. "And who might you be?"

Feeling a flush rising in her cheeks, suddenly feeling shy, Daisy struggled to maintain as much composure over her features as possible. "I am Miss Margaret Pembroke, but everyone calls me Daisy."

"Ah, there must be someone French in your family if that is the case, Miss Daisy," the viscount surmised.

"How could you possibly know that? No one ever guesses."

"Marguerite, eye of the day, the sunniest flower to bless the earth," he declared with all the aplomb of a professor before adding with a grin, "My mother's gardener is an eloquent man."

A genuine smile stretched across Daisy's face for the first time since she had been accosted by the viscount. She could not, however, identify the strange look that crossed the gentleman's face. Her breath caught in her throat; she thought it could be admiration, but she dismissed the wayward idea as foolish nonsense.

Smiling shyly, Daisy was surprised at how quickly her opinion of the viscount had changed, despite all that her father had always said of the aristocracy. His lordship had seemed like an intoxicated idiot moments earlier. Now she was feeling a trifle more relaxed in his company. And she really would enjoy the refreshment of an ice before she figured out her personal dilemma.

While it was kind of the nobleman to offer her assistance, she really could not see how it would be possible. *Unless he has young children in need of a governess.* She turned to examine him speculatively. He seemed a little young. She had a hard time imagining him as a proud papa, but it was a possibility, she reasoned, otherwise why would he have been outside the employment office? But then she remembered the obvious evidence of his drinking. Despite her unfavorable experience with noblemen, she strongly doubted they would go looking to hire household staff after having been carousing. But her unfortunate experience did tell her that it was impossible to predict what a nobleman would do. She resolved to hear what the man had to say and reserve judgment for later. Loving to look on the bright side, she reasoned that she would at least get an ice out of the conversation.

"What are you thinking, Miss Daisy? You have the most interesting face, but I cannot fathom what is going through your head."

Daisy allowed a good natured giggle to spill from her mouth. "I was thinking, my lord, that I have never had a chance to visit Gunter's on the arm of a viscount, and I am anticipating that it will be a singular experience."

Jasper grinned along with her. "Have you ever been to Gunter's before?"

"When I was a little girl," Daisy answered without looking at him, continuing to gaze about as though she had never seen the neighborhood they were passing through.

"Do you live in London, Miss Daisy?" Jasper tried again to draw her into conversation.

"Not exactly, my lord," she replied.

"What is that supposed to mean?" he asked, allowing his frustration to come through in his tone.

Daisy looked at the nobleman beside her with surprise. "Pardon me, my lord, I was not attending. I was distracted by looking at all the charming houses. I have not been in this part of London for many years and am quite enjoying the view. But you are quite correct; it is intolerably rude of me to not attend you, as you have been kind enough to invite me for a treat. My mother would have apoplexy if she were to witness such behavior. What were you asking me?"

Jasper frowned as he took in her grin, wondering what was going on in her pretty head. It appeared as though her feelings changed with every gust of wind. Just a few moments earlier he clearly read suspicion written all over her face, but now she was gazing about, seemingly without a care in the world. He was still feeling the effects of too much whiskey and port, had in fact been on his way home when he walked by her, so he had allowed his thoughts to come out of his mouth.

Jasper gazed in wonder at the woman by his side. He tried not to be an overbearing buffoon, but it had never happened to him that a young lady did not hang upon his every word, at least not since he had been let out of the schoolroom. He couldn't help the grin that split his face over the novel experience.

"No need to apologize, my dear. I was merely trying to make conversation. I had asked you where you live," he reminded her.

He watched in fascination as her cheeks suffused with colour. Why would she be blushing over his efforts at conversation? It should be an innocuous question, but it was one that caused her consternation. "I am staying with a friend in Bloomsbury, my lord.

I am currently without a permanent address," she answered him with as much dignity as she could muster, but then her natural optimism buoyed her and she smiled. "It is a charming little house, and I am delighted to be staying with her, although I really do need to make arrangements for myself as quickly as possible."

"You are fortunate to have such a friend." Jasper could not help replying stiffly, wondering if any of his friends would house him if he ever was truly down on his luck.

"I am, my lord. I do realize that. But of course, I am hoping to not overstay my welcome, which was why you found me standing in front of Miss Holstein's establishment. That fine woman has already arranged a situation for me, but unfortunately, that did not work out so well, so I was hoping some other arrangements could be made."

"What kind of work are you looking for?" the viscount asked, puzzled.

"My first position was one of governess. It would be ideal if I could find another. I could also be a lady's companion. If neither of those positions are available, I have the necessary skills to be a housekeeper." A note of pride in her tone belied the worry that was also there.

The viscount cleared his throat in discomfort. "Pardon me for asking such an indelicate question, miss, but why are you searching for a position? It is clear to me that you are gently born. Why are you not getting married and arranging a more secure position for yourself?"

Daisy grinned at the viscount's choice of words. "That is not as easily done as said, my lord. One cannot snap one's fingers and have a groom appear before her eyes." She then looked at Jasper with widened, twinkling eyes. "Or do you have that ability, my lord? It would be wondrous if you did."

Jasper returned her grin. "Alas, not so easily, but it probably isn't all that hard, is it?"

Daisy did not wish to dwell upon how impossible what he suggested really was so she merely shrugged and smiled. "Never mind, my lord, you need not trouble yourself with my problems."

By this time they had reached Berkley Square, and the viscount ushered her into Gunter's. Daisy struggled to contain her glee over the proffered treat as she sniffed the sweet air appreciatively. Looking around at the well-dressed patrons, she was glad she had worn her best dress for the expected interview with Miss Holstein. Her eyes darted about the room, barely taking in the details, overwhelming her with the air of decadence that permeated the room. It was nothing less than sumptuous from the chandeliers hanging above, down to the fancy shoes worn by the ladies seated on the velvet-covered chairs. Part of her wanted to run from the shop and never look back, but she was so close to tasting a cream ice once more that she could not bring her feet to turn away.

As she gazed about, it seemed to Daisy that everyone in the room was nobly born. She tried to dismiss from her mind the thought that she was not supposed to be there. She lifted her chin, refusing to be cowed by anyone looking down their noses at her. She reminded herself that the viscount had invited her, and he wasn't put out by her apparent less than noble heritage. Stiffening her spine, she called to mind her parents' often-stated opinion that aristocracy is nothing but an accident of birth and certainly did not make these people any better than her. In fact, as her father would often mutter when her mother was out of earshot, it often made them far worse than average folks.

"What do you think you would like to have, Miss Daisy?" the viscount asked solicitously.

Shaking her head to rid it of her uncomfortable thoughts and stiffening her spine further, Daisy dithered another moment before making her selection. They were soon seated in the high-backed, comfortable seats and she was daintily picking at the treat. Grinning once more at the viscount, she expressed her appreciation. "Thank you ever so much, my lord. I had no idea I was wishing for just such a treat."

"It is my pleasure, my dear. It does a heart good to see someone as easily pleased as you seem to be. I find it difficult to fathom how utterly sunny your disposition appears to be."

ꕥ

Daisy grinned again, and Jasper's eyes darkened as they lingered on her sweetly upturned lips. He had never before met a person like her and was unsure how to proceed. He watched with appreciation as she enjoyed her ice before he broached his unorthodox proposal.

Licking the last of the treat from her spoon, Daisy sighed her enjoyment. "That was delicious, my lord. Thank you ever so much. Now, if you would be so kind as to get on with whatever discussion you were hoping to have, I would appreciate it, as I have my own affairs to figure out."

Jasper blinked at her straightforward prompting. The chit was unique, he would give her that. He felt a niggle of doubt over his outrageous idea. He was quite certain she would make waves in his circles. But, a grin broke over his face as he was again convinced it was a brilliant idea.

"I would like you to accompany me to a party at my parents' estate," he stated, his voice calm and sure. He enjoyed watching Daisy's eyes widen as her lips parted on her gasp of shock.

She glanced around hoping no one was overhearing their conversation. She leaned forward, keeping her voice low. "I was so sure you were no longer inebriated, my lord, but surely you must still be foxed if you are making such a daft suggestion. There are so many things that make your suggestion impossible, not the least of which is that your mother is unacquainted with me and would no doubt not be delighted to receive a stranger at her party. An untitled stranger at that," she concluded, as if it were an afterthought, but he heard the bitterness in her voice. He wondered about the strange tone but forged ahead anyway.

"Well, that is where you are wrong, my dear. If I were to tell my mother that I was bringing a female guest with me, I can assure you she would be beside herself with delight."

Daisy eyed the viscount with suspicion. After a moment of hesitation she asked, "Why is that the case, my lord? I find it highly doubtful."

"I am the firstborn son. My parents, well, my mother anyway, would like nothing better than for me to settle down, get married, and produce the next Abernathy heir. If I told them I had a particular friend I wanted invited to their party, you would receive an invitation delivered to your door before the ink had even dried on it."

"Even if your parents are desperate, surely they cannot be so despairing of you that I would be considered acceptable, my lord. You do recall that you met me outside an employment office, do you not?"

"That is what makes it so deliciously perfect," the viscount grinned, which made Daisy all the more determined not to give in to the temptation she was feeling as the butterflies in her midsection took flight.

"And you cannot be seriously trying to convince me that you are hard up for options. You are handsome and a viscount and not near your dotage. Surely you have your choice of debutantes who would be delighted to accompany you to a party at your family's estate."

"Well, of course, but they would all be expecting an actual proposal," Jasper explained, weary patience dripping from his tones.

It began to dawn on Daisy as to what he was proposing. "So you want me to accompany you on the pretense of a courtship that shall never culminate in an actual proposal, is that what you mean, my lord?"

Jasper could tell from her tone that Daisy was not completely pleased with his idea but he plowed on, ignoring the warning bell clanging in his head. "It is absolutely perfect, Miss Daisy. You will have somewhere to go for a week, and maybe you can even make contacts with people who are looking to hire someone."

"My lord, surely you must realize it cannot work both ways. Either I am a servant looking for employment, who would not be welcome in your mother's sitting room, or I am a fellow guest. We cannot combine our two situations."

The viscount grinned over Daisy's precise words and voice. She sounded as though she was wondering if he was always daft or if he was still suffering the effects of excessive drink. It was obvious to him that she was losing patience with him, as though she were his governess. His grin widened over the image that called to his mind. His governesses had always been aged, pinch-faced women, nothing like the lovely creature that sat in front of him. He foresaw a challenge before her for finding employment. From what he knew of society matrons, none of them would welcome her into their home.

Deciding to make conversation to find out a little more about his new friend, in order to figure out how to convince her, he asked a few more questions. "How well do you know Miss Holstein? And what went wrong with your previous post? And what kind of a name is Miss Holstein, anyway? It cannot be real. It puts me in mind of a good bovine."

Daisy giggled over Jasper's words, but put her hand up to stem the flow of his questions. "Wait, wait, my lord," she gasped through her laughter. "I can only answer one question at a time." She paused for a moment to allow her giggles to abate.

"Miss Holstein is a lovely, kind soul who works hard to find appropriate positions for her clients. Surely her name must be real because no one would make up such a dreadful name. I cannot say that I know her well, it is more that she is a friend of the friend I am currently staying with."

"Ah, so the good woman has a vested interest in finding you somewhere so that you will no longer be taking up space in Bloombsbury?" Jasper inquired.

"Do not be beastly, my lord," Daisy admonished. "Charlotte is my dearest friend in the entire world. She has offered that I could live with her indefinitely. It is my own sense of independence which is insisting I need to make my own arrangements. Neither she nor Miss Holstein could have known that things were going to turn out the way they did with my previous position. And I would prefer not to tell you what went wrong with my first post."

"Well, if you do not think you could try to arrange another employment while at my mother's house party, perhaps we could look about for a suitable husband for you while we are there," Jasper stated with a reasonable tone, unsure why that seemed so distasteful to him all of a sudden.

Jasper felt twitchy under Daisy's assessing gaze, but he managed not to fidget. He saw her trying to figure out what he was thinking and implying. He waited to see what she would say next. He didn't have to wait long. To his surprise the young woman burst into laughter, which she kept as quiet as possible so as to not draw undue attention to their conversation.

"Oh, my lord, you are a complete hand. That was a delightfully ridiculous suggestion. If I were to arrive on the arm of a viscount, and the son of the hostess at that, do you really believe any of the other gentlemen would even consider trying to fix my interest?"

Blinking at the logic of her question, Jasper refused to back down. "I understand what you are saying, Miss Daisy, but you are a very taking young woman, and I am quite certain the gentlemen will feel moved to pay you their addresses, whether I am present or not."

She shot him a shrewd glance. "Would you ever consider doing such a thing to a friend of yours?"

He only shrugged. She grinned.

"You are a rake, aren't you, my lord? I ought to be scandalized to be in your presence. But I find you much too amusing to dredge up any sort of reprimand."

Daisy was still grinning, unable to put away her amusement so quickly, but she still offered a dismissive shrug. "It really matters very little if there are to be eligible gentlemen present, my lord. I cannot accompany you to your house party. It really is important that I get on with making my own arrangements for my future."

Jasper gazed at his companion, nonplussed. "I cannot understand why you are being so stubborn about this. I promise you, if you do this for me, I will make sure you are taken care of when it is over."

Daisy stiffened her already perfectly straight posture and gazed at the viscount with dignity as her cheeks warmed with embarrassment. "You really are a rake, aren't you? I do not wish to be taken care of by any gentleman, my lord. I am a proper sort of female and have not yet sunk to such a level, nor will I ever."

Jasper grinned at her discomfort. "Is that your confounded independence talking or have you perhaps misunderstood what I meant?"

"I guess that would depend on what you meant," Daisy's reply was guarded.

Jasper realized that she distrusted him. He wondered absently if he ought to take it personally or if she just distrusted all men. Or perhaps it was aristocratic men she had an issue with. He tried to placate her as he replied.

"I merely meant that I will ensure you are protected and have a suitable position when our charade is complete."

Jasper was quite certain the chit didn't believe him and struggled to keep the amusement from his face as she gazed at him with skepticism shining from the eyes she now had slightly squinted at him. He waited to see what she would say. It was clear from her expressive face that she was trying to decide how best to handle him.

"It has been a pleasure to meet you, my lord, but I really must be going."

The viscount was surprised at the level of disappointment he felt over her obvious dismissal. His hand shot out to grab her arm, almost of its own volition.

"Please do not leave yet, Miss Daisy. I implore you. What will it take to convince you to accompany me? I can assure you that no harm will come to you." Jasper cringed inwardly at the sound of his begging, but he really was near to desperation.

Feeling Daisy's scrutiny sharpen further, Jasper kept his features as impassive as possible.

"It would appear my perspective needs broadening, my lord," Daisy commented, her nonchalant tone belying her shrewd focus upon his face. "What could you possibly have to gain from having me accompany you to visit your family's estate? Why do you want your parents to think you are pursuing a courtship?"

Jasper cursed his drink-addled brain as he worked to come up with something believable that did not include telling her the truth. Although he liked people to think he was an open book, the thought of actually allowing someone into his personal space was almost enough to give him hives. He needed to think fast because the girl was coming to all sorts of conclusions on her own.

"Why would a viscount need to bring a sham eligible *parti* to his parents' house party? Why not just court some young lady for real? What would he hope to gain?" Daisy studied Jasper with widening eyes. "You are under the hatches, and your parents are plump in the pocket. Is that it, my lord? You do not wish to actually become leg shackled, which is why you do not wish to invite someone of your acquaintance to accompany you. But you are hoping that if your parents think you have finally stopped sowing your wild oats, they might be more willing to frank you than if you turn up on your own and make your request."

Feeling the heat rising in his cheeks, Jasper willed the hot colour to recede. He refused to blush like a schoolgirl. "You think you have it all figured out, don't you, Miss Pembroke?" he tried but failed to keep the bitter sarcasm from his voice. "You don't know anything about my family, or me, so I pray you stay out of my head."

"I will gladly stay out of your head, my lord. I have no interest in entering this charade with you. You need not fly up in the boughs. I will bid you a good day."

Once again Jasper grasped her arm and held her in her place as gently as he could. "I apologize, Miss Daisy. I am acting the cad. You do have every right to depart, but I beg that you do not do so. You are quite correct. I have run into difficulty with my finances, but my parents have been tight fisted up until now. As you say, I have been sowing my oats. But I am making an attempt to turn things around. Unfortunately, my father does not believe I can change my ways. I wish to turn them up sweet by bringing a suitable young lady to meet them, one who will not actually have expectations.

Chapter Two

Jasper stared at Daisy, wondering how else to respond. *How could the chit have been so accurate in her assessment?* he asked himself blankly as he struggled once more to control his fidgets as Daisy's perceptive gaze raked over him.

The viscount had never met anybody like her. Her independence baffled him. Why would she not take him up on his offer? He couldn't imagine any other woman of his acquaintance refusing such an opportunity. Did the chit not realize how important he was and what he could do for her? He tried not to be overly high in the instep, but he was the Viscount of Hawthorn after all.

Daisy gazed at Jasper, seeing more than he would like. She knew it was important to him that she accompany him, but she didn't know how she possibly could. There was no way his mother would consider a governess to be a good potential wife for her son.

"I will pay you," Jasper said in desperation.

Daisy's jaw dropped open in shock.

"I beg your pardon," she demanded, her tone indignant, while her mind began to churn with curiosity.

Jasper knew he had caught her attention so he pressed home his advantage. "Really, we could be of benefit to one another," he pleaded. "I know you need money, and if my plan works, I will have plenty. Don't you see?" he asked with a curious tilt of his head.

Daisy blinked rapidly, nonplussed by his argument. "But, my lord, I abhor lying. How can you ask me to participate in this dishonest bargain?"

Jasper's head remained tilted, and he studied her with caution. "You could regard it as a paid job, just like an actress. But the stage would be my parents' estate rather than a theater. Actresses are not lying — they are merely pretending." He saw her indignation rising, and he hastened to add, "I can assure you, I am not calling your morality into question. I am merely offering you a post. Did you not assure me that you need a paid position?"

"Do you truly think it might work, my lord?" It was Daisy's turn to study her companion with dubious question. "I am not convinced I could play the part."

Now Jasper warmed to his subject without hesitation. "No one would know any different, Miss Daisy, I can assure you."

Daisy blushed over the audacity of considering his proposition. "I will have to think about it, my lord."

Jasper grinned, sensing his victory was near.

"Do not look so smug, my lord, I have not yet accepted your ridiculous offer."

The viscount wiped the grin off his face with effort. Daisy couldn't help the rise of her own amusement. Lord Jasper Seaton was such a gamester. It was obvious to Daisy that the viscount had never grown accustomed to being denied. She wished fervently she was not so tempted to accept his offer. It would be a good experience for him to learn to hear the word *no.*

With a small sigh, she realized that lesson would not be coming from her. The viscount was right, there was potential for her to find an alternate solution to her problems. And she was willing to admit, at least to herself, that she didn't mind putting off returning to the servants' quarters for a fortnight. She was about to concede to his request, but then her mind began scanning through all the complications.

Jasper heard another soft sigh escape her lips as she parted them to speak. Thinking she was going to once more deny his request, he began to protest. Her raised hand stemmed the flow of his words. He realized he might not be able to get his way in this matter. Resigned, he waited to hear what she had to say.

"My lord, I will admit to you that I would actually like to accept your offer or invitation or whatever you might like to call it. But there are too many problems to overcome, especially with both of our pockets to let. The gown I am currently wearing is the best I own. It will not do for a week at a country estate. And I certainly do not have the time to make enough clothes to be able to pull this off in a couple of days, besides needing to buy the cloth and such. There is also the matter of my maid. I could not possibly turn up without a lady's maid to lend me countenance."

Daisy's earnest expression changed to one of amusement as she observed the viscount's impassive face. "My lord, that is a remarkable skill." Her smile widened as his face broke into a grin.

Jasper cleared his throat before he replied. He was beginning to enjoy the young woman's company and was eager to get on with his plans.

"Miss Daisy, have no fear. We shall find solutions to all these dilemmas. The matter of gowns is easy enough to solve. My sister left behind entire rooms full of gowns you could help yourself to, and I am quite certain you could open an account at any dress maker. We need not worry about the bill until after I have secured my funds."

A flush climbed up her neck, but she was unable to stop the hot colour from flooding her cheeks. "My lord, I cannot take your sister's clothes," she began, her embarrassment preventing her from objecting even more forcefully to the thought of the viscount buying her gowns.

"Actresses require a wardrobe, Miss Daisy, would you not agree?" Jasper brushed the matter aside, moving on to the other issue she had raised. "Do you not know anyone who could possibly play the role of your maid? I had thought to say you could get away without one and just use a maid of my mother's, but if we are to travel there together, you will, of course, require a maid."

Daisy brightened at his words, happy to see he had at least a semblance of a sense of propriety. "Thank you, my lord, I do believe I know of someone who might do the trick quite nicely."

"How quickly do you think you would be able to get everything ready?" the viscount asked, his intelligent gaze making Daisy inexplicably uncomfortable.

"How soon do you wish to depart?" Daisy countered with a question of her own, holding back her hysteria with decided effort.

Jasper reached out and took his companion's cold, trembling hand into his own. He tried not to be moved by how tiny hers was when compared with his own. He had never considered himself to be a large man, but the young woman before him was little more than a waif. He found that so surprising. The force of her personality gave one the impression of a larger individual. Shaking his head to rid it of distraction, he hoped his smile was reassuring.

"Are you nervous?" he asked as he chafed her hand in an effort to warm her. "You are not going to back out on me, are you?" he asked, feeling like a cad for forcing his scheme upon her and uncomfortable with the first pang of conscience he had felt in ages.

The viscount grinned as his companion stiffened her spine. "No, I am not going to back out on you." She nearly spat the words. "Pembrokes do not go back on their word. Although, if I recall, I have not yet actually given you my word, have I? Very well, my lord, I will accompany you. Of course, I am nervous. I would have to be a complete imbecile not to be. I have much more to lose than you do if this scheme does not work out."

Jasper was about to object to her words, but seeing her haughty look, he paused and allowed her to continue. "I will acknowledge that you are hoping to benefit greatly from this scheme, but it is ridiculous to consider that there will be terribly unpleasant consequences for you if it fails. Even if we are found out, it will not be you who is deported."

Jasper's concerns turned to amusement as he guffawed over her words. He quickly hushed as he saw the eyes turned towards them with speculation.

"My lord, do control yourself, we do not need any attention brought upon us." Daisy was trying not to let her discomfort show as she did her best to ignore the interested eyes regarding them.

"I am sorry to argue with you, my dear lady, but a bit of attention will lend credence to our story. If my parents hear that a young lady has fixed my interest from someone other than me, it will be all the better, would you not think?" Jasper's enthusiasm was quick to fire. "It is absolutely ideal, in fact. I will call round for you tomorrow and take you shopping. It is perfectly acceptable for a gentleman to escort a lady friend upon her errands."

"But I am not perfectly sure if I will have my maid arranged by tomorrow, my lord. If I do not, that would be stretching the proprieties somewhat, would it not?"

Jasper considered her words, not wanting to give up on his plan. He snapped his fingers as he determined a compromise. "I will take you riding in the Park at the fashionable hour. Then I can drop you off on Bond Street after our ride. That will give us an opportunity to discuss the rest of our plans. In fact, I see nothing wrong with my accompanying you into some of the shops. I am fairly certain gentlemen do it all the time."

Daisy felt as though her life were spinning out of control. She had been wishing for some excitement, but this seemed like it was going to be a whole lot more than she had bargained for. But her word given was sacred to her, and she would not now go back on it, no matter how lily livered she was feeling.

"Very well, my lord. That will give me this evening to see whether or not I can arrange for the maid we had discussed."

"Excellent. Now allow me to see you home." Jasper stood and bowed over Daisy's hand, making her cheeks warm once more.

Daisy took herself to task for the shiver of awareness that slithered down her spine at his show of gallantry. The viscount's behavior was all for show, she reminded herself, realizing that was going to be something she would have to remind herself over and over in the coming days. Plastering what she hoped looked like a genuine smile upon her face, Daisy allowed his lordship to assist her from her seat and place her hand through his elbow.

"I would really rather you not escort me home." She managed to keep her face looking pleasant, but her tone must have revealed that she wished not to hear any argument on the subject.

"And why ever not, my dear?" Jasper heard the amusement in his voice and regretted it as his companion all but radiated her discomfort.

"Bloomsbury is hardly the place for you to be seen, my lord," Daisy explained, her voice revealing her embarrassment.

Jasper wished he could put her at ease. "It is hardly beyond the pale, Miss Pembroke."

"Have you ever been there before, my lord?"

Jasper should have seen that trap coming. With effort, he managed to keep a snarl off his face as they made their way out of the sweet shop and into the fresh air. "That is neither here nor there, my dear girl. I am going to escort you home."

"If you are seen escorting me home to Bloomsbury, my lord," Daisy began, her patient tone setting the viscount's teeth on edge, "we will hardly be able to convince anyone that I am an eligible *parti*, would you not agree?"

Stubbornly, Jasper refused to accept her logic. "While you are a part of this scheme, as you have called it, you are under my protection. You are my responsibility now, Miss Pembroke, and I cannot, as a gentleman, allow you to be wandering around the city on your own without protection of any sort. You are not even in the company of a maid," he pointed out reasonably. Seeing that she was about to protest further, he stalled her with a point of logic she could not refute. "If it is as déclassé as you say, surely you must realize that no one of significance will see me there, so your protesting is for naught."

Jasper's lips twitched as he struggled to hold back his laughter while he watched Daisy's lips part in protest but no words followed. Looking disgruntled, Daisy had to acquiesce. "Very well, my lord. I ought to be gracious and thank you, but I find that I cannot."

Now Jasper gave up the struggle as he threw back his head and guffawed. He knew he was going to have an entertaining time with the girl. For the first time in ages he was looking forward to the future, and even his dread of returning to his ancestral home had diminished somewhat. He had a feeling that anything would be easier with Daisy by his side.

Daisy wasn't as convinced as the viscount seemed to be that all would be well. Her usually sunny disposition was a trifle dimmed as she pondered all the difficulties needing to be overcome in such a short time.

Jasper must have noticed her preoccupation as he began questioning her. "What has you so blue devilled, my dear girl?" he asked, leaning toward her with a grin belying the concern showing in his eyes.

Daisy tried to shrug away his question. "I am hardly blue devilled, my lord. I am merely summarizing the lists of things I need to accomplish."

Jasper blinked as he gazed at his companion. "Are you one of those highly organized females that like to manage everyone and everything around them?"

Daisy's grin returned with full force. "Mayhap, my lord," was all that she would allow, but the viscount was satisfied that her worrying seemed to have been brought under control, at least for the moment.

"If you have a maid in tow by morning, you could come to the house and look through my sister's old gowns to see if you thought any of them would serve our purposes."

Daisy protested. "But, my lord, I do not feel comfortable taking your sister's clothes without her leave. Will she not be at your mother's party? Do you not think she might notice that I am wearing her gowns? For that matter, your mother is likely to notice."

"I hardly think they will be taking that much notice of your clothes, my dear. They will have other things to occupy their minds. Besides, my sister barely wore each gown more than once. I doubt she would recognize any of them, even if we were to tell her they had been hers. And now that she is a married lady, she has disavowed any interest in her old wardrobe. They are merely gathering dust in her old dressing room. I can assure you, no one shall begrudge you any of those gowns."

Daisy was dubious over some of his words but saw the logic in others. She felt the need to protest. "Surely you jest if you think any of the ladies at the house party will not be analyzing everything about me when I show up in your company. Every stitch of my clothing will be assessed in an effort to ascertain my standing and my wealth down to the last farthing."

"I doubt it will be so bad as that, my dear girl."

"Have you not spent any amount of time with the ladies of your station, my lord?"

Daisy's sceptical tone brought amusement to the viscount's face as he replied, "I am beginning to wonder whether or not I have," he admitted. "Although, I find myself wondering how you have come to this knowledge," he commented.

With a dismissive shrug, Daisy sidestepped his question. "If you are absolutely certain your sister will not be collecting those gowns for her own use at some point in the future, perhaps I will make use of some of them. With the help of my maid we should be able to alter them sufficiently to suit the current fashions and avoid detection."

"Detection of what?" Jasper was suspicious.

"Of our deception," Daisy explained in exasperation. "Have you not been paying attention?"

Jasper had the grace to blush, much to Daisy's amusement. "My dear, I feel as though I ought to apologize, but I am not entirely certain for what."

Daisy giggled over his words. "No apology required. In fact, I probably owe you one. I was less than gracious in accepting your offer of assistance. Mayhap you are correct, and this scheme shall benefit the both of us. If nothing else, it shall be an adventure I can reminisce upon when I am near to perishing from the boredom of life as a governess in the future."

She said these last words with such a degree of laughter in her tone that Jasper joined her in her amusement.

They were still laughing when Daisy stopped and pointed to a small house squeezed in between two larger ones. "This is my temporary abode, my lord. I thank you for your escort. I will see you on the morrow with my maid in tow. It would be best if you do not stand here over long, my lord. I do not wish to draw attention to our association."

Jasper tipped his hat to her gallantly and turned on his heel without argument; he had his own arrangements to make before they met again.

Chapter Three

After closing the door quietly behind her, Daisy leaned against it and gnawed her lip in indecision, wondering how much of her adventure to share with her hostess. Charlotte was her oldest and dearest friend; she really ought to tell her everything. Pushing away from the door, she went in search of her, glad for once that Charlotte had only a few servants.

Charlotte looked up from the needlework she had been toiling over as her young charge bustled into the room. "How did it go with Miss Holstein, my dear?"

Daisy sat down across from her friend, perching delicately on the edge of the aging settee, and allowed a sigh to escape her lips before she shook her head in denial. "She was not there. The shop was closed up tight."

"Really?" Charlotte asked, her brow wrinkling with surprise. "She rarely closes her office. Are you quite certain you had the correct address?"

Daisy grinned indulgently at her old governess who had never quite accepted that she had grown up. "Yes, Charlotte, it said Miss Holstein's Employment Office on the sign. I am quite certain it was the correct place."

Charlotte returned her smile. "Oh, yes, of course. I had quite forgotten she had such a sign. Well, I rarely ever visit her office, you know."

"I know, my dear, pay it no mind."

"Well, you can just go tomorrow, then. Or you could give up on your idea of gaining employment and stay here with me. You know I enjoy having you here, and you are no trouble at all."

Daisy smiled her appreciation. "I know, and you are a dear for offering, but I cannot abuse your hospitality by staying any longer than necessary."

Charlotte began to argue. "There is absolutely no abuse. Everything here is really yours by right." She would have continued on the topic, but Daisy cut her off.

"My dearest Charlotte…" Daisy kneeled before her friend, clasping her hands warmly between her own. She hated to see her former governess aging, knowing that Charlotte's concerns for Daisy's future did nothing to aid her failing health. "Everything here is not rightly mine. You served my family well. You have rightly earned your retirement years. I know my parents were generous, but I am certain whatever they may have settled upon you is not sufficient for the two of us. Besides, at my age I need to be gainfully employed. And you know I hate needlework. I could not bear to sit here with you stitching away. It would drive me mad."

Charlotte smiled indulgently at her companion. "But you can stay a while longer. I so love having you here."

"And it is a pleasure for me to be with you." Daisy squeezed her friend's hand again before continuing in a lighter tone. "I will actually take you up on the offer of staying a few more days. I have been offered a temporary, paid position, but it will not commence until next week."

"Oh, how nice. What kind of job is it? It must not be another governess position. No one wants the governess to be only temporary."

"It is a bit like a paid companion," Daisy began evasively before blurting out the entire story. "I met a viscount while standing in front of Miss Holstein's closed shop. His name is Lord Jasper Seaton, the Viscount of Hawthorne. His father is the Marquis of Abernathy."

"And you are going to be his companion?" Charlotte demanded, her tone of disgust conveying her thoughts quite clearly.

"How long have you known me, Charlotte? Do not jump to conclusions until you have heard the entire story. I will admit I had my reservations when he first proposed his scheme, but while it is a trifle havey cavey, it is most certainly not that type of position."

Daisy strove for indignation, but she knew from the warmth in her cheeks, she was probably looking guiltier than she should.

Charlotte settled back in her chair, only slightly mollified. "You are right, my dear. I trust you completely. I should let you finish your tale before I jump to my conclusions. Please, carry on."

"Well, the viscount seems to be the black sheep of his family. I am not sure what the history is, but I got the impression there is bad blood between him and his father. He strikes me as a good enough fellow, but he has been making an effort to maintain the feud up until now. I think he has sailed rather far up the River Tick and needs his parents' money to get straight once more. He does not wish to get leg shackled, but he thinks if he gets his parents to believe he is pursuing a courtship they will open their purse strings to him."

"So you are going to help him deceive his parents? Why would you even consider such a thing?" Charlotte's tone of disapproval left no room for doubt over her thoughts on the subject.

Daisy shrugged again, which brought a censorious look from her former governess. "The viscount thinks I might be able to find another position through the connections I will make at his mother's house party."

Charlotte's dubious expression was comment enough. Daisy continued. "I know, I told him the same thing. There is no way a lady is going to hire someone she has met socially to be her governess. But there is the possibility of finding a position as a paid companion, which when I think about it, might be much more to my liking."

"Do you really think you could tolerate being at the beck and call of some aging lady who is no doubt unhappy and unpleasant?"

"Why must she be unhappy and unpleasant?"

"If she was a joy to be around, her family would happily be providing the services she is hiring out," Charlotte pointed out reasonably.

"Or mayhap, she is a spinster with no family to speak of," Daisy countered. "And even if she is a cranky old thing, it can hardly be worse than tending to the spoiled babies of noblemen."

"There are probably more similarities than you would imagine," Charlotte replied with a grin. "But do you seriously expect me to believe you think you are going to find suitable employment while accompanying a viscount to his mother's party at a country estate? There must be some other reason you are even considering accepting this strange man's preposterous offer. You have not suddenly developed a tendre for the man, have you?"

Daisy blushed hotly but shook her head firmly in denial. She stared rather defiantly at her former governess for a moment before giving in and admitting the full truth. "If you must know, I want to see what it is like, being a part of that world, even if only for a week. I know I should not wish it, that it will no doubt lead to frustration and heartache since the aristocracy is nothing but a bunch of dressed up fools as my papa would say." Daisy shrugged helplessly once more. "But I cannot help myself, Charlotte, I just want to see it."

Charlotte's face softened instantly upon this admission. "Of course you do, my dear. Very well, what can I do to assist you in this harebrained scheme?"

With a whoop of laughter, Daisy threw her arms around her friend for a fierce but brief embrace. "Thank you, my dear, I knew I could count on you. There is actually something that would be a huge help," she said as she eyed the discarded needlework.

Charlotte caught on immediately. "You will need appropriate attire. How long do we have? I could stitch you up enough gowns in a couple of weeks."

"We do not have that long. The viscount wishes to depart for the country in a few days."

"What? But you cannot possibly be ready that quickly. Is the man daft?"

"It is a possibility." Daisy smiled. "But he is thinking of buying me a couple of gowns from a proper modiste as well as giving me some of his sister's old gowns. That is what you could help me with — they will need to be altered to fit as well as to bring them up to date and make them unrecognizable to his mother and sister."

Charlotte stared at Daisy with chagrin shining on her lined face. "It is highly inappropriate for this gentleman to buy you gowns, my dear girl."

"He said to think of it as though I am an actress playing a role, and he is merely buying me some costumes."

Charlotte hmmed noncommittally.

"It may not even be necessary if there are sufficient gowns from his sister. But taking those dresses does not leave me entirely comfortable either," Daisy admitted.

"Perhaps you ought to rethink your plans," was Charlotte's quiet suggestion.

"No, I gave his lordship my word. I am determined to help him. He said he wishes to straighten out his life and I find that I believe him. All he needs is access to his funds in order to do so. And he has promised to help me ensure my situation is established before we part ways at the end of this escapade."

Charlotte again sniffed with disapproval. "A young, single nobleman is in no position to be arranging your affairs, my dear girl. But I understand your desire to catch a glimpse of what might have been, and I will stand by my offer to help you."

"Thank you, my dear Charlotte." Daisy smiled before changing the subject. "Besides clothes, there is one other vital component in order for me to play the role of a lady."

"You will need a maid," Charlotte surmised immediately.

"Exactly! I was thinking about asking Kate from up the street. Do you think she would be willing and able?"

Charlotte smiled her appreciation. "I think that is a wonderful idea. You are a dear, good girl for thinking of her. Even if things do not go as well as you planned with your viscount, the experience will be wonderful for Kate. Perhaps it will make it possible for her to be able to get a proper position and be able to help her family."

"It may not, though, Charlotte, and I would hate to get her hopes up on an empty promise. If this scheme does not work out as we hope, neither the viscount nor I will be in any position to give her a letter of reference."

"That's true, and you should be sure to mention that to her when you're discussing the plans with her, but regardless of how it turns out, it will be just the polish Kate needs."

Daisy wrinkled her nose. "Is she that unpolished, Charlotte? I do need someone who is going to be able to help me pull off this role. It needs to be believable that she is my maid. I do not want to draw any more attention to myself than necessary."

"I do not think you will have a lot of choice, for one thing. You can trust her to keep your secrets, which is more than you can say for some stranger that you might hire. And you would be no more sure with a stranger of their skills. I say, speak to her about it and decide for yourself if you think she can pull it off. You are fully aware of what is required. If your viscount will be footing the bills, if you think she will suit, hire her on the spot and get her to help us get you ready. That will show what skills she might have and give the both of you some experience together."

Daisy leaned over and kissed her old governess' cheek. "You always had the best ideas, my dear. I shall go down the street and have a quiet word with her right away." She glanced down at her skirt. "Since this is currently the best dress I own, perhaps I ought to change it for something else before I go traipsing about the street."

With a grin, she hurried from the room. Within a very short time she was knocking on the front door of a slightly shabby cottage up the street. A small girl answered the door.

"Hello. Are you Gina? My name is Miss Pembroke. I am staying with Charlotte Johnston three doors down from you. Would your sister Kate be available to speak with me?"

Little Gina's eyes were round saucers of curiosity by the end of Daisy's question, but without a word, she nodded her head and scampered off in search of her sister, leaving Daisy standing on the stoop. A boy of about ten years, who had witnessed the exchange, made a sound of disgust and strode forward to welcome their guest.

"Gina can't hold two thoughts in her head at the same time. Sorry she left you standing there, miss, please come in, if you don't mind."

Daisy stepped into the dimly lit hallway and allowed the youngster to shut the door. "I'm Walter, miss. Kate won't be a moment, I'm sure. Would you like to have a seat?"

Smiling over the boy's gallantry, Daisy accepted the proffered chair. Just as she perched gingerly on its edge, they heard the flurry of approaching footsteps. Suddenly the small hallway was filled with people as Gina and Kate entered, followed by several other youngsters of varying ages.

Daisy stood to greet Kate, who didn't bother introducing all her siblings.

"Gina said you wished to speak with me, miss?" Kate made the statement sound like a question, as though she doubted her sister's words.

"I do hope I have not disturbed you. If you have a few moments, I would appreciate discussing a matter with you."

Kate blushed and bobbed a small curtsy. "It's no bother at all, miss, thank you. But if it's privacy you might be wanting, that is in short supply around here. We could maybe go step outside to talk, if that's all right with you."

"That is a wonderful idea, thank you. It is a lovely day. Perhaps we could walk down to that small park at the end of the street. I believe there is a bench there where we could sit and talk for a few moments." Turning to smile at Walter and Gina, Daisy continued speaking to Kate. "Your brother and sister made me quite welcome, but it is a matter of some delicacy that I would prefer to discuss just with you for the moment."

"Don't worry about them, miss, they don't mind." Kate turned to her siblings with admonition. "You'd best have your chores done by the time I get back." She quickly wrapped a shawl around herself and stepped out the door after Daisy.

"Thank you for taking a few minutes to talk with me, Kate, I am sure with that many of you under one roof there is never a shortage of things to do."

"That's very true, miss, which is why it's a pleasure to be able to get away from it for a wee spell. There wasn't anything that can't wait for me to return." Kate drew a deep breath and looked around. "You were right — it is a lovely day, and I'm right glad for the opportunity to get out and enjoy it for a few minutes."

They quickly reached the little park Daisy had mentioned and sat down on the bench. Daisy was glad to see that it was empty and was wondering how best to broach the subject when Kate eagerly demanded information.

"So what did you want to ask me, miss? I have to tell you that I'm fair to perishing from the suspense."

This broke the ice nicely, as it made Daisy giggle. "I am not quite sure how to explain everything. I have a chance to go to a house party that a marchioness is hosting at a country estate for her wellborn guests. But in order to fit in with the crowd of people who will be there, I need to have a lady's maid. I was wondering if you would possibly be able to play the role."

Daisy clearly saw the family resemblance as Kate's eyes grew as round as Gina's as she listened in silence to Daisy's scant explanation. She didn't respond immediately, merely gazing at Daisy with her mouth slightly agape.

"Do you think you might be able to do it? It would require you to be away from your family for about two weeks." When there was still silence, Daisy continued, "You would, of course, be paid."

Those final words must have been the last straw for Kate's endurance. She clasped her hands to her chest and grinned at Daisy while tears slid down her cheeks. "Oh, Miss Pembroke, I would be right honored to be your maid. It's exactly what I've been hoping for."

"I need you to realize that this position is only temporary. I will not be able to keep you on after the two weeks is up. Do you understand that?"

"That's all right, miss. My cousin, who is in service in Bath, might be able to get me a proper job after that. She has been telling me that she could if I only had some exposure. I wasn't certain what exposure was, but now I'm thinking this might just be it. She needs me to be sure that I know what I'm doing." Realizing this might not paint her in the most favorable light, Kate was quick to add. "That don't mean that I don't know what I'm doing, I can assure you, miss. I've been studying as much as I can, asking questions of everyone I know who is in service and, I promise you, I won't let you down. I'm going to be the very best lady's maid you could ever wish for. And I thank you deeply for the opportunity."

Daisy was unable to hold back her laughter over the girl's enthusiastic words. "I am feeling very reassured, Kate, thank you for your ready acceptance. Will you be able to keep my secrets?" She threw that question out, wanting to get an unguarded response from her new maid.

"I'm an excellent secret keeper, miss. The things I know, but will never tell, could curl your hair for you."

Daisy smiled once more over the girl's choice of words. "And do you suppose you would be able to start right away?"

"For sure I can. You did see how many of us were trying to squeeze into the hall at my house, didn't you, miss? And that wasn't even all of us. They'll barely notice that I'm gone."

"That I find hard to believe, Kate, but thank you again for your ready acceptance. You see, I will also be playing a role. I do not usually mingle with the sort who will be at this party. In the next couple of days, before we depart for the country, I need to get ready. If you are available to start right away, you will be a big help with that."

"I can start immediately, miss. I don't mean to brag, but I have a very steady hand with the needle. I could make you whatever you would like."

"Excellent. Thank you, Kate. We should be able to manage without making anything from scratch, but if you are able to help with alterations that will be very helpful. Your duties will begin on the morrow. Let us say nine o'clock. Please come to Charlotte's house at that time and we will begin."

"I look forward to it, miss."

The two girls parted ways, and Daisy returned to discuss the latest development with Charlotte. That night, she doubted if she would sleep a wink but surprisingly sleep claimed her as soon as her head hit the pillow. It had been an eventful day.

Chapter Four

"Oh, Charlotte, it is lovely." Daisy fingered the soft fabric of the elegant day gown, marvelling at the fine stitching and lovely colour. "How did you get it done so quickly? You must have worked all night!" She said this last with an almost angry tone. "My dear, I would not have asked such sacrifice from you."

"I know that, you silly widgeon. That is why I wanted to do it. You cannot go shopping for fancy new garb if you aren't dressed the part. It will never do to have a modiste looking down her nose at you."

Daisy threw her arms around her oldest friend. "You are a dear. Thank you, it will do perfectly for the errands I have to do today, and for the party. No one will ever know that I am an imposter."

"You are not an imposter," Charlotte declared, fiercely loyal. "You have as much right as anyone to be rubbing elbows with a marchioness, or even a roomful of dukes and duchesses."

"You know what I mean, Charlotte." Daisy rolled her eyes, dismissing the topic. "I was trying to compliment you. You did a spectacular job with this gown, Charlotte. I really appreciate it. It will be that much less work for Kate and me later."

"Well, I have no intention of stopping now. You are going to need a ridiculous number of gowns and all the accoutrements that go with them. And it was actually rather enjoyable. When you return this afternoon we will get the rest figured out."

Daisy blew her a kiss as she glided from the room, on her way to meet Kate and the viscount.

꧁꧂

Daisy felt conspicuous standing on the viscount's front step, waiting for the door to be opened. It was good they had agreed for her to arrive early. It would be terrible if she were seen and their plans ruined before they even got under way. Her nerves stretched taut, and she wondered if she would be able to pull this off. The servants would be in a better position to spot her pretense if she wasn't able to pull off the deception. As the door opened, Daisy's chin rose and her backbone stiffened into position. She was Miss Margaret Pembroke, and she had been invited to visit the Viscount of Hawthorn.

As the butler ushered them into the front receiving room, Daisy was relieved she had a maid in tow, she was sure that was why the butler had accepted her so readily.

"His lordship will be with you momentarily, miss. Please be seated."

Daisy avoided meeting Kate's eyes, afraid they would both burst into a fit of nervous giggles. The ornate clock on the mantle ticked by blessedly few minutes while they waited in tense silence.

"Miss Pembroke, I am glad you were able to make it," Jasper greeted her in a loud voice. For her ears only, as he bent over her hand gallantly he continued, "I was not completely certain you would show up."

Daisy was torn between feeling offended that he thought she would not keep her word and delight over his warm greeting, reminding herself it was all part of their act. "Thank you for seeing us, my lord, I know you are a busy man," she said politely, ignoring the flutters in her stomach when he pressed a kiss to the space on her wrist where her sleeve had ridden up above her glove.

Pulling her hand from his grasp and pressing it to her waist to prevent it from trembling, Daisy turned to smile at Kate. "My lord, I have brought my maid with me, and we are ready to get to work."

Jasper blinked for a moment. He had been so absorbed in welcoming her, he had quite failed to notice anyone else was in the room. It was very unlike him. One could not dance on the edge of respectability as he did without being constantly aware of his surroundings. Even when he was in his cups, he never allowed his senses to be dulled. This realization caused him to grow wary of his association with this girl.

"Very well, miss, let us proceed."

Daisy looked at him questioningly, but Jasper ignored her searching gaze. "Is aught amiss, my lord?" she asked.

"Of course not, why do you ask?" he replied, his polite tone at odds with the warmth with which he had greeted her earlier.

Daisy hesitated, wondering if voicing her thoughts might be considered inappropriate. "You have become all starchy all of a sudden," she finally blurted.

Jasper couldn't help but laugh at her observation. "You are definitely an original, my dear girl. Now come along, we have plenty to do before we go for our ride."

Feeling uncertain and shy, Daisy hesitated for a moment before she noticed Kate's anxious gaze upon her. She felt responsible for reassuring the other girl, and now she owed her the promised position as well. Bracing her shoulders, she smiled at Kate, lifted her chin to a proud angle, and strode after the viscount, climbing the stairs in his wake.

They found themselves in a small room overflowing with fabrics of every colour and shade.

"You will have to excuse the tight quarters. My housekeeper did not think it appropriate for me to be together with you in a bedchamber so she had all my sister's gowns brought to this room."

"I am sorry that she had to go to so much trouble on my behalf." Daisy began to apologize but Jasper interrupted her.

"I am sure you will agree that since it is my idea to have you accompany me, it is really on my behalf, so you need not trouble yourself."

Daisy's brows rose toward her hairline at his overbearing manner, but she was sidetracked by Kate's delight before she could question the viscount further.

"Oh, Miss Daisy, isn't it marvelous? Have you ever, in all your days seen so many gowns?" The other girl was gazing about her with rapt attention.

"I surely have not, Kate. It is a wonder indeed." Turning to Jasper with a smile, she added, "I can see now why you can be certain your mother and sister will not notice the gowns being familiar. If she has this many to choose from, she certainly cannot miss a few."

"Let this be a lesson to you not to doubt my word in the future." Jasper said that with a straight face but couldn't contain his mirth when he saw the myriad emotions crossing Daisy's face over his domineering tone.

"Are you attempting to make me cry off from our arrangement, my lord?" she asked in a quiet voice.

"No, my dear, I apologize for being a buffoon, please disregard my fidgets, I have not yet had sufficient tea this morning." He nearly rolled his eyes at his weak excuse, but Daisy took him at his word.

Jasper almost laughed at the look of relief that chased the concern from her face. "My father was the same way, my lord. He could barely face the day without at least three cups each morning. It used to drive my mother to distraction. Perhaps you should ring for a pot to be brought so we can get through the task at hand."

"I shall be fine for now," he said, feeling warmth creep up his cheeks when he realized his housekeeper was gazing at him as though he had lost his mind. He was wondering if maybe he had.

"Have you any idea what sorts of activities your mother has planned for the week? It might help us narrow down our search for appropriate things."

"I am not fully informed of all her plans, but I have been to enough of these events to be able to guide you, I am sure. You will need day dresses for each day, at least one riding habit, evening attire for supper, and there will probably be a ball at the end and perhaps even one in the middle, so be sure to bring two ball gowns."

"Gracious, my lord, how will we get all the necessary gowns packed and transported? And how many guests are your parents inviting, do you suppose? Will the house be able to contain that many fripperies?"

Jasper laughed. "Have no fear, we shall manage. That is why we will be traveling by coach, not curricle, even though it is only a couple hours to Abernathy."

Daisy exchanged a glance with Kate, and then both girls plunged into the mass of colours. Jasper couldn't help admiring Daisy's managing ways. He was surprised how quickly she was able to assess the situation and make her selections. He had to reassure her a couple more times that there would be no trouble with her taking the gowns.

When the housekeeper left to attend to some household matter, Daisy took the opportunity to voice a concern that had been niggling at her mind throughout the morning. "Are you sure word is not going to reach your family about this? With your housekeeper involved, does that not guarantee that your parents will be informed?"

"No, Mrs. Marks has been devoted to me since I was a boy. She can be trusted implicitly. She thinks this is a great joke and is not troubled in the least to keep my secret."

Daisy cast Jasper a dubious look. He heaved a long suffering sigh and explained further. "It is in Mrs. Marks' best interests to keep my secret. If she wants to maintain her position in this household even after I inherit, she needs to remain in my good books. Mrs. Marks is far from stupid."

His cynicism was unnerving for Daisy. "I preferred it when you said she was doing it as a favor to you, my lord."

Jasper chuckled. "You may continue to look at the bright side if you wish, but reality always creeps in."

Daisy would rather not consider such dark thoughts, so she changed the subject back to the matter at hand before the housekeeper returned. "It is a piece of good fortune that your sister and I are both on the shorter side. If she had a tendency to take after you, we would have a great deal more work to do. As it is, most of these gowns will not need many alterations for them to suit."

"Mayhap not, but you must keep in mind that these are all last year's styles. You shall have to make a few adjustments to bring them up to date. Some of this trim is really ghastly — I do wonder what she was thinking."

"That is no matter, my lord. I am sorry to ask again, but I just need to confirm that you are absolutely certain it is all above board for me to take these gowns. If you are sure, I think I will be able to make do with these and shall not need any gowns from a modiste. I shall merely need new ribbons and trimmings and such. Between Kate, Charlotte, and I we should be able to get all of this ready in a couple of days."

"Excellent," the viscount replied, looking satisfied and self-congratulatory. "Now let us leave the servants to box everything up. You and I can have a spot of tea before we leave for our drive. You made quick work of that, so there is little need for us to rush."

Chapter Five

Jasper had left Daisy to tidy herself up before they went driving while he oversaw the preparation of the horses.

"You look ravishing," Jasper greeted her as he helped Daisy climb up into his curricle, and then handed in her maid after her.

Daisy snorted and rolled her eyes. "You are a complete hand, Hawthorn." She grew serious. "You are more experienced in these matters than I am, while I think my dear Charlotte did lovely work, making me this gown, is it truly going to pass muster for your escort?"

"Absolutely, I can assure you, it will do nicely," Jasper answered, his tone serious and his eyes searching. She was the least self-conscious woman he had ever met. She truly seemed to have no concept of her own loveliness. He wondered for a moment if it was unwise to expose her to the aristocratic company that would be gathering for the party. He pushed the thought from his mind with the reassurance that he would be there to look after her.

"Your horses are quite handsome, my lord," Daisy commented with a delighted grin as she looked about while they rolled along the cobblestoned street. "They look as though they would be quite fast if they were able to have their head."

"Are you wishing to see me put them through their paces?" Jasper was pleasantly surprised. No young lady of the *ton* would ever pass up an opportunity to be seen riding around the Park at the fashionable hour in favor of such sport.

"I would love that, my lord, but I know you wished to be seen in the Park, so you need not bother with my whims."

"I can assure you I would much rather go for a gallop through the countryside than take part in the Parade through Hyde Park." Jasper paused, undecided, remembering their plans. "But it would be best if we are seen together before we head to Abernathy. I tell you what, let us make one pass around the ring and then we can leave. I will tool us around and out through Cumberland Gate, and we can take the Uxbridge Road. At this time of the day there should not be too many others on the road, and we shall be able to feel the wind for a few minutes before we swing round to Bond Street for a spot of shopping."

Daisy pulled a face at the thought of shopping but she approved his plan. "Very good, my lord, let us make it so."

Jasper threw back his head and laughed, looking forward to seeing *ton* events through her eyes, beginning with the Parade through Hyde Park.

He was not going to be disappointed. With her wide, eager gaze flitting about, she soon had her observations to share.

"Gracious, my lord, you certainly knew of which you spoke when you said we would be able to be seen here. Why are there so very many people here? Do they not have other things to do?"

The viscount chuckled as he nodded in acknowledgement to a greeting being called to him from one of his acquaintances riding by. "For ladies of the *ton*, this is what they have to do, Daisy." He failed to notice that he had begun addressing her with such familiarity. "To see and be seen is the sole purpose in life for most of the debutantes."

Daisy wrinkled her nose at this. "Sounds deadly dull to me."

"Most of the time it is," Jasper agreed. "But there are times that it is all worthwhile."

"Like when?"

Jasper turned to her, taken aback by her direct gaze focused so fully upon him. She was so often distracted by her delight in her surroundings, he rarely got trapped by her concentrated focus. He quite enjoyed the experience of being the object of her fascination. He almost forgot what they had been discussing.

"Like right this moment when I am riding out on such a lovely, sunny day with a beautiful young lady beside me. What could be better than this?"

Daisy again snorted dismissively. "I thought you were going to be serious for once," she complained, turning her attention back to observing the crowds.

"I was," Jasper muttered under his voice, but Daisy barely noticed.

"Oh, my lord," she chortled. "Do look at that woman over there wearing the purple habit in the white carriage. The feathers in her hat are so long they are going to get tangled in the trees. Did no one tell her what a bad idea those were?"

Jasper followed the direction of her discreetly pointing finger, glad that she was not such a bumpkin as to be pointing outright. He stifled his own laughter when he realized who she was talking about. "That is Lady Lucretia Foxworth. She is this season's *diamond* and she would not take kindly to your mockery."

Daisy tore her eyes away from the ridiculous sight and searched Jasper's face for signs that he was funning her. "Are you perfectly serious, my lord? I will not deny that she is a beautiful woman, but surely no one would want to emulate her style choices."

"Look around and come to your own conclusions."

"Oh good heavens, my lord. Why are there so many foolish ladies amongst the *ton*? Please tell me you will not be expecting me to imitate her, as well. I can assure you I will not be able to pull it off creditably."

Jasper's gaze searched hers for a moment before he gave in to his amusement. "You are perfectly correct, my dear girl. I do not believe you could play the role of society jade. No, I will not expect you to imitate Lady Lucretia. You do a creditable job of being Miss Daisy Pembroke, and that is sufficient for our plans, have no fear."

Daisy was undecided whether she was relieved or disappointed over his words. She looked back at the beautiful *diamond*. Shaking her head, Daisy acknowledged to herself that no matter if she wanted to, she would never be other than she was, and that was a far cry from the leader of the *ton* that the beautiful young debutante was. After one last wistful glance and a small sigh, Daisy tore her eyes away and allowed them to roam about over the rest of the milling crowds.

Jasper amused himself by watching the myriad expressions chasing themselves over her mobile face. It crossed his mind that the next fortnight was going to be highly diverting.

Daisy turned to him, her expression bright. "It truly is fascinating to watch all these people. I wish I could sit on a bench all day and watch them, but I suppose we ought to get on about our business. Thank you so much for bringing me here, my lord. It has given me a better picture of what I shall be in for during your mother's house party."

"It has been my pleasure to have you with me, for certain, my dear. But what do you mean that it has given you a picture of what to expect?"

"Seeing the interactions, I realize that much of it is acting, so I have less qualms about the role I shall be playing. And seeing that everyone is playing a role has reminded me that I must not take anything that is said to me as sworn truth."

Jasper gazed at her with amazed admiration. "That is very true, but how did you come up with that by watching the Parade?"

Daisy shrugged. "It was simple really. Take for example your *diamond.* Surely if she had the least sense, she would realize how silly she looks driving around in an open carriage with such tall feathers sprouting from her head. And everyone else must realize it is ridiculous as well, but other ladies are imitating her choice of headwear. This tells me that appearance is everything to these people, it matters not how foolish that appearance might be."

Daisy looked around some more before inclining her head slightly. "Did you notice that carriage just over there?"

"The one with the matched bays?"

"Exactly." Daisy beamed at her companion before continuing. "The two ladies in that carriage seemed to be so polite to the lady on horseback with whom they were just speaking, but as soon as the mounted lady rode away, they began whispering fiercely to one another. It seems to me as though they are speaking unpleasantly about the lady they just professed friendship with."

The viscount's eyebrows were inching up his forehead. "You should be in the employ of the Home Office, my dear girl. Your talents are being wasted in any profession other than that of a spy."

Daisy grinned at the compliment. "Thank you, my lord. Others would see the same things if they were not so absorbed in themselves."

Her words were so full of the truth there was no answer Jasper could offer. He merely flicked the leads on his horses and headed away from the crowds, ready to show Daisy the abilities of his favorite pair. She laughed and held on to her seat as they picked up speed.

Before long they were tooling along the road, with few other carriages in sight. Jasper allowed the powerful horses to lengthen their paces, and he grinned as he heard Daisy's laughter ringing out. Before long he slowed them back down to a more demure pace as he steered them toward the busier traffic and they returned to the fashionable part of Town.

"That was smashing, my lord," Daisy declared with glee.

"I am happy to have pleased you, my dear." He kept his face grave, but his eyes sparkled with enjoyment.

Daisy huffed a sigh. "It seems rather dull to go shopping after such fun."

"Do you wish to be conveyed home instead?" Jasper offered solicitously.

"Do not be daft, my lord," Daisy reprimanded. "We do not have the time for me to be missish. This shopping needs to get done and the alterations finished so we can get our little expedition over with."

Jasper felt a rare pinch of guilt over how obviously she was dreading the process. "I ought to release you from your promise," he began before Daisy interrupted.

"Oh no, my lord, I apologize if I sounded as though I am trying to wriggle out of our deal. I am not, I can assure you. While I am terribly nervous about the whole thing, I truly do not want to back out of it. In fact, I am looking forward to it. It shall be an adventure. A bit of excitement to reminisce about to prevent me turning to dust from boredom as a governess or companion in the future."

"I shall do my best to make it a memorable adventure then, Miss Daisy."

As they turned onto Bond Street, Jasper brought his horses to a stop. "Do you think I ought to come in with you and help you make your choices?"

"Only if you want everyone to be searching the papers for an announcement on the morrow, my lord." Daisy laughed at his incredulous expression. "Your driving and presence here has drawn enough attention to us for our purposes. From what I have learned about you in the past two days, it would be a first for you to be in such an establishment. If you were to turn up there with me on your arm, it might be just a little too much for some to take in, would you not agree?"

"How did you get so smart?" Jasper asked, shaking his head. "Very well, my dear, I shall wait for you. But do make sure you make the right choices."

Daisy rolled her eyes in exasperation. "I shall do my poor best, my lord," she replied, her tone dry. "Come along, Kate, you must surely be bored to tears."

"Oh no, miss, it has been one of the funnest days of my life so far."

The girls exchanged happy smiles as they headed for the shops. Daisy was grateful that the viscount had discretely pressed some guineas into her hand earlier in the day. She was highly uncomfortable taking his money, but she was unsure how much she would need and knew her meager funds would not stretch far.

"It is for your costumes." He had been matter of fact, keeping her embarrassment to a minimum.

Daisy and Kate were momentarily overwhelmed by the volume of fabrics, ribbons, and trinkets within the first shop they entered. But before long, they were happily engaged in picking out the necessities. They made swift work of making the necessary purchases and were soon striding toward the viscount, who was walking his horses along the street.

"Are you sure you have everything you need?" Jasper had never known a female to complete her shopping in such a short time. "You surely cannot be finished already."

"We are indeed. Thank you for your patience in waiting for us, my lord. Now if you would be so kind, you could drop us off in our neighborhood so we can get on with the rest of the preparations."

"You are a strange woman, Miss Daisy Pembroke," Jasper remarked as he handed her and the maid into his carriage before clicking his tongue to his horses and setting out for Bloomsbury.

Daisy's only response was a low chuckle.

The viscount dropped his passengers in front of Charlotte's tidy house, promising to call 'round the following afternoon.

"I do not think it advisable, my lord. This is not the right environment for you, for one thing, and you shall be interrupting our work, for another. We shall have to arrange tea for you, and it will just be a lot of bother for nothing."

"That is certainly putting me in my place nicely, my dear."

Daisy blushed over Jasper's sarcastic tone but did not relent. "If we are to be ready to leave in two days, we need all the time we have in order to make all the necessary preparations. And it would be terrible to have our charade exposed by someone finding out that your intended resides in Bloomsbury. No matter how eager your parents are to marry you off, even they might hesitate over that."

"Why Margaret Pembroke, you are a terrible snob," Jasper declared. "I do believe it is you who is looking down your nose at this neighborhood, not me." Daisy did not relent in the face of his accusation. "Very well, I see your point about needing all the time you have. But you do realize I shall have to come here with my carriage to pick up you and your baggage."

Daisy shrugged and inclined her head. "Surely it will be early, and we will be quick."

Jasper sighed. "Very well, my dear. I shall be here early, two days hence. Send around a note if you hit any snags or wish for my assistance in any way."

"Thank you, my lord, we shall do our level best not to need you, but I appreciate the offer."

With those words, Daisy hopped down from the carriage and followed her maid into the house.

The next days and nights were a whirl of activity. Daisy found she quite enjoyed the camaraderie of Charlotte and Kate as they bent over their needles and made all the necessary alterations.

She was trying on the last gown and Charlotte was putting in a couple last stitches while Daisy watched in the small looking glass. "It has been so long since I have felt this pampered, Charlotte. Thank you so much for all that you are doing to help."

"How can you possibly feel pampered? You have been working just as hard as Kate and me." Charlotte looked up from her stitches to search the younger woman's face.

Daisy laughed and shrugged. "But we have been working for me rather than for someone else's benefit. And it has actually been such fun. I have never had the opportunity to sit around with other women sewing. Even as a girl my needlework was a solitary drudgery. This reminds me of the lovely times I had while I was away at school for such a short time."

Charlotte's smile was indulgent. "You always did hate anything to do with needle and thread."

"But when you can sit around and giggle with others, it turns into a game rather than a dreaded ordeal. I never would have thought it possible."

They shared a laugh before Charlotte nodded and stood. "I do believe you are finished, my dear."

"Once again you have produced a masterpiece. I have no need to fear being found out from my clothes. Any misstep will be of my own making."

Charlotte hugged her friend close. "You know you don't have to do this, don't you?"

"Oh, Charlotte, of course I do. But while I am terrified, there is an equal amount of excitement thrown in to make it all worthwhile."

"Very well, if you are certain, you ought to be in bed. The viscount will be calling round to collect you before you know it."

"I doubt I shall sleep a wink," Daisy declared. Once again she was mistaken. Despite her anxieties, the busyness of the past couple days took their toll on her and she fell asleep within moments.

Chapter Six

Jasper grumbled as his valet shook him awake.

"You did ask to be up early, my lord," he reminded respectfully.

The viscount cracked his eyelids open. "You are, no doubt, quite correct," he drawled.

"You are supposed to be heading to your parents' party, my lord," Henry reminded his master calmly, which elicited a disconsolate groan from the bed. "Did you try to drown the memory away last night, my lord?"

"I can hear the grin in your voice, Henry, even though I am refusing to look at you."

Unrepentant, Henry bustled about, opening the heavy curtains and laying out the viscount's traveling clothes. "Would you like me to ring for something to be brought for you to break your fast, my lord?"

Jasper cocked a shocked eyebrow at his valet. "At this hour, Henry?" he asked, reproachful.

Henry's face displayed his apology. "You really ought to eat something before you face the rigours of your travel, my lord. And you will be picking up Miss Pembroke," he reminded. "Do you not think it would be wise to fortify yourself first?"

With a dry chuckle, Jasper forced himself to sit up and swing his feet over the side. Sighing, he acknowledged the wisdom of his valet's words. "Very well, Henry, ring away. But I beg of you, coffee and toast only. I could not stomach anything more than that at this ungodly hour."

Henry's grin remained firmly in place as he bustled around the room. His efficient movements had the viscount fed, shaved, and dressed before too many moments had passed. By the time he was dressed, Jasper's gaze was as sharp-eyed as usual.

"Thank you, Henry. You are as proficient as ever. I trust that all has been arranged, and my baggage is properly stowed."

"Of course, my lord. I shall be riding in the second carriage with your and Miss Pembroke's luggage. If you have no further need of me, I will leave now to ride over and get on with collecting the rest of the luggage."

"Very well, Henry. That would be best."

ཐ

Within a short time, Jasper was handing Daisy and her maid into his carriage, and they were making their way out of the city.

Jasper was chagrined to see the sympathetic expression Daisy was sending his way. "Was it terribly difficult for you to get up this early, my lord?"

"It is not so very strange for me, Daisy, my dear." Jasper made an attempt to brazen it out.

However, Daisy wasn't about to fall for his tales. She rolled her eyes at him but failed to comment. She had her own anxieties to concentrate on and allowed him to maintain his claim.

A few minutes of silence were interrupted by her yawning. Quickly covering her mouth, Daisy blushed to her hairline. "I do apologize, my lord. It was a short night, as we worked late making certain all was in readiness for today."

"Do not trouble yourself, my dear girl, it is perfectly understandable. You might as well put your head back and try to get a bit of sleep. We have several hours of driving ahead of us."

"Oh, my lord, I doubt if I could sleep a wink. I am far too excited."

Jasper looked at her and observed the anxiety shining in her bright eyes. He was swept with an overwhelming desire to pull her into his arms and comfort her as best he could. Feeling the maid's suspicious gaze focused on him, Jasper squelched the impulse and merely reiterated his suggestion that she try to get some rest.

"I will not pester you with chatter or questions. Close your eyes and at least get a little rest."

"Very well, my lord, I will do as you bid," was Daisy's cheeky reply. She followed his directions, and before long, the motion of the vehicle had soothed her nerves. Her breathing evened out and her head began to nod.

Jasper took a moment to study his companion. In repose, she looked even younger than she usually did. He wondered how she could possibly be responsible for herself. He realized there was much he did not know about her and determined to get to know her a little better when she awoke. Chastising himself for his usual self-absorption, he resolved to spend the time during the drive after she awoke learning as much as he could. They needed to establish their story so that it would stand up to the scrutiny they were sure to face once they arrived at his parents' estate.

He was surprised how enjoyable it was to sit and watch her sleep. Jasper could have done it for hours, but then he caught Kate's fierce eyes upon him. Jasper tried to charm her with a smile, but it seemed she was not going to be so easily beguiled. He wasn't sure if he should endeavor to engage the young woman in conversation. To solve his dilemma, he decided to follow his own advice. Closing his eyes, he thought he would just rest them a few minutes.

Expecting he would be too aware of his surroundings to actually fall asleep, he was shocked to open them what felt like a moment later to realize that he had been sleeping. Across from him, Daisy and Kate were whispering quietly to each other. Daisy caught his eye upon her.

"Good morning, my lord," she greeted him cheerfully. "I would like to thank you for the suggestion to close my eyes. I thought it could not possibly do any good, but I actually slept and now I feel much more the thing."

Jasper tried not to glare at her. He was not feeling at all the thing. He hated falling asleep in a carriage. The crick it always placed in his neck was such an irritant.

Daisy's sharp gaze searched his face briefly before she let slip a light giggle. "Oh dear, my lord, you are not feeling nearly as refreshed as I am, are you? Do you need a wee bit more sleep? Would you prefer if Kate and I remain silent so you can get a bit more rest?"

"Not at all, my dear, but I thank you for your solicitous offer." His begrudging reply was polite, causing another giggle to escape his companion.

A moment of silence stretched through the carriage before Daisy cleared her throat delicately. "I was far too anxious this morning to eat very much. Did you by chance think to pack some refreshments?"

Jasper looked at her blankly for a moment before Kate piped up from her corner.

"Perhaps that basket could be an answer, my lord," she offered, wry amusement lurking in her low voice.

Surprised, Jasper grabbed the basket, blessing his valet at the back of his mind. "No doubt my servants arranged for our comfort."

Daisy tried to maintain a polite, social façade, but it had been so long since she had been pampered or provided for. She found she was far more excited to see what was in the basket than was surely seemly for a lady of the *ton*.

Jasper felt her curious gaze upon him and decided to tease her for a moment. He feigned peeking into the basket but then closed it, putting it aside with a shrug.

After another moment of taut silence, Daisy prompted, "Well? Was there anything in there for us to eat, my lord?"

"Oh, did you wish to eat?" he asked. Seeing her incredulous face, he was unable to contain his mirth. With a bark of laughter, he relented. "Yes, my dear girl, there is plenty to keep you satisfied in this basket. Please, help yourself."

"Allow me, miss," Kate insisted, taking on her roll of lady's maid with enthusiasm.

A few moments later, Daisy sat back with a sigh. "Thank you, Kate, and thank you, Lord Seaton, I was beginning to fear I would perish from my hunger before we reached our destination."

"I find that doubtful," Jasper began before Daisy's tinkle of laughter rang out.

"My lord, you are a complete hand," she declared, as was her wont. She waited a beat before asking solicitously, "What sort of traveller are you, my lord? Would you prefer silence to think your own thoughts or do you prefer to pass the time with light conversation?"

"I am glad you have asked. I was thinking there is much I do not know about you. While you were sleeping, I realized there are many things I ought to have found out before now."

Daisy's stomach knotted at his words. She hated lying and had been so relieved that he seemed uninterested in her past. She had not yet decided how much to tell him. Resolving to wait and see what he asked before she panicked, she offered what she hoped was an encouraging smile and waited expectantly for his questions.

"What is your family situation, Miss Pembroke? I assume you do not have any family or you would not be seeking employment."

"You are quite correct, my lord. I am sadly an orphan. My parents both died a year and a half ago."

"You have my sympathies, my dear. How tragic that must have been for you. And there were no extended family who could take you in?"

"Unfortunately, not really. Neither of my parents came from large families. There are, of course, some cousins and various other extended relatives, but no one was overly anxious to have me join their families, and I decided I would prefer to fend for myself rather than be beholden to them."

"But surely they would have welcomed you." Jasper could not conceive of the lovely young woman being abandoned to her fate.

Daisy did not wish to dwell upon the painful subject. Trying for a light tone, she lifted her chin to a proud angle. "Their circumstances made it challenging to be very welcoming, and I did not wish to impose. I can assure you, my lord, being a governess is far preferable to being a poor relation."

Jasper searched her face, his ears catching the fact that there was much being left unsaid. "Did your relations by any chance have some unattractive, unmarried daughters?"

Daisy's tinkling laughter filled the small space of the carriage, causing the viscount to catch his breath over the instant pull of attraction. He studiously ignored the sensation, waiting for her reply.

"I beg leave to say that had nothing to do with the situation, my lord," Daisy insisted.

"Did you truly enjoy being a governess?" Jasper asked, curious to see how she would answer.

"Well..." Daisy hesitated, wondering how best to reply. "The children were actually not monstrous. There were four, two boys and two girls. They were varying in age from three to eight. It was very busy, to say the least."

"You were on your own with four small children?" Jasper was aghast.

Kate just barely managed to keep her gasp to herself. It was not so strange to her. She had been responsible for her younger siblings for years. Daisy cast her a sympathetic glance before turning her attention to the viscount.

"It is not so very strange, my lord. But no, I was very rarely completely on my own with the four children. Usually a maid was assigned to assist in the nursery. She would keep the baby occupied while I was busy with the children in the schoolroom. And when we went out of doors, a maid or a groom would accompany us in order to help keep the children safe. There was a small lake on the property, and I was always terrified the boys would try to go for a swim."

"Were they the rambunctious sort?"

"Very much so," Daisy said, smiling in memory.

"How long were you with that family?"

"Fifteen months."

"So you sought a position within three months of your parents' death?"

"That is correct. It was all a stressful muddle at first, as I am sure you can imagine. But when I came to terms with the situation, I decided being a governess would be the answer for me." Daisy sighed. "I never thought it would be possible, but I actually find that I miss the children."

Jasper tilted his head to examine his companion, trying to see into her thoughts, wondering how to pry the truth out of her. "How did you have the necessary qualifications?"

Now we are getting to the tricky parts, Daisy thought, as she smiled nervously. "I have received a rather excellent education, my lord," she began to explain.

Kate, who hadn't been paying much attention to the conversation but had been gazing raptly out the window, as she had never been anywhere outside of Bloomsbury, gasped suddenly. "Oh look, miss, it is the prettiest thing you have ever seen, I'm sure."

Daisy followed Kate's pointing finger and had to agree with her assessment. It was a beautiful sight. The field full of woolly, white sheep surrounded by the vivid green of the hedgerow was the epitome of bucolic charm, but for the city-born-and-bred young maid, it was a sight to behold.

Looking at the viscount to see how he was taking the interruption, she was surprised to see the look of compassion upon his face. He was watching Kate's enjoyment of the scenery with such indulgence displayed in his eyes.

"Have you truly never been outside of the city before now, Kate?" he asked, leaning forward, kindly interested in her reply.

The usually hostile Kate now smiled shyly at Jasper. "No, my lord, my family has always lived in London."

Jasper was surprised by the information. They had yet to travel very far. His parents' estate was less than a day's travel from the centre of Town. It was hard to imagine never having been outside the City. He had a new thought.

"Have you ever been outside of London, Miss Daisy?"

"Well, of course, my lord. The family I worked for spent most of their time on their country estate. I am actually still quite fascinated with the city as I have less experience with London than I do with the countryside."

"Ah, yes, of course."

Daisy mistrusted his speculative gaze and hastened to steer the conversation along the same vein, hoping the viscount would not return to wondering about her circumstances.

"What about you, my lord? Do you spend much of your time in the City or out?"

"I, of course, grew up on my parents' estate, the one to which we are travelling. My father has other properties that we visited from time to time, and he would sometimes bring the whole family to London when he would sit down in the House. But in recent years, I have spent most of my time in London. There is so much more to do in the City than there is while rusticating upon the estate."

"To be sure," Daisy nearly drawled, just imagining the type of shenanigans the handsome young lord was likely to get up to.

She watched in fascination as the viscount threw back his head and laughed heartily.

"Your sarcasm is strangely appealing, Miss Margaret Pembroke. Are you very sure you have not made your curtsy to Society? I am convinced the patronesses would be enamored with you."

"Are you funning me, my lord?"

"Perhaps a little, my dear girl. Now why do you not go back to telling me how you were so excellently educated?"

Daisy felt the blush rising in her cheeks, and she silently cursed the fairness of her complexion that gave away nearly every emotion. She braced herself, as she watched his gaze sharpening over her hesitation to answer the question.

"This should not be a difficult question, my dear," the viscount drawled.

Daisy knew his lazy tone was deceptive as his gaze remained bright, but she lifted her chin, refusing to be cowed. "I spent one year at Ponder's End with Mrs. Tyler. She was perfectly lovely, although I hated being away from home and missed my governess and parents terribly. But my parents thought it would be good for me to have the exposure to other girls, since I was the only child."

Trying not to squirm under the viscount's unblinking gaze, Daisy made an effort to keep her smile in place and unaffected.

She had not realized she was holding her breath until she let it out in a puff she had to control so it was not a gasp when Jasper finally responded.

"Intriguing, my dear," he finally offered. "I find it so curious that you would find yourself in need of employment when your childhood was so obviously idyllic."

Daisy offered a dainty shrug. "Circumstances change, my lord, surely you must be well aware of that. We would not be on this errand otherwise." Daisy decided she had told him enough for now and turned the questions on him. "Were you able to find out who will be present when we arrive?"

"No, my mother was decidedly uninformative, I must say. She was effusive, as I expected, in her delight that you would be accompanying me. She urged us to arrive with all haste."

Jasper's smile widened to reveal the dimple in his cheek. Daisy wanted to stare at it but forced her eyes away. Clearly his smiles were hardly ever genuine as the dimple so rarely peeped through. If she were not made of sterner stuff, she surmised that looking at the viscount would be enough to turn her head. As it was, despite her best efforts to remain firm, butterflies fluttered in her midsection. Studiously ignoring the ridiculous sensation, she reminded herself that this entire situation was all make believe.

"Does your mother host house parties often, my lord?"

"Oh yes, inexplicably it would seem it is one of her favorite things. She hosts them as often as my father will allow, I believe."

"So do you usually attend?"

"I used to, of course, when I still lived with them. For a time I was unsure if I was even welcome to attend. Of late my mother has started sending me invitations."

"And do you reply?" Daisy asked with a trill of laughter.

Jasper shrugged. "Usually."

Daisy tried not to be annoyed with the effort required to pull the information out of him. She was torn between enjoying the back and forth conversation and wishing he would just tell her everything she needed to know.

"Have you been to any of her parties of late?" She struggled to contain her annoyance, as she could see that it amused the wretched man.

"It has been some time since I attended. My mother seemed to be using her parties as an opportunity to try to match make, you see.

I found that it was much more ideal to have previous plans whenever she got it into her head to have another party."

Daisy's smile widened in amusement. "And now here you are, bringing your own match. Will your mother be terribly disappointed when it turns out that we will not suit?"

"It is hard to say, my dear. It will depend on how attached you allow her to get to you over the next se'ennight."

Guilt rose up in Daisy's heart. It must have been written on her features, as Jasper was quick to chuckle. "Have no fear, my dear girl. Even if my mother grows quite attached to you, she will weather the disappointment easily. It will at least give her the opportunity to redouble her efforts to match me up herself. While I am certain she shall be delighted with you, there will be one obvious flaw about you."

"And what, pray tell, is that?"

"She did not pick you out herself."

Daisy's delighted chuckle rang out in the confines of the small space before she quickly clapped her hand over her mouth. "I am so sorry, my lord, I should be containing myself, should I not? Proper ladies do not laugh so loud, do they?"

"Where do you get your ideas from? Was Mrs. Tyler terribly strict?"

"The lady for whom I was the governess had very clear rules about such things. I was supposed to be passing these instructions on to the children. No, Mrs. Tyler was lovely and did not try to crush our spirits."

"I can see why you had such difficulty being a governess. It would seem that it is not in your nature to crush the spirits of youngsters. Is that why you left the position?"

"Not exactly." Daisy did not wish to dwell on her reasons for leaving her post. "Of which school of thought do you suppose your mother is, my lord? Should I be prim and proper, as Lady Sadbury would prefer?"

"I think you need only be yourself, Miss Daisy, and you will be a success."

"Well, myself is a governess making an effort to get another position. I highly doubt that will be acceptable in your mother's drawing room." Seeing the viscount about to object to her words, Daisy hurried to interrupt. "I know what you are saying, though, my lord. You meant I should be natural, right?" At his nod, she plowed on. "That is a relief, my lord, as I suspect it would be difficult for me to prevaricate for an entire week. Now tell me, my lord, what sorts of activities do you suppose your mother has planned for us?"

Chapter Seven

"Are you getting nervous at this late stage?" Jasper stared at the lovely lady across from him. He was unsure how to manage the silly chit. She was such a contradiction. If he wasn't quite convinced that she hated untruths, he would wonder if she was lying to him. It was hard to figure her out. He watched her emotions chase themselves across her face and waited for her answer.

"Well, of course I am nervous, my lord," she declared, not bothering to hide her feelings. "I will not know anyone except you and my maid, and I am beginning to feel that we are endeavoring to defraud your parents in some way. I am wondering how I ever allowed myself to be talked into entering this charade."

Jasper grew concerned as his companion looked to be on the verge of tears, but then his admiration for her grew once more as she regained her composure. He watched in fascination as she pulled her tattered feelings back into herself and she offered him a tremulous but warm smile. "I apologize, my lord, I promise not to fall apart on you," she laughed. "But yes, I am a trifle nervous."

"You have every right to your feelings, Daisy. I can understand your being nervous. I will admit to you that I am a little nervous myself. I have a lot hanging on our success. But I am fully confident that we will be a smashing success. My parents are going to love you — I am sure of it. And if they love you, they will be quite willing to part with some of their blunt in order to aid me in my efforts to set up a proper life for you."

Jasper knew he had gone too far when he saw her tilt her head in that adorable way she had when she wanted to analyze him further.

He held his breath, knowing her inquisitive questions were to follow. He didn't have long to wait.

"How are they going to react when no relationship develops between us?"

"We already have a relationship of sorts," Jasper argued.

Jasper had to bite his lip to contain his grin as he watched her roll her eyes in exasperation. "You know what I mean, my lord," she huffed.

"I suppose I do." He laughed at her for a moment. "You mean, how will they react when they do not read any interesting announcements in the paper, correct?"

"Exactly! Will they want their money back, do you suppose?" Daisy worried.

"It is rather unlikely."

"How can you be certain?" she persisted.

"You are a worrier, aren't you, my dear Miss Daisy?"

"I have found it to be a very practical quality, Lord Seaton, I must say."

"Now I beg of you, do not go getting all starchy on me, my dear. I did not intend my question as a criticism. I merely think you ought to concern yourself a little less about certain things. I know my parents rather well, and I can assure you, they would never ask for their money back. In fact, if you break my heart, they might be inclined to give me a little more."

Jasper had to exercise considerable control over his emotions not to burst into laughter at the serious scrutiny she subjected him to. "I am beginning to wonder if your entire family is quite daft, my lord."

"No doubt we are, Miss Daisy. Be sure to have a care, although I doubt it is contagious."

Daisy began to giggle. "Mayhap it is, my lord. Very well, I will leave you to concern yourself about your parents. I shall exert myself to enjoy the experience to the fullest, whatever the marchioness might have planned for us."

Jasper was left wondering for a few moments what was going through her mind as he watched her follow Kate's gaze out the window to the passing scenery. She brought one more concern to him. "You do not suppose there is any chance your mother might have invited the Sadburys, is there?"

"As I have never heard of them, I find it highly improbable," Jasper offered, thinking to reassure her.

"That is hardly a noteworthy explanation, my lord. Until a few days ago, you had never heard of me either, and here I am, a guest in your carriage."

Jasper gazed at her nonplussed. "I do see your point. However, do keep in mind that my father is the Marquis of Abernathy. While he is not overly high in the instep, I am quite certain that neither he nor my mother will wish to associate with a toad such as Sadbury."

Daisy blinked a few times before asking quietly, "Why would you call Lord Sadbury a toad? You just said you had never heard of them, and I have told you nothing."

"If they were all that was attractive and good, you would not have left their employ."

"They were not all that horrible, certainly not bad enough to call him a toad, since you have never even met him."

Jasper gazed at her, his eyebrows elevated. "Then why did you leave them? Since you were at Miss Holstein's fine establishment hoping for another position, I am fairly certain it was not that you no longer needed the employment."

"It is really none of your affair, my lord, and has naught to do with our current adventure." Daisy's reply was prim but resolved. Jasper refrained from pressing the subject, although his curiosity ratcheted up another notch.

Jasper watched in fascination as Daisy pulled a book from her pocket and began to read. He surmised she was done with his questions for now. As she feigned interest in her reading, he studied her curiously, wondering what was going through her mind. He would allow her to evade him for now but was determined to learn her secrets.

Chapter Eight

Charlotte was surprised to open the door to her friend's frantic knocking. "Miss Holstein, do come in, whatever is the matter?"

"Oh Charlotte, hurry and shut the door. I am quite certain I was not followed, but one can never be too sure."

"I beg your pardon?" Charlotte wondered if her friend had taken leave of her senses. "What has happened to put you in such a taking?"

"Is your charge here?" Miss Holstein ignored Charlotte's question, glancing around frantically.

"Do you mean Daisy? I should say rather Miss Pembroke?"

"Yes, yes, is Miss Pembroke here? Hurry and call her, this is quite an urgent matter."

Charlotte grabbed her friend's hand and pulled her into her small, tidy sitting room. "Sit down, Jane. Should I pour you a cup of tea or perhaps something a touch stronger? You look as though you are going to fall over."

"Where is Miss Pembroke, Charlotte? This is important." Miss Holstein's fierce tone brought a flutter of nerves to Charlotte's stomach.

"She is not here. What is this about?" Now Charlotte was torn between fear and amusement. "Have you found her a position? She was quite anxious to speak with you, but you were not in your shop when she called around. I did not think you even knew she was looking for another post."

"I found out this morning by different means," Miss Holstein replied, her tone ominous, her face nervous and pinched. She took the offered seat and smiled faintly at her friend as Charlotte poured her a small glass of whiskey. "Thank you, my dear, perhaps that is just what I need."

Charlotte waited with barely restrained impatience as her friend gathered her composure. "Are you ready to explain what has you in such a taking? And how is it connected with Miss Pembroke?"

Miss Holstein placed the now empty glass on the table beside her chair, took a fortifying, deep breath, leaned toward her friend, and declared in a fierce whisper, "Your dear Miss Pembroke is in some sort of danger and must be warned immediately."

Charlotte's initial reaction was to laugh at her friend's strange dramatics, but seeing how earnest she was, she quelled the impulse and strove for logic. "Why ever would you say that? She is perfectly safe. What sort of danger do you think she is in?" Charlotte had her misgivings about Daisy's decision to accompany Lord Seaton, but she begged leave to doubt that he posed a threat to her, besides the fact that as far as she knew no one was aware of her scheme to accompany him.

"Lord Sadbury and some weasely faced friend of his visited me at my shop this morning looking for Miss Pembroke. When I expressed my surprise that she was no longer in his employ, he became quite threatening. I had no idea she had left her post with Lady Sadbury's children and was quite taken aback at the situation, but I had the presence of mind not to mention you. But as soon as they left my shop, I came here as quickly as I could, whilst making every effort to ensure I was not being followed."

Charlotte gazed at her visitor with a mixture of horror and admiration. "Did they say why they were looking for her?" she asked cautiously.

"That is partially why I am so concerned. They could not seem to agree on a reason why they were asking after her. The weasel was insisting that it was a matter of grave importance, while Lord Sadbury merely said the children missed her and he wished to hire her back. When I told them I had no idea she had left their home, Lord Sadbury became quite ugly and began threatening me if I did not tell him her whereabouts. Well, I can tell you I was mighty put out by his behavior, and I made myself quite clear on the subject. He must have realized he was not going to get any information out of me right then because he finally left and took his friend with him, but as he was going he promised to return and declared I had better come up with some ideas where she could be. I hope I have not brought trouble to your door, Charlotte, but I did not know what else to do. I do not know anything about this. Do you know what these scoundrels could want with her? She seemed like a decent young woman when I interviewed her." Now Miss Holstein, having recovered from her shock of being threatened, began to question her association with her client.

"She **is** a decent young woman," Charlotte declared, fiercely loyal. "I am grateful that you have come to me with this. Daisy came to see you several days ago to tell you she had left the Sadburys and to ask if you could arrange another position for her, but your shop was closed. I can assure you there is nothing unseemly about the situation from her standpoint. While she did not go into very much detail about why she left, I can vouch for her that she is a good person and not up to anything havey cavey. I have no idea why Sadbury would be so fierce or even why he would be looking for her. While I am sure losing their governess made them a little uncomfortable, Daisy's dealings were always with Lady Sadbury, and I am certain the lady will be able to hire someone else in no time."

Miss Holstein looked unconvinced but subsided sufficiently for Charlotte to ask for more details. By the time she had her friend's ruffled feathers soothed, she had all the information she could get out of her. When Miss Holstein was ready to leave, she took with her Charlotte's assurance that if the gentlemen returned to question her she was free to disclose Charlotte's address. She would handle their questions comfortably.

"Do have a care, though, my friend. They made me highly uncomfortable, which is why I did not wish to direct them to you."

"I will have a care, thank you, and I am certain all will be well. I appreciate your concern. I will take care of this matter smartly."

Miss Holstein left Charlotte's small house with a clear conscience and a lift back in her step, free of the concerns that had sent her scurrying there barely an hour earlier. She left a worried Charlotte in her wake.

Charlotte nibbled the end of her pen as she wondered how to word the missive she would send to warn Daisy about her pursuers. There was no guarantee it would not be read along the way, and she did not wish to give away Daisy's secrets. She could not write that her former employer was seeking her.

Dear Miss Pembroke:

I hope this note finds you well. I wished to inform you that acquaintances from your former residence have been looking for you with some rigor. Please advise.

Sincerely, Charlotte

Charlotte reread the note. She was not quite satisfied with it, but it was the best she could do. Daisy would have to make of it what she did. *If the girl was not so ridiculously independent that she kept all her secrets to herself, perhaps she would not find herself in this strange predicament,* Charlotte thought rather fiercely. Perhaps this will be a lesson to the girl to let her friends care for her a little more than she would usually allow.

Charlotte worried herself into some fidgets, but she could not come up with any explanation that would have Lord Sadbury searching for his former governess. She forced herself to set the concerns aside with a mental shrug. If Miss Holstein sends them to her, she will have the opportunity to question them herself. In the meantime, she should hurry to post the letter to Abernathy.

❧

"A letter has arrived for you, Miss Pembroke."

Daisy was surprised to hear the softly modulated voice of the Marquis of Abernathy addressing her as she crossed to the stairs.

"For me, my lord? How exciting. I do love receiving correspondence, and I did not think to receive any while I was in residence." She kept a friendly smile on her lips while her mind was whirling with questions. The only person who knew her location was Charlotte, and she strongly doubted her old governess would risk her charade by writing to her.

The marquis looked almost reluctant to pass the missive to her. His intelligent eyes, so like his son's, searched her face before he handed it over. Daisy smiled as cheerfully as possible, hoping it masked the guilt she felt over their deception.

She was having a lovely time whenever she was able to forget that she was there under false pretences. Mind you, she had difficulty putting that troublesome thought from her mind most of the time, but she really was enjoying herself quite immensely. The difficulty her conscience insisted on causing her was a small price to pay for this brief glimpse of what might have been.

The marquis looked at her expectantly as she took the paper from his hands. Unsure what he was waiting for and hoping he did not wish for her to read the note in front of him, she glanced at the writing on the front, verifying for herself that it was indeed Charlotte's hand.

"Oh, how delightful, it is from my very dearest friend. Thank you so much for ensuring it got to me, my lord." Daisy hoped that was sufficient as she turned to continue on her way up to her chamber. It was nearly time to prepare for the evening meal.

The marquis' voice stopped her once more as her foot was about to reach the bottom stair. "If you have any need of assistance, I trust you will come to me," he began, as his piercing gaze again appraised her intently. "My wife has taken it into her head to be quite attached to you, and I do not trust that my son would have the wherewithal to be able to help, should you be in any kind of trouble. So you are stuck with me to assist you, should you have the need."

Daisy looked back at the marquis with her own assessing gaze. She felt a multitude of emotions vying for her attention at his words. She was gratified by the thought that the marchioness liked her, but her pleasure was negated by the obvious fact that the marquis did not share his wife's joy at her company. And she could not abide his opinion of the viscount.

She hoped her tone would remain polite, even though she heard the coolness in it as she said, "I thank you for your hospitality, my lord, and I will keep in mind your offer of assistance should I be in need, but my friendship with Lord Seaton will ensure that it is to him I will turn first, should I find myself in trouble."

Daisy was surprised to see respect flare in Abernathy's eyes as he continued gazing at her steadily. He bowed slightly to her and left the room on a soft tread. Shaking her head over the vagaries of the nobility, Daisy began the climb to her room. She knew the marquis would never admit to how alike he was to his son. She wished she could see some way of bridging the obvious gap that existed between Jasper and his father. Pushing such thoughts from her mind, she turned her attention back to the paper in her hand. She didn't know why, but just looking at it made her nervous. She hurried up the stairs, determined to open it in the privacy of her room.

Staring at the few, sparse words Daisy felt the bottom drop out of her stomach. The worst she had feared was about to befall her. She really ought to have changed her name and found another post. But it was obviously a little late to have such thoughts at this point and she set her mind to determining the best course of action. She was still sitting at the dressing table, staring off into space, when Kate arrived to help her get ready for dinner.

Kate entered the room babbling away, so excited to be in the privileged position of lady's maid to the honored guest of the heir of the house. After a moment, she realized her mistress was not attending her. "I'm sorry, miss, is my chatter boring you? You seem troubled."

Daisy shook herself out of her troubled thoughts. "No, no, Kate, I love hearing your chatter. I am delighted to know you are enjoying yourself as much as I am. I am merely finding the rigors of a house party to be more tiring than I had expected." Plastering a convincing smile to her face, Daisy asked the maid, "What do you think I should wear this evening?"

Kate was easy to convince to return to the duties she was apparently enjoying so much. Daisy laughed despite her worries. "You certainly look as though you do not mind being my maid, Kate. Are you sure you are all right with all of this?"

"Oh miss, I am more than all right. I am enjoying myself immensely. I'm hoping that when you don't need me anymore I'll be able to get another position in a house like this. Even if I'm a chambermaid, I think it will be great fun."

Daisy was glad that she had at least one less thing to be concerned about. She allowed the girl to dress her however she wished and was glad that she was ready well in advance of the appointed time to gather. She hurried to the drawing room where she knew there was an escritoire for the guests to use. Since she had already composed the note in her head, Daisy was able to quickly pen the letter she planned to send back to Charlotte as soon as possible.

My very dear Charlotte,

Thank you so much for your note. I hope this missive finds you well. I am having a wonderful time here. The weather is lovely. We have been spending time out of doors and there is to be a dance at the end of the week.

I cannot imagine why my former acquaintances might be looking for me, but surely it cannot be so urgent that it cannot wait until sometime after my return.

With warmest regards,

Miss Margaret Pembroke

After sanding the paper and carefully folding it, Daisy went in search of the butler. "Mr. Bloom, would it be possible for this to be posted at the earliest convenience?"

"Absolutely, Miss Pembroke, I will see to it right away." The butler gestured for an attentive footman to see to the matter.

"Thank you, Mr. Bloom." Daisy was grateful to have the matter settled as well as possible under the circumstances.

Settling herself in the parlour where the houseguests gathered before meals, Daisy was doing her best not to fidget when the viscount strolled into the room. Seeing her already there, he raised his eyebrows in surprise and made his way toward her.

"You are remarkably prompt for a young lady," he commented with something resembling censure in his voice.

"I find myself remarkably hungry this evening," she offered as way of an excuse while the heat rose in her cheeks. Daisy suspected she ought not mention the state of her stomach, despite the fact that she was so nervous she doubted she would feel hungry again until this week was well behind her.

Feeling the viscount's steady gaze searching her face, she launched into a convincing dialogue on the delights she had enjoyed that day.

Jasper gazed at her with skepticism. "Until this moment, you have never struck me as the type to babble. Whatever is wrong with you?"

The colour rose in Daisy's cheeks once more, but she made every effort to maintain a neutral expression upon her face. "I am not sure what you mean, my lord."

Jasper did not wish to press her, especially as he saw that the room had begun to fill. He was worried about the chit, a thought that brought a degree of disgust to his mind. This scheme was supposed to have been simple — spend a few days in the country with his family, get his money, and go home. She was supposed to just be a tool in his effort to get what he wanted. Of course, he never wanted her to get hurt in the process, but he hadn't intended to really care about her feelings. Here he was hoping it wasn't too much for her. *Clearly I have been spending too much time with ladies of late,* he thought with disdain, he was becoming missish. He was relieved when the butler announced that dinner was served.

Being a viscount, even though they were in the country and everything was much more relaxed than at a London dinner party, he was obviously not going to be able to escort Daisy in to the table. He found himself looking at her once more to ensure she would be all right, while he left her side to escort the lady his mother was indicating with her raised eyebrows.

Daisy, intercepting his look and correctly interpreting the concern she read there, smiled and waved him away. "My lord, do be serious, I shall be perfectly fine with whomever your mother pairs me. Now get on with you."

Jasper turned and offered his elbow to a dowager countess of somewhere he could not at the moment remember, grateful that she was a chatty sort and did not require his full attention. When they got to the dining room, he was relieved to see that his mother had seated him next to Daisy. He could not monopolize her conversation for the evening, but he would be able to keep his eye on her and help her out if she needed.

ꕥ

Finally, the marchioness stood to signal for the ladies to leave the gentlemen to their port. Daisy felt as though her nerves were strung tighter than the strings of the harp in the parlour. It was sitting there for anyone to use if they so wished. The night before, Daisy had found this time between dinner and bed to be enchanting and had delighted in the games and laughter that had made the time fly by. Now all she wanted to do was be alone in her room to ponder her options.

"Do you play, my dear?" Daisy had been too preoccupied to notice the marchioness approach.

Daisy shook her head ruefully. "I am rather more conventional than that. I only play the pianoforte, I am afraid."

"That is perfectly all right, my dear," Lady Abernathy replied. "You will have all the more appreciation for my daughter's skills."

Daisy giggled over the marchioness' words. "I am sure it will be delightful to hear," she managed to reply politely.

A few minutes later, when Jasper's sister sat down behind the large instrument, Daisy discovered it was not just parental pride behind the marchioness' words. The countess played beautifully. Daisy found it mesmerizing to watch the other woman pluck the strings, bringing forth a haunting melody that filled the entire room. Emotion stung the back of her throat.

"Have you never heard the harp played before, Miss Pembroke?" Lady Abernathy asked, peering closely as a tear slipped down Daisy's cheek.

Blushing furiously, Daisy hurried to wipe the moisture away with a watery chuckle. "I have not," she admitted. "I am uncertain if I consider it a pleasure or not," she continued with a laugh.

"You must feel deeply to have it affect you so," the marchioness commented with approval as she patted Daisy's arm before bustling away to check on her other guests.

Daisy watched her circulate the room seeing to the comfort of her many guests. "Our mother is a wonder, is she not?" Daisy frowned over her lack of attention that evening. Once again she was surprised by a member of Jasper's family approaching her.

"Lady Welland, that was beautifully done," Daisy complimented.

"Thank you, but please, you must call me Elizabeth, or Bess if you would like. And if I may, I would like to call you Margaret." Jasper's sister was ready to be friends, making the guilt churn a little stronger in Daisy's belly.

"To be honest with you, I may not answer if you call me Margaret. All my friends call me Daisy."

"Very well, Daisy. How does it come to pass that you have never had the pleasure of hearing the harp being played?" Both of them turned to gaze at the instrument in question, which was now being plucked by another young lady with far less skill than Bess had demonstrated. "Well, perhaps it could not be referred to as a pleasure at the moment." They shared a quiet chuckle at the other girl's expense.

"At least she has the bravery to make an attempt." Daisy, always the peace keeper, felt the need to excuse the other girl's lack of skill.

"I would beg leave to point out that is not bravery, that is foolhardiness. But never mind about her. I would like to hear all about you. Surely you realize my brother has never asked our mother to invite anyone to one of these parties, let alone a young lady."

Now Daisy's cheeks were on fire. She looked around the room, wondering how best to handle the countess. This brought a giggle to the other woman.

"Oh, do not look so nervous, my dear. I promise I have no intention of interrogating you. In all honesty, I am delighted to have made your acquaintance. We had all despaired of Jasper ever settling down. I never thought I would see the day that he actually seems to be concerning himself about another person. I applaud you."

Once again, when a member of Jasper's family disparaged him, Daisy could not stand for it idly. "I have found your brother to be a very caring gentleman. He has even been all that is kind to my maid, who is a rather shy girl. I find he manages to make himself smaller when he speaks to her. I am not sure how he does it, since he is such a large man, but it does set her at ease a trifle."

Bess was gazing at Daisy in fascination. "You have been watching him rather closely, have you not, Miss Daisy?" she teased. "Very well, if you do not wish to tell me about yourself, and you also do not wish to hear me speak ill of my brother, let us play a game. I see my darling earl is helping to set up the table for a game of loo. Do you think my brother would be willing to make up a foursome with us?"

Jasper had just sidled up to them and thus heard his sister's question. "Are you not afraid I shall trounce you, Bessy?"

His sister stuck her tongue out at him, causing the trio to join in good natured laughter.

"It has been years since I have played, but I would love to try," Daisy exclaimed after the laughter subsided, causing both siblings to look at her as though she had two heads. "Is aught amiss?" she did not understand their dubious expressions.

"You played loo as a child?" Bess asked, her surprise making the question hesitant.

Daisy's features settled into what she hoped was a face of indifference but she feared was the look of a frightened doe. Unsure of why they were both looking at her in such a way, Daisy forced a nonchalant shrug. "Did you not learn to play as children?"

Jasper, the one who usually wanted all around him to think he was so worldly and blasé, shook his head pompously and said, his voice prim, "Our parents did not think it seemly for their children to gamble."

Daisy burst into laughter. "You are too droll, my lord. I did not have anyone to play with, so my parents spent time with me. They found the nursery games too dull after a time, so they taught me their favorite games. Of course, we played for buttons rather than money. So I would not say it was gambling precisely, but yes, I did spend many evenings of my childhood gaming with my parents."

Daisy was so pleased by the pleasant memory of her parents that she heaved a sigh. She could see from the dual looks of sympathy upon Jasper and Bess' faces that her own features had turned to melancholy. Forcing a cheerful smile to her lips, Daisy asked, "So shall we play? I fear I am rusty, and I wonder if my winning streak the last time I played was merely because my parents were cajoling a child, but I am ready to find out."

Jasper held a chair for her as she took her seat at the table. The earl was fussing with the cards and complaining good naturedly that he would prefer to be partnered with Jasper, as he was certain his wife's skills had not improved since the last time they had played.

Daisy smiled as she watched Bess swat her husband playfully. "You are not gallant, my lord," she declared with a pout as the earl wiggled his eyebrows at her. Until this moment, Daisy had thought the earl to be severe and cold, but now she realized why Jasper had declared his sister's marriage to be a love match. Of course, being a man, he had said it with such a tone of disgust. But Daisy was happy to see that, although it was not the fashion, it was still possible to witness a happy marriage. She contained the small sigh that wished to escape her lips.

She must not have been entirely successful, as Jasper turned to her with half a smile tilting his face. "They are rather disgustingly happy together, are they not? It almost gives one a toothache to look at them."

Daisy smiled back at him. "It does a heart good to see," she insisted.

"Maybe a girl's heart," Jasper teased before turning to his brother in law. "Are you going to deal or make calf's eyes at my sister all night?"

Obviously the earl was used to the viscount's ribbing, as he merely glanced at Jasper with a haughty eyebrow raised before he began to spread out the cards to the players.

Much to Daisy's surprise, the evening passed quickly. What felt like a couple minutes later, Lady Abernathy was standing to indicate the time had arrived for the guests to retire for the night. Looking around, Daisy noticed that several of the guests had already left the room.

"Thank you for a delightful evening, my lady," Daisy said to the marchioness as she was taking her leave.

"I am pleased to hear you have been enjoying yourself, Miss Pembroke. I wish you a good night."

Daisy curtsied to the room at large before making her way to her chamber.

ꟿ

"Your friend is quite delightful, my son," Lady Abernathy declared without preamble. "I do wonder at her judgment, as she is here as your guest," she began to tease before growing serious once more. "It is a wonder that I have never met her before, as she is clearly not fresh from the schoolroom."

"Her parents' death prevented her from having her Season," Jasper explained.

"Ah, that might explain it," his mother accepted. "She is very well mannered and seems comfortable with her surroundings, which is a relief. When you asked me to invite someone I had never heard of, I will admit to you I was worried she was going to be some country bumpkin you had picked up just to be annoying."

Jasper was surprised by his mother's words, and heat rose in his cheeks at realizing how close to the truth she had come. While Daisy was not a country bumpkin, he had picked her up, not to be annoying, but his motivations were not at all noble. Daisy's dislike of falsehood must be contagious; he hesitated to lie to his mother and smiled at her instead.

"I do agree with you — Miss Daisy is a delight. I am happy you are enjoying her company nearly as much as I am," he finally managed to reply.

"The only trouble is, my son, I do believe the young lady sees you too clearly. I have my doubts that she will marry you."

Jasper felt the blood draining from his head. He actually felt faint for a brief second and knew he had paled. He hated for his parents to ever be aware when they hurt him. Feeling his father's sharp gaze, Jasper held onto his composure by a thread.

"Have no fear, Mother, I can be very convincing." He allowed his lips to form into a lecherous smile, knowing full well it would shock her, wholeheartedly glad that Daisy was not here to witness this exchange.

As he expected, his mother gasped her shock, but she was not actually overly surprised. The marquis, on the other hand, kept his cold gaze steady on Jasper. "Do not speak in such a way in front of your mother," he declared firmly.

"I did not say anything untoward, my lord," Jasper replied, his chin rising to a proud angle, his flinty gaze matching his father's.

Bess' eyes flitted from face to face of her gathered family, and she uttered a nervous laugh. "Come now everyone, it is late and we are all tired. We must not be so shocked that Jasper has finally found a young lady to take an interest in. Should we not be grateful and supportive? Surely it is about time, would you not agree?"

The marquis and marchioness shared a glance before turning their twin stares of disappointment at their only son. Answering

Bess, they acknowledged her words, "You are no doubt correct, Elizabeth, it is about time." The marquis' drawl was haughty, hinting that even this the viscount could not do correctly.

Jasper knew his smile was bordering on a snarl but he couldn't bring himself to straighten it out.

"We ought to ensure his financial situation is sorted out so the poor girl does not lose interest in him," the marchioness said to her husband.

He knew he should be happy about her words, it was why they were here after all, but it felt like one more slap across the face, and he was unsure if he would be able to swallow it.

"Daisy, did you need something?" Bess asked, louder than necessary, hoping the other girl hadn't heard the exchange.

Daisy stood just inside the doorway, looking from one face to the other of Jasper and his family. "I hope I am not interrupting, my lady, I forgot my shawl when I left."

Jasper was surprised to see the generous smile gracing his mother's lips. "Not at all my dear, come right in."

Daisy scurried over to the chair she had been sitting upon, snatching up her wrap hastily, while keeping a worried eye on Jasper. He offered her a reassuring smile, but he could tell from the look in her eyes that she was not fully convinced.

"I was just heading above stairs, allow me to walk with you." The marchioness was all graciousness.

His lovely little companion, who knew nothing of the two-faced world his parents inhabited, smiled with delight over the attentions of the older woman. They bade the others another goodnight, and Jasper watched as the two women drifted from the room arm in arm.

Bess shot her brother a sympathetic glance before she took her father's arm and stole his attention so Jasper could quit the room before any more words were exchanged.

Chapter Nine

hat was that I walked into last night?"

Jasper tried to feign ignorance, but it was impossible in the face of Daisy's warm concern.

"That was my loving, maladjusted family showing their concern that you would come to your senses and realize what a terrible catch I am. The good news is I am to get the money. My mother fears you will recognize me as a terrible bargain if I am not better situated."

"Oh Jasper," Daisy began, sympathy oozing from each syllable before she caught herself on the familiarity and drew back. "I mean, my lord," she corrected herself but continued in her caring tones. "Are you all right? I am sure you are relieved about the money, but that was not exactly how you intended to accomplish it."

Jasper patted the small hand tucked into the crook of his elbow. His stomach turned over at how right it felt to have her there at his side. She was little more than a stranger he had hired to play a role, but she offered him more emotional care than anyone in his family. It would be easy to get used to. He shook himself from such a ridiculous notion. He had absolutely no interest in getting himself leg shackled. And the young woman had been quite clear that she had no intention of involving herself in any other type of association.

"I am perfectly fine. It is exactly what we came here for. I knew you were the perfect accessory."

The pained look that crossed Daisy's expressive face made Jasper feel like something that ought to be scraped off the stable floor, but it would not do to allow the chit to get overly concerned about him.

He admired her composure, as she accepted his words with a blink and turned her attention back to their surroundings.

They were taking the air in his mother's well-manicured garden. Other couples were also perambulating about the walkways. Some young ladies were sitting on the benches, giggling and gossiping. It was a tranquil scene. Jasper was almost enjoying himself. With Daisy on his arm looking around with such obvious delight, he recognized the attraction to such a gathering.

"Is it as good as you had hoped?" he asked her, careful that they were not overheard.

Her smile was as bright as the midday sun. "Oh yes, my lord, aside from worrying about you. That I would never have expected. But the party itself is a delight. And I would think your mother was absolutely lovely if she weren't so mean to you."

"You need not have any qualms about enjoying her company. I shall not consider it disloyal of you."

Daisy chuckled, and Jasper's chest tightened at the sound. "Thank you, my lord, I appreciate your offer. Your father on the other hand…" Her voice trailed off as she thought better of her words.

"Go ahead, my dear. I can promise you I shan't take offence."

Daisy's nose wrinkled endearingly. "As my host, I ought not to speak ill of him."

Jasper kept his silence, hoping she would express herself, knowing it would be amusing and light compared to most of the thoughts he had entertained about his sire.

"It is just that he makes me so nervous. How could you bear it as a boy, my lord?"

Jasper smiled his amusement. He had been right in his assessment. "I did not know any better, if you must know the truth. His coldness predates my birth, I do believe, so until I was an adult, I didn't even realize that not all noblemen were like him. My only concern as a boy was that I was unable to imitate him perfectly. I thought I would never qualify to be his heir. According to my father, I still do not, but I now realize it is for entirely different reasons."

He had tried to be light and flippant, but he must not have succeeded as his soft-hearted companion made a small noise of sympathetic distress and clutched his arm a little tighter. Jasper could not look at her for fear the warm concern in her eyes would unman him. He changed the subject away from himself.

"What exposure have you had to his coldness to make you so nervous of him? It has seemed to me that he has been surprisingly gracious whenever he has been in your company."

Daisy started. Jasper could see that she had not meant to discuss it with him. A charming pink suffused her cheeks as he gazed at her. She nibbled her lip nervously, looking at him from beneath her eyelashes. If he were with any other female, he would consider her behaviour coquettish, but this was Daisy, and he knew it was all unconscious, which made it all the more appealing.

Forcing himself to remain impassive, he raised a quizzical eyebrow. Her blush deepened, but she did begin to speak.

"A note arrived yesterday from Charlotte, and your father approached me about it while I was going up to change for dinner." Daisy lowered her voice as though she were about to reveal a dreadful secret. "I believe he might have read the missive."

Jasper tried to appear shocked but was not actually surprised, and Daisy's concerns were amusing. He tried not to smile as he responded. "What makes you think he read it? Was there anything very dreadful in the letter?"

"Well, no, Charlotte was very circumspect in her choice of words, aware that it could be read any number of times on its way to me. It was merely the way the marquis looked at me as he was giving it to me. And he offered to assist me in any way, should I require it."

"Well that was generous of him, was it not?" Jasper could not quite understand why this was causing her concern.

"A proper young lady should not have concerns for which she would need assistance," Daisy insisted, causing Jasper to throw back his head and guffaw, drawing many eyes to examine them speculatively.

"Hush, my lord," Daisy admonished, making it difficult for Jasper to obey, but he realized she was genuinely distressed by the attention directed their way, so he did his best to control his mirth.

"I do apologize, my dear, but your notions are, on occasion, quite ridiculous."

Jasper's amusement would not abate under her efforts to quell him, but he did stop laughing long enough to ask her where she came by such an idea. "Everyone has concerns, Daisy, even proper young ladies. Perhaps proper young ladies have even more concerns than others, if you think about it for a moment. What about orphans or heiresses? They can be quite proper but they would have plenty to concern them."

Daisy cast her eyes downward, realizing the sense of what he was saying. She did not want him to know about her concerns and how very improper she considered them. She would rather he think her ridiculous instead, although she hated the thought of that as well. So, she held her silence, hoping Jasper would let the subject drop. Her hopes were in vain.

"So, it seems to me that you did not want the marquis to know about your concerns. What did Charlotte write to you about? What was so urgent that it could not wait a few days until you return?"

"It is really none of your concern, my lord," she answered repressively.

"You are here as my guest — everything about you is my concern, for the next few days at least." Seeing that his words were not softening her resolve, Jasper tried a different tactic. "Come on, Daisy, I thought we were friends. Why will you not confide in me?"

Daisy was struggling to find an appropriate answer that would not require her to reveal her secrets when the butler announced that tea was ready to be served.

The smile of relief that graced Daisy's face did not reassure Jasper. "Do not think that this is over, Daisy." His parting words brought a startled look to Daisy's face, which she quickly smothered with a gracious smile as she joined the other young ladies.

Chapter Ten

Charlotte was just sitting down with a cup of tea when there was a loud banging on her door. With a shiver of dread, she went to open it.

There on her doorstep was her friend Miss Jane Holstein, accompanied by two rather rough-looking characters. One of the men had a veneer of refinement clinging to his edges, despite the ugly look in his eyes. Charlotte gripped the doorframe tightly as she waited to hear what her visitors had to say.

"I am so sorry, Charlotte, they were quite insistent on meeting you, and you did say not to concern myself about it, so I brought them here. I hope I have not caused you any trouble. These are the gentlemen who are searching for Miss Pembroke." Jane's tone expressed just how little she thought of the gentlemen in question, but she kept her words and face polite.

Charlotte did not want to invite any of them into the sanctuary of her small home and so stood her ground, holding the door tightly while she turned her attention to the men.

"What is your business with Miss Pembroke?" she asked, keeping her tone as neutral as possible. She did not want to give away any information to any of her callers.

"It is urgent business that is of a private nature, miss. We must speak with her as soon as possible." The smaller of the two, the one who looked as though he once knew what respectable was, spoke in a refined voice that had been abused by excessive drink.

"Well, Miss Pembroke is not here at the moment. She has actually left Town for a few days. If you were to call around next week, you should be able to speak with her then."

The larger of the two men growled low and menacing, making the two ladies step backward involuntarily. The smaller one cast him a quelling look before turning to Charlotte. "As I mentioned, the matter is of some urgency. Perhaps we could travel to speak with her wherever she might be found."

Charlotte knew he was making an attempt to keep his tone conciliatory, but it was not at all reassuring. "Excuse me, but I do not even know who you are. I am not about to give you my friend's direction. She will be home next week — you can speak with her then."

She was about to shut the door firmly, but the man put his foot in the way, making it impossible. Dread trickled down Charlotte's back, but she stiffened her resolve and kept her chin high.

"I apologize, miss, I did not introduce myself. I fear I have forgotten my manners in the urgency of the situation I face. I am Lord Sadbury, the Baron of Clifton. Miss Pembroke was in my employ until two weeks ago. I really need to speak with her." He made an attempt at being gracious but merely sounded as though he was growling the words.

"Why?" Charlotte asked baldly. "Are you wishing to take her back into your employ?"

Lord Sadbury looked blankly at her for a moment before he began to nod. "Yes, exactly that. My wife finds that she just cannot manage without the girl. And the children miss her, of course. Yes, we really must find her and bring her back to the children."

Charlotte could see that the baron was warming to his subject even though he was lying through his teeth. She was more determined than ever to keep Daisy's whereabouts a secret. She hoped there was some way she could prevent her young friend from returning to Bloomsbury at all. Charlotte sensed danger for the young woman emanating from these two men.

Plastering what she hoped was a convincing smile of regret onto her face, Charlotte answered the baron. "I am sorry to inconvenience you, my lord, but I cannot give you her direction. I am sure she will be happy to hear from you upon her return to Town. If you would care to leave your card, she can call on you as soon as she is back."

An ugly look crossed the man's face as he regarded her with cold anger. Fear trickled through Charlotte's veins once more. She glanced at Jane, wondering if she would be of any help should the situation get more difficult. The fear shining in her friend's eyes made her heart sink. She tightened her grip on the front door to her house.

"Once again, I apologize that I could not be of more help, but now I must bid you a good day as I have my own affairs to attend to today." With that, Charlotte pushed the door closed. She heard the men grumbling and then Jane's shrill voice before the clomp of footsteps allowed her to relax as she wilted against the door. *What has my darling Daisy gotten herself into?* she wondered as she composed another note.

My dear Miss Pembroke:

Your acquaintances called around looking for you quite enthusiastically. I assured them you would be happy to meet with them upon your return to Town, but it would seem they are disappointed by the delay. I felt certain you would wish to be informed.

I hope you are having a good time and your arrangements are coming along. I trust you will keep me apprised of any developments.

Sincerely,

Charlotte Johnston

Daisy's hand shook as the marquis handed her another note. "You look a trifle pale, Miss Pembroke, are you feeling well?"

"Quite well, thank you, my lord. Your generous hospitality here in the country has been just what I needed. I am having a delightful time. Thank you for passing this along. I should sit down to read it somewhere quiet."

"Why do you not have a seat here?" Lord Abernathy indicated the large chairs situated in front of his own desk. She was standing there, feeling so very small after he had summoned her to his library to receive this latest message from Charlotte.

"Oh no, my lord, I would not want to intrude on your space. You surely have work to do. I will just leave you in peace. Thank you so much for passing on the message." Daisy realized she was babbling but could not stop herself. She knew she could not read the message with his watchful eyes upon her no matter what it contained. She curtsied deeply and quickly headed for the door.

"My offer still stands, Miss Pembroke," the marquis called after her, his voice low but carrying.

Daisy pretended that she had not heard, almost breaking into a run in her haste to be free of the haughty man's enervating presence. Seeing that the morning room was empty, she slipped in there to have a quiet moment and examine Charlotte's latest missive.

Her hands were cold and clammy as she folded the paper back up. *What shall I do?* she asked herself rather desperately. *What could they possibly want with me? Lord and Lady Sadbury were perfectly clear when they terminated my employment that I was 'no longer welcome in their home. Surely his lordship's search for me could mean nothing but trouble. And* my *poor dear Charlotte must be beside herself with worry for me and concern for her own safety. Considering the friends the wretched man kept, who knows who had presented themselves at her house.*

Feeling tears of indecision welling in her eyes, Daisy dashed them away with an impatient hand. *Tears will be of no use to me,* she thought with disgust.

"What seems to be the trouble, my dear?" The deep voice from the doorway sent shivers down Daisy's neck. She should have known he was there; she could usually sense his presence.

Daisy had managed to avoid him for most of the day. Since their conversation in the garden the day prior, Daisy had been keenly uncomfortable in his presence. Happy for him that the purpose of their visit had been accomplished, Daisy was torn with her own disappointment that their time together was going to come to an end. She realized it was rather contradictory to avoid his presence when she was so sorry over the end to their arrangement, but she couldn't seem to make sense around the handsome nobleman.

"Naught, my lord, all is well." She told the boldfaced lie without even batting an eyelash. Much to her shame, the viscount saw through her words and merely gazed at her knowingly.

"I hate to accuse a lady of being a liar, but surely you must be jesting with me," he drawled lazily, delighted to see she was not unaffected by his presence.

She determined to tell him a version of the truth. "I am worrying about my future, if you must know."

"I told you that you had no need to concern yourself about that."

"That is easy for you to say, my lord. Your affairs have been sorting themselves out rather nicely." She could not help the waspish tone of her voice.

"Do you not trust me to keep my word?"

Daisy searched the viscount's warm gaze to find the meaning behind his words. She was covered in confusion, unsure how to answer. "Of course, I trust you. I know as a gentleman you will do all in your power to keep your word. But we have not yet come up with a plan, and I am unable to stop myself from worrying."

It was now Jasper's turn to search Daisy's trembling gaze. "I think there are things you are leaving out, my dear. Why do you not confide in me? I truly believe that two minds are better than one. If you share your troubles, they will be lessened."

Daisy was not yet desperate enough to confide her troubles to the rake before her. He might know about trouble, but it was of a whole different variety than she was dealing with. That thought brought a smile to her face.

"Thank you, my lord, you are perfectly correct." She stepped forward and linked arms with him. "Now I must confide in you that part of my troubles is that I am perfectly famished. Do you suppose your mother will be serving a luncheon today?"

Jasper looked as though she had just slapped him. Daisy was unsure what could have caused such a reaction, but could not bring herself to ask.

"You really do not trust me, do you?" he asked, his lips pinched into a thin line.

"Sure I do," Daisy replied promptly, her eyes widening in surprise over his strong reaction.

"If you did, you would tell me why Charlotte is writing to you and why you look so worried about it."

"I did tell you what is worrying me," Daisy insisted.

"In the very vaguest sense, not in any way that is any different than before," Jasper insisted. "You look far more concerned than you did when we were still in London, before we set out on this adventure. Something has happened, and I fail to understand why you will not tell me about it."

"Why should I confide in you, my lord, when you have not seen fit to do so with me?"

Jasper stilled. The confirmation that she was keeping something from him was not nearly as satisfying as he had expected it to be. He watched Daisy with sad, serious eyes. "Very well, Miss Daisy, I will tell you whatever you would like to know. But not here. Let us go riding — we can bring along a groom to keep it all perfectly above board," he concluded, seeing the protest that was forming on her face.

"Did I pack a riding habit?" Daisy asked herself out loud. "It has been an age since last I rode. I wonder if I shall remember how it is done."

This brought laughter to them both, breaking the terrible tension that had held them in its grip. "Once you have learned you can never forget," Jasper assured her. "And I am absolutely certain there was a habit in that mountain of clothing you packed for our week here."

Daisy's impish grin was a welcome sight, and Jasper sucked in his breath, eager to be off with her. "How quickly can you be ready?"

Daisy tossed him a saucy glance as she teased him. "If I were a proper lady, it would no doubt take me an hour to get ready, but since I am not, I could probably meet you by the front door in about fifteen minutes."

Jasper rolled his eyes at her. "I will believe that when I see it. Should I have a maid bring you a tray? You did mention how hungry you are." He knew she had been trying to distract him, but he didn't feel right making her miss a meal if she really was hungry.

"Thank you for thinking of it, my lord, that would be a lovely idea, but you had best allow me twenty minutes in that case," she replied as she dashed off to make her preparations.

True to her word, Daisy met the viscount at the front door just as the clock chimed the hour, exactly when she had promised to be ready.

"You are a rare woman, Miss Pembroke," Jasper complimented as he handed her up onto the horse he had arranged for her use.

Daisy felt like a cat with the cream, ready to preen under the unexpected attention. Before she could purr, she forced her attention to the task at hand, gaining control over the spirited mare the viscount had selected for her ride.

"She is a beauty, my lord, but perhaps a trifle too energetic for my lack of experience," she complimented and worried all in the same breath.

"You shall be absolutely fine," Jasper soothed. "She has perfect manners, have no fear."

Daisy was delighted and pleased to find that the viscount was correct when he said you never forget how to ride a horse. Even though the young mare pranced and fidgeted, Daisy was able to gain control of her mount, and they set off in the direction the viscount indicated, a groom following discreetly in their wake.

"I forgot how different everything looks from the perspective of a horse's back," Daisy commented, looking around at the passing scenery with shining eyes and prettily flushed cheeks.

Looking at her made Jasper tighten his grip on the reins. His horse objected, reminding the viscount to relax. Regaining control, he brought the gelding alongside Daisy, and they rode along in silence for a few companionable moments.

Once they were well away from the house, Jasper reopened the conversation they had not finished. He was reluctant to open up so completely to another person but was well aware that Daisy would not confide in him if he did not trust her with his own secrets.

"When I was fourteen, the headmaster at Eton accused me of cheating," he began in a low, serious tone, feeling Daisy's warm gaze boring into his face but refusing to meet her eyes. "I had most certainly not cheated and was highly offended by the accusation and refused to defend myself. In my opinion, at the time, a Seaton of Abernathy would never sink so low as to cheat, and therefore, the accusation was ludicrous. I expected my parents to be of the same mind. They were not. Ever since then, I have done my best to live down to their low opinion of me."

"Oh Jasper, I am so very sorry!" Daisy's soft heart bled for the young man he once had been. And for the pain that he so obviously still carried for the harm his parents had done to him. "Do you have any idea why the headmaster made such a ridiculous accusation?"

"There was a sudden and marked improvement in my school accomplishments. Apparently, with my previous academic progress the only plausible explanation was cheating. No one thought it possible that I was capable of making such achievements on my own."

"That is why you were so very angry the other night when I entered the room. Your parents were once again accusing you of not being able to do something on your own, like find and keep a lady's affections."

"How could you tell I was angry? No one else seemed to notice."

Daisy shrugged shyly. "I know you." Seeing he was about to object, no doubt thinking that his family ought to know him even better than she did on only two weeks acquaintance she explained, "Perhaps not having known you all your life gives me a clearer perspective. And we are allies, my lord, which does alter the situation, would you not agree?"

"I would wholeheartedly agree," he answered immediately. "Which is why I am insistent that you must share with me what is troubling you."

Daisy sighed in defeat; she would have to tell him everything. "I hardly know where to begin." There was so much she had not told him. But there was not time, and she doubted he was looking to hear her entire history. He was asking about her most recent troubles, she supposed. The ones that could impact him if Charlotte was not able to prevent Sadbury from coming to Abernathy in search of her.

"I have received two missives from Charlotte. It would seem my former employer is searching for me."

"And why does this trouble you? Perhaps they are wishing to offer you your old position."

"Perhaps, but that is rather unlikely. Our parting was not the most amicable."

"Are you afraid of them?" Jasper asked the question with a tone of voice Daisy had never heard from him before. Gone entirely was the rebellious rake who was forever feigning boredom. In that moment, for the first time in what seemed like eons, she felt as though she could lay all her burdens down for someone else to carry for a while. It was a heady sensation, tears sprang to her eyes. It took a supreme effort not to bend over and wail her grief and worry. Nonetheless, she pulled herself together, again hoping to keep as many details as possible to herself.

"I am afraid of what a mess they will cause for you and our adventure if they find me here and inform your parents that they are searching for their former governess."

Jasper shrugged. "Do not trouble yourself over such a trivial matter, my dear. Being a governess certainly does not put you beyond the pale, as I have pointed out to you on more than one occasion. It would be a singular experience for my parents, but I can assure you, considering their opinion of me, I am certain they would think it quite fitting."

Daisy's concerns had been making her feel as though she might never laugh again, but to her surprised delight, the viscount's words caused her to pitch into a fit of giggles. When she was able to catch her breath, she could not help saying, "Oh my lord, you are a complete hand. I so wish I could deny your words, but unfortunately I heard what your parents said the other night. It is quite possible you are correct in your assessment. They might even welcome my profession in the hopes that a governess might be able to keep you in line." The ridiculousness of this notion sent her off in more gales of laughter.

The viscount examined her features as she settled down from her mirth. "You are still concerned over something, though, are you not?"

"I fear that I am. While we have laughed over your parents and their potential acceptance, I will admit that it does still concern me." Daisy sighed. "But I am particularly concerned over why exactly Lord Sadbury would be searching for me. He never paid me any mind. Of course, he could be searching on behalf of his wife, but she hardly cared about me either. The children loved me, but even they were not so attached to me that they would have any trouble finding another governess to take over. Why would they be searching for me? It strikes me as rather ominous."

Jasper searched her eyes to gauge the depth of her worry. He found himself reaching out to cover her hands where they held the reins tightly. "Are you afraid?" he asked again, shocked at the thought. What he knew of this young woman boggled at the idea that she could be in fear of someone. She trembled beneath his touch.

Daisy smiled at him. "My lord, of course I am afraid. I am a woman on her own, trying to make my own way. Sadbury has the power to harm my ability to find another position. Lady Sadbury wrote me a lovely recommendation despite the fact that we agreed that I would leave their employ. If they are no longer willing to vouch for me, it could cause me a great deal of difficulty."

"My dear, after this week, I have a strong feeling that you will not be searching for another position. Your destiny is not to be a governess." He had meant it to be reassuring , so he was unprepared for the anger he saw instantly radiating from her narrowed eyes.

She was fiercely cold in her indignation. "I am quite sure that we agreed before we embarked upon this adventure that you were not going to be having any impact on my life. You cannot change my future, my lord. This is one week out of my life in which I get to play at being a member of your Society. I will be returning to my independent life when this is over, and you will not be altering that."

Jasper's cheeks heated as though she had slapped him. "I can assure you I was not trying to control you, Miss Pembroke. I was trying to be kind, which would seem to be a concept that is foreign to you." He paused for a moment, catching himself in his seemingly righteous anger and stared at her, trying to see inside the workings of her head. "Has no one ever tried to look out for you before? Is that why you are so dead set against accepting assistance from anyone? Why would you not want my help to make your life a little easier?"

Daisy took a deep breath, taken aback by the vehemence he exhibited. Chagrin and concern chased each other across her features. "I do apologize, my lord, I did not wish to be offensive. You may be right about my independence being a liability at times. It is why I am in the circumstances in which I find myself." She paused, searched his eyes for his sincerity, and then fixed her eyes back on the road ahead. "Thank you for your generous offer of helping me. I know you have extended it before, and I will be happy to consider accepting if you have any actual, concrete ideas. I will not allow my pride to get in the way, and I will make every effort to reel in my independent tendencies as well."

She tried for humor, and although it fell a little flat, Jasper smiled at her effort. "Very well, my dear, I accept your apology and will exert my efforts to come up with some ideas, but let us first deal with the matter at hand. You are still anxious despite agreeing to consider accepting my help." His tone was dry over the bland nature of her acceptance. He continued, "What troubles you, lass?"

Daisy blushed fiercely, unable to meet his eye. "Are you absolutely certain you cannot be persuaded to drop this matter, my lord?"

Now there was absolutely no way Jasper was going to allow the matter to drop. "Quite convinced, my dear, now get on with the telling. It will not get any easier by putting it off any longer."

"I cannot feel easy about Sadbury searching for me because of the reason for my departure." She took another deep, shuddering breath while Jasper nodded at her encouragingly, trying not to allow his impatience to show at her obvious reluctance. "Lord Sadbury often had disreputable friends about the house. I made every effort to keep the children and myself away whenever he was entertaining. We would usually remain in the school room and the nursery, but one time his friends stuck around for several days."

Daisy's voice had become so low that the viscount had to strain to hear her words over the plodding of the horses' hooves. He now had a terrible feeling he knew where this tale was going, and an uncharacteristic rage began building in the pit of his stomach. He forced himself to wait for her to tell the rest of the story, knowing it would do her good to get it off her chest. Jasper had a feeling that she had not told anyone the true reason for leaving her employer.

"The children were so restless after being cooped up for so long. They could no longer be contained. The servants had told me that the master and his cronies had ridden to the neighboring estate for some hunting, so I was certain the way would be clear for me and the children to play in the gardens for a little while." Another shuddering breath was required before she continued. "One particularly unpleasant character returned early. I never did find out why. He claimed he just wanted some sport with me. I believed his intentions were violent and unsavory. When he accosted me, I gave him a black eye and kicked him in a particularly sensitive spot. This, of course, set the children to crying, and the maid and I quickly bundled them back to the nursery while he was bellowing vile things behind us."

Jasper let out the breath he had been holding in a great rush. He was relieved beyond all belief to hear that she had managed to extricate herself from the untenable position. "Were you too unnerved to see that garden ever again? Is that why you left?"

Daisy's incredulous stare was answer enough. "How ridiculous, my lord. I was actually somewhat proud of my handling of the situation. With the maid and the children standing by, in hindsight I realize he would not have been able to accomplish much, whatever his intentions were, and I feel that even if I had been alone, the methods I employed would have made good my escape. The trouble came when the dastard told Lord Sadbury. I was called to his library and put on the spot in front of the man. It was humiliating and unnecessary. I informed Lord Sadbury of my opinion of him and his employ in no uncertain terms. I left the next day. It was only Lady Sadbury's intervention that allowed me to leave in some degree of comfort. She arranged for my transport and wrote me a letter of recommendation so that I would be able to find another position. I am absolutely certain Sadbury is not searching for me to ask me to return. He may be a foolish rapscallion, but even he is not that dense."

Once again Jasper realized she was trying to lighten her fear through humor, but he also heard the underlying worry her words tried to hide. The foolish thought went through his head that he would like to put his arms around her and offer her the warm comfort of a hug. He could just imagine how well she would take that. He reached out and squeezed her hand again.

"I promise you, you will be fine. I will not abandon you to your fate. Whether you want certain types of assistance from me or not, I will not leave you to be terrorized." He paused for a moment, seeing that she was looking at him expectantly. He wished to offer further assurances. "I am fairly certain he will not have the temerity to call here, at any rate. You have met my father. He has been at his most relaxed here in his own home, but his reputation amongst the *ton* is such that I can assure you a baron of no note will not be calling unannounced."

Finally Daisy's laughter was sincere. "I never would have thought there would be reason to be happy that someone is an arrogant curmudgeon. Thank you, my lord, I do find that to be strangely reassuring. Now I only have to concern myself with what I shall do once I return to Bloomsbury."

Jasper felt a strange twist in the region he suspected was his heart. "We shall think of something, Daisy," he promised her solemnly. "I shall make sure nothing happens to you."

Daisy's smile revealed her gratitude combined with her disbelief. She did not bother saying a word in denial. Instead she expressed her gratitude. "My lord, I can hardly fathom it, but I feel profound relief after laying my burdens bare. Thank you so much for insisting that I tell you my secrets. I do not know why you are not more successful with your life, my lord, as it strikes me that you are always right. Does it not become tedious?"

Jasper laughed over her words. "What makes you say I am not successful? Perhaps my life is exactly how I planned it to be."

Daisy lifted her eyebrow in an almost exact imitation of the marquis' sardonic inquisition. "My lord, do you expect me to believe you planned to be in a position to have to trick your parents into giving you money? Money that by rights will be yours one day anyway, so it is rather ridiculous that you have to connive to get it."

Jasper's heart swelled at her lecture combined with her defense of him. Clearly the lady respected him despite the questionable choices he had made in his life. It was a heady thought. Very few respected much about him, other than his skills at the card table or in the ring. He had not even realized he wished to be respected for more than that. Certainly he had never received such sentiments from his family. It made her all the more delicious. His appreciation for her grew as he contemplated her. He did not bother contradicting her words. She would never be able to understand his reasons for doing just as she had described. But then when he contemplated her own fierce independence, he thought perhaps she would. He would think on it some more before he indulged in any more confidences.

Daisy's small sigh was the only indication that she did not fully look forward to complying with her following words. Her smile was cheerfully delightful as she said, "We ought to return to the house, my lord. The hour is advancing, and I should be getting myself ready for the evening meal. Did I understand correctly that this evening there is to be a ball?"

Jasper smiled at her enthusiasm increasing dramatically as he nodded his acknowledgement of her words. "Yes, my dear, your understanding was correct. The marchioness has invited some of the gentry from the area to join us as well. That is why we were left to our own devices for the afternoon. She and her staff have been absorbed in the preparations."

"How perfectly marvelous," she crowed. "I have never been to a ball."

"Do you know how to dance? Should we take a few minutes for me to show you some of the steps?"

"Thank you for the kind offer, my lord, but yes, I do know how to dance. Not the waltz, of course, because that had not yet made its way to our shores when I was a girl, but the country dances I know quite well. Mind you, I will be rather rusty, but if you would be kind enough to lead me out, I do not think I will disgrace you."

"I think there is still much you have not told me," Jasper complained as they neared the stables to return their mounts.

Daisy's tinkling laughter sounded from behind him, but she did not offer any further explanation.

Chapter Eleven

"The witch is lying." Lord Sadbury spat on the floor of the rough tap room he and his henchman had retired to after their fruitless search for the girl.

"What're you gonna do guv'nor?" Elton scratched his greasy head absently as he watched the baron seething beside him. "I have a few skills what could make her talk." The large man rubbed his hands together in anticipation of how much he would enjoy extracting the information.

Lord Sadbury had not yet sunk to that level. "We are not going to torture anyone," he declared, unsure how he had found himself in this position. He had been an honorable man at some point, he was sure. Shaking his head, it was of no matter now. He had to find the girl.

They were joined by another man, this one more finely dressed and far more sophisticated than Sadbury would ever be. "Did you manage to discover anything?" he asked, his voice hard and cold as his diction declared his wellborn ancestry.

Sadbury shook his head dully, his eyes disclosing his fear, despite his efforts to remain composed.

"Well then it is lucky for you that I figured you would be incompetent and set someone to watch the woman's place. She sent a note advising the girl of our search for her. I have her direction. She is at Abernathy. Do you suppose the marquis has need of a governess?" He paused and allowed a mirthless laugh to fall from his lips. "Or perhaps the chit has decided to find a different form of employment. Mayhap my attentions gave her a taste for exploration." His leer was unnerving, even to his companions.

Sadbury swallowed the lump in his throat, despairing of the wretched moment that had brought him into contact with the lecherous nobleman before him. "What do you intend to do, my lord?"

"We," he said with deceptive, gentle emphasis, "are going to find and question the girl. We need to know what your precious Miss Pembroke knows. And if need be, we are going to eliminate the threat she poses."

Sadbury couldn't even swallow now and could barely speak around the despair choking him. "You aren't going to kill the girl, are you?" He tried to gather the courage to have a backbone. "I do not know as that I would be able to allow it, my lord."

The devilish man before him laughed wickedly. "You do not think you could allow me to do as I wish? I hardly think you would be able to stop me, you miserable toad. Now come along, we need to be on our way to Abernathy."

"We cannot go to Abernathy, my lord. We truly ought to follow that woman's advice and wait a couple days until she returns."

The steady, cold gaze of the other man settled on the baron, and he fought the desire to fidget under his stare. "I have no desire to wait. We need to get this matter sorted immediately. I am fairly certain I was invited to a soiree at Abernathy this week. There is no trouble whatsoever about turning up there." Turning to Elton he said, "You will not be welcome, I am sure." He then turned back to Sadbury. "But you should be able to pass as a potential guest. Did you bring something better to wear than what you have on? It would not do to turn up in front of the marchioness looking like you have been working in a barnyard."

Sadbury felt the heat rising in his cheeks and bristled at the man's words. The other man always looked as though he had just left the gentle ministrations of his valet moments before, no matter what he was doing. *It is one more reason to hate the man,* the baron thought as he looked down at his own rumpled appearance and grimaced. "Aye, I have other clothes with me, but I really must protest, my lord. I do not feel comfortable arriving unannounced at Abernathy. Surely you are aware of the marquis' reputation. I cannot think he will take it lightly if we arrive and inconvenience him while his wife is entertaining, much less if we make an attempt to carry off one of her guests."

"You shall have to be particularly persuasive, then, will you not, Sadbury?"

The blood drained from Sadbury's face, and it pooled in his feet as he began to sweat. He discovered he was more afraid of his companion than he was of Abernathy. Wondering if it would be worth surviving this experience, he swallowed painfully and then took a gulp of the brown liquid Elton had poured into his glass, grateful that the ruffian had not abandoned him yet.

The wellborn man stood, signalling it was time to be on their way. As they stepped onto the street, it crossed Sadbury's mind that perhaps he should throw himself beneath the hooves of the next equipage that passed them by. He realized he was too cowardly to take that way out. He followed along in the wake of other man as he took off quickly and haughtily.

ᘓᘐ

Charlotte had no desire to even approach the door when she heard a loud knocking.

"Charlotte, it's me, Jane Holstein, could you please open the door? I am alone."

The words did not motivate her overmuch. She was unsure how she could face the woman she had thought was her friend.

"Please, Charlotte, I really need to explain to you. I know you are probably quite angry with me, and I cannot say that I blame you, but could you please hear me out?"

With a resigned sigh Charlotte wrenched open the door, peered around quickly before grabbing her guest by the arm, pulling her into the house, and then banging the door closed forcefully and barring it shut.

"What do you want, Jane?" she asked, weary all of a sudden. "It has been a trying few days, and I do not think I have it in me to make small talk."

"I came to apologize, Charlotte. I know I should not have brought Lord Sadbury here, but I did not know what else to do. He and his friend were quite insistent that they needed to speak with

Miss Pembroke. While they were in my office, I did not feel so threatened by them until after I had given them your address. By then it was too late. I would have sent a message to you, but they planned to come straight away, so it would not have arrived in time. And then they insisted that I accompany them. I will admit to you that I was terrified. I was so afraid they were going to become violent with us when you refused to give them Miss Pembroke's direction. I still do not know how you mustered up the gumption. I can tell you, I would not have been able to stick to my resolve as well as you did."

Charlotte smiled wanly at her friend's compliment. "While I was nervous for myself, I am terrified of what they might want with Daisy. I absolutely could not tell them where she is, and I hope that by warning her about them she will be able to find somewhere else to go instead of coming back here. If they are going to be returning to speak with her, I would rather neither she nor I are here when they turn up."

"Do you think she has somewhere else she could go?"

Charlotte looked at her friend with cold assessment. "I do not blame you for bringing those cretins to my home, but I do not think I will entrust any more information into your care. I am sure you will understand."

Miss Holstein's cheeks burned with her humiliation. "I do understand, Miss Johnston, and I appreciate your generosity in accepting my apology. Is there anything I can do to assist you and Miss Pembroke?"

Charlotte had never been one to hold a grudge, and she wasn't about to start at this point in her life. She eased up on the coolness of her replies, but she would never confide in her friend when Daisy's safety was at stake. "Thank you for your offer, Jane. I am sorry to seem so angry with you. I know you were put in an untenable situation. If I can think of anything you can do to help, I will let you know, but at this point I am afraid I do not know what to do. I do not know where either of us will go. I cannot upend my life on a moment's notice." She nibbled her finger as she worried about the problem.

Miss Holstein looked at her helplessly. She had a few ideas, but she realized she would not be able to help. Charlotte was right not to share the information with her. It was safer for all of them. She sighed. "It is best if you can stay angry with me for now, Charlotte. Then I will be able to honestly tell them when they return that you would never trust me with your whereabouts after I took them to see you."

Charlotte found she was able to smile at her friend after that. "Would you care for a cup of tea before you go?"

"Thank you, my dear, but it seems to me that you have rather more on your plate than you need. It would be better if you do not have to entertain company as well. Besides, in case either one of us is being followed, it be much more convincing if I am not seen to be staying overly long."

Charlotte blanched. "Do you really think you were followed? Oh good heavens, I posted a letter to Daisy as soon as those cretins left here. It never even crossed my mind to worry about being watched."

Jane tried to soothe her friend. "I am probably being overly dramatic. You need not worry. They walked with me back to my office, quarreling the whole way. I can safely say they were not watching your house whenever you sent your letter."

Charlotte was unconvinced but did not press the matter, merely escorting her guest to the front door and shutting it firmly behind her. When she was once more alone, she sank into the nearest chair and wracked her brain for ideas what to do next.

"The only good thing that I am sure of is that Abernathy is well guarded. She shall be safe as long as she is there. And Lord Seaton, as foppish as he may appear to be, seemed able to protect her should the need arise." Charlotte was aware that it was a sign of a troubled mind to be speaking to oneself, but she could not seem to stop herself. "So I am left with trying to figure out how to protect her and myself when she is done with Seaton." Charlotte sighed and applied herself to coming up with attainable ideas.

Chapter Twelve

Daisy smiled at Kate in the mirror as she put the finishing touches to her deceptively simple hairstyle. "You have worked wonders, Kate. I barely recognize myself."

Kate blushed bashfully. "Get on with you, miss. You would be beautiful wearing a burlap sack and your hair in pigtails. It's easy to make you look nice, since you are so lovely to begin with. And these gowns. I have never seen such beautiful garments, have you, miss?"

"Not in a very long time, Kate. I feel like a very lucky girl to be sure."

"Are you nervous about tonight, miss? I just felt you shiver."

Daisy did not wish to burden her young friend with her woes. She searched for a reasonable explanation that would also be true. "I have never been to a ball, and there will be many more guests here than usual. I worry that it has all been going too well up to now and that something will happen to reveal that I do not really belong here."

Ever loyal, Kate gasped. "Of course you belong here, miss. You are just as deserving to be here as any one of those hoity toity lords or ladies. Just because you don't have a title don't, I mean, doesn't mean you don't belong in their company. Everyone can see you're Quality."

Now it was Daisy's turn to blush. "Thank you for your expression of confidence, Kate. Are you having a fine time? Are the other maids treating you well?"

"Oh yes, Miss Daisy, I am having a very fine time. The other servants are ever so nice. We have our own parties while you all are having yours. There are some handsome footmen who sure know how to dance."

Daisy laughed as her maid's face took on a dreamy cast. "Do make certain you do not lose your heart to any of those young men, Kate, my dear."

"My heart is in no danger, Miss Daisy, I am merely having a good time for the first time in my life. I have my head solid enough on my shoulders, don't you worry none about that."

"Very well." She stood and stepped back from the looking glass, endeavoring to see herself from all angles. "Is anything out of place, Kate? Will all our stitches hold, do you suppose?"

Kate gasped teasingly. "Are you calling mine and Charlotte's skilled efforts into question, miss?"

Daisy laughed and answered drily. "I rather think I had a hand in some of these gowns, and it is my poor skills that are being questioned as well."

Kate grabbed Daisy's hand as she twitched to and fro. "Stop your fidgets, miss. Everything is in its proper place, you look lovely, all the stitches will hold, you are going to have a lovely evening, and all will be well. Now get on with you. I know you hate to be late, so you had best be getting along."

It was exactly the right thing to say. Daisy's eyes flew to the clock on the mantel. She grabbed the shawl Kate was holding out for her and dashed for the door with barely a backward glance.

The first person Daisy saw when she entered the drawing room was Jasper. He was standing by the mantle holding a small glass of amber liquid, talking with his brother in law, the earl. Her breath caught in her throat. He really was a most deliciously handsome man, with his high cheekbones, firm jaw, and that stubborn lock of chestnut hair that always threatened to tumble onto his forehead. She had been trying studiously to ignore her attraction since she met him, but it just snuck up on her and could not be denied. She thought rather absently that she hoped her feelings were not displayed on her face for all to see. She dragged her eyes away from him just to be safe. They collided with Lady Bess' watchful gaze.

Bess smiled and sidled up to Daisy. "You look lovely this evening, my dear. I love that colour, it suits you perfectly. In fact, if I recall properly, I had a gown in that same colour for one of my first Seasons, but it certainly did not suit me as well as it does you."

Daisy felt the colour ebb and flow on her face at the countess' words. She made every effort to remain impassive despite her desire to run and hide. She decided to brazen it out. "Thank you for your kind words, my lady. It is one of my favorite gowns as well. You are looking breathtaking this evening, if I may say so, my lady. You must have been extremely popular during your Seasons."

Seeing the countess' positive reaction to her words, Daisy continued in the same vein. "Did you become betrothed to the earl during your first Season or did you have the opportunity to enjoy multiple Seasons?"

"Oh I lead the earl on a merry chase, to be sure," was her reply as she flashed her dimples in a delighted smile. "Before I ever set foot in London for my first Season, I made my parents promise me that I could have a second. I told them I wanted to have fun the first year and then settle down to make a decision during my second Season. I was right to do so, although for a time I worried that I would pass up certain opportunities. Some of the gentlemen did not wish to be dallying in the City any longer than necessary. And some of the ladies I became friends with did not have the luxury of being able to postpone their choice, so they were no longer there the following year. But I did not regret my decision. I did have a wonderful time during both my Seasons."

"What was the best part?" Daisy hoped she did not sound too eager. She did not want it to become overly obvious that she pined for a Season herself, nor that she had never had one.

Bess did not seem to notice that there was anything amiss. She was more than happy to reminisce about the happy memories. "Oh, it would be difficult to pinpoint what I enjoyed the most. I would not say it was the Marriage Mart. At first I found it terribly droll that some of the gentlemen thought my declaration that I would not make a decision during my first Season to be a challenge of some sort. There were various gentlemen who vied for my attention, who made every effort to change my mind. Some were most insistent. I found that to be a trifle distressing. The very best part was the dancing, I would say. Meeting so many lovely people and attending a different entertainment every evening, and sometimes during the day too, was far too diverting. Oh and the theatre, that is still one of the best parts about going to London. Now as a married lady, the Season has an entirely different aspect. I am undecided about which is better. Of course, being out of the Marriage Mart makes it far less fraught, to be sure." Bess laughed for a moment. "But enough about me, tell me what has been your favorite?"

Daisy blinked in surprise at her words. Did the lady not realize she had not had her own Season? She was just opening her mouth, trying to come up with an explanation that would not embarrass either of them, when she heard a voice just behind her shoulder.

"There you are, my dear, I was wondering where you had gotten to." Daisy had been far too engrossed in the countess' tales to notice Jasper's approach. Now the usual prickles on the back of her neck whenever the viscount was near were making themselves known with a vengeance, and she had to struggle to suppress the frisson of awareness that threatened to shiver her spine.

Pasting a relaxed smile to her lips, Daisy turned to Jasper saying, "Your sister and I were engrossed in conversation. I apologize if I was supposed to be somewhere."

"Not at all, my dear, I was just longing for your company." Daisy blushed at Jasper's flirtatious words, which made Jasper grin before he asked her, "Are you acquainted with the Viscount of Rosemeade, Lord Jack Worth and his lovely wife, Susan?"

Daisy blinked and struggled for composure, grateful that Jasper's casual attitude had caused him to leave out her name in the introductions. Jack looked just like his father. Daisy would have recognized him anywhere, even though it had been most of her lifespan since she had seen him. Obviously, she had changed significantly. There wasn't an ounce of recognition in his gaze. Daisy's smile felt a trifle crooked, but she did her best. "How do you do?"

"It is a pleasure to make your acquaintance," Lady Worth said with enthusiasm. "My husband has been friends with Lord Seaton since they were boys. We have quite despaired of him ever meeting someone sufficiently appropriate to introduce to his family and friends. You shall have to tell us all about yourself and how the two of you met, and most especially how you managed to convince him to leave behind his bachelor ways long enough to bring you to a house party."

Daisy kept her smile in place through sheer strength of will. Her eyes flicked to Jasper's gaze for a second to see how he was taking his friend's wife's words. From the lady's tone, Daisy was unsure if she were in earnest, whether she were teasing Jasper, or if she were instead sensing there was something amiss with Daisy and Jasper's relationship. She decided to take Lady Worth's words at face value and answered politely. She had no intention of revealing anything about her own history, and she hoped to keep this conversation brief.

"There is very little to tell about myself, my lady. I have lived a rather dull life up until now. Lord Seaton and I struck up an unlikely friendship when we met quite by accident on the street in London. When we realized we were each the only ones we knew who abhorred blancmange, we just knew we had to be friends."

Jasper was proud of her handling of the situation. He could tell she was uncertain about Susan's question, but she managed it with aplomb. Her reply was perfect. He felt like applauding, but managed to contain his reaction to grinning like a simpleton at her. It crossed his mind that he probably looked like a fool in love. But that was to their advantage, he supposed, as long as he managed not to actually hand his heart over to the chit. Their eyes met once more, and he wondered if he might have already done the foolish deed.

He watched in wonder as the group around Daisy oohed and aahed over her words. Lady Worth's question must have been sincere as she seemed to accept Daisy's answer happily. They all began pelting her with questions, but they barely waited for her to respond. Everyone was laughing and talking over one another. Jasper felt rather helpless watching the scene unfold. He wished he could protect her from the attentions of his family and friends, but there was naught that could be done. In fact, it seemed as though Daisy did not wish to be rescued. She looked at him with a grin and her face aglow with delight. He was relieved to see that she had gotten over her moment of discomfort. The desire to take her in his arms and kiss that smiling mouth surged anew, and he turned away momentarily.

His father's eyes were boring into him. Jasper was surprised that he had not sensed the marquis' attention. It was rarely a good thing, and he had developed a sixth sense about it as a form of self preservation as a child. Jasper lifted his eyebrow in inquiry, smiled slightly, and lifted his glass in salute. The marquis' face remained inscrutable as he nodded in acknowledgement and then turned to speak to someone who had just hailed his attention.

Once again Jasper congratulated himself on the brilliant idea of bringing Daisy to accompany him to his mother's house party. She was a hit with everyone she met. He wondered if it was a skill born of being a governess that she was able to sail so serenely through the social gauntlet or if it was a skill she had learned during that mysterious childhood of hers. He resolved to solve the mystery of his little friend, the governess.

Despite the commotion around her, Daisy had witnessed the exchange of glances between Jasper and his father. It bothered her that there was so little warmth between the two men. It was very different with Jasper's sister and their parents. While the marquis would never be called a gregarious man, there was certainly much more warmth between him and his daughter. She wondered if it would be possible to mend the rift between father and son. Daisy would give anything to have her parents back; she hated to see someone throwing away the opportunity to enjoy their family. She pushed the thoughts to the back of her head as her attention was again demanded by one of the other guests.

There were so many more people this evening than on previous days. The marchioness had outdone herself. While Daisy suspected it would be far from a crush by London standards, for her it was the closest thing she was going to experience, and she was nearly beside herself with excitement. She gathered she was too old to clap her hands and do a little dance of joy, so she maintained her composure on the outside as best as she could but that was what was going on inside her head. Once again her eyes met Jasper's, and they shared a delighted smile. They were both getting exactly what they wanted out of this week. She turned her attention back to getting the most out of the experience.

Just as the butler announced dinner, Daisy wondered who would be her escort into the dining room. She was surprised when Jasper came to take her arm.

"There are enough people here we need not stand so much on ceremony. I shall be your escort for the very short walk, my dear."

"Delightful," was Daisy's reply. She wondered if the marchioness would be dismayed. Looking around, she was surprised to catch Jasper's mother looking at them with approval. "Your mother looks happy, my lord," she murmured.

"You have that effect on everyone," he said, smiling disarmingly.

Daisy dismissed his words with a roll of her eyes. "You could charm a snake from its skin, my lord."

They sat down and were introduced to the people closest, with whom they could converse. Jasper was on Daisy's left; to her right was a rakish looking young buck. Daisy had heard the other young ladies chattering about Lord Ethan Hawkridge. He was the indolent heir to the Earl of Welland, Jasper's brother in law. That is to say, he is the heir until the earl and his new bride manage to produce offspring of their own. Daisy anticipated some fascinating conversation from him.

Across from her was Lord Justin Fulton, his wife was to his right, in front of Jasper. Daisy had heard a few rumors about them and how they had come to be married. Of course, she would never be able to ask them about it, but she wondered if they would volunteer anything interesting.

The final guest with whom Daisy could reasonably converse was in front of Lord Hawkridge. A pretty young woman from a neighboring estate, Miss Margaret Ecklestone appeared to be overwhelmed with the company she found herself in. Daisy wondered if this was the first time she had been included in the Abernathys' entertainments. It would seem the girl had not had a London Season to polish off her air of fascination. Daisy's eyes flicked to Lord Hawkridge's face to see how he was taking the prospect of being seated in front of a country miss. She was surprised to see a look of pleasant amusement on his normally bored visage. Daisy knew it was going to be an interesting dinner even before any food was served.

Daisy applied herself to making polite conversation with the people around her. She began with Lord Fulton, surmising he would be the easiest to talk to besides Jasper, but it would not do to allow themselves to monopolize each other all night.

"Did you have far to travel to arrive at Abernathy this evening, my lord?"

"No, Miss Pembroke, we were already at one of our nearby properties. It was a convenient invitation to accept. We had no idea Abernathy had such grand entertainment planned. It is a good thing one always dresses appropriately when dining with a marquis."

Daisy grinned over the earl's wry joke and watched with a pinch of envy as he exchanged a private glance with his wife. She almost sighed over the evidence that theirs was obviously a love match. The whispers she had heard indicated that it had not started out that way, but it was clear that it was now. Daisy swallowed the lump in her throat and pushed aside the wish that she was an adoring wife on the receiving end of just such a look. She took a sip of her wine to wash down the sour taste suddenly in her mouth and decided that Lord Fulton was NOT the safest first conversationalist for the evening and turned to the gentleman on her right.

"Did you have far to travel this evening Lord Hawkridge? I do believe I heard Lady Bess mentioning you would be staying on for a couple of days after this evening."

"That is correct, Miss Pembroke, you shall not be rid of me quite so quickly as some of the other new additions to the party."

"Why would I wish to be rid of you, my lord?" Daisy was intrigued by the young man's choice of words.

"Are you not loyal to the Abernathy plots?"

Daisy felt her eyes widen at his words. She tried to maintain a façade of nonchalance, but his words were far too surprising. She had no idea what he was talking about and refused to look to Jasper for assistance. She smiled brightly and pointed out to him, "I hope it is not gauche of me to point out that you did not answer my first question, my lord."

Now Lord Hawkridge smiled with genuine amusement. "Ah yes, did I travel far? My dear Miss Pembroke, such a question reveals your ignorance about matters of the *ton*. You should be more careful what you ask."

Daisy refused to be intimidated by his tactics of evasion. She stood her ground, unconsciously raising her chin and an imperious eyebrow. "Really, my lord?" she drawled, her tone implying boredom. "I thought it merely revealed polite interest and the fact that I do not follow the gossip too closely. As a young, unmarried lady I would consider it unseemly for me to be aware of your movements."

She was happy to see that her words had gained her a modicum of respect in his eyes. He inclined his head to her. "Very well, my dear, you might have a valid point there. No, I did not have overly far to travel to arrive. In anticipation of the event ,I was visiting friends in the vicinity. But as Abernathy is rather far from my usual abode, I will be staying for a couple of days here as an additional house guest." He paused for a moment before commenting, "If I understand correctly, you and the viscount will be heading back to London in two days."

"That is correct. Many of the guests will be leaving on the morrow, but his lordship wished to spend a little bit of time with his family while there were fewer people about and his parents would be more available."

"Reasonable sentiment, I suppose." He nodded as though she had asked his opinion. "How do you feel about staying at Abernathy when there are fewer people as a buffer between you and the marquis?"

Daisy was astounded at the ill-mannered question and again wondered what the baron's motivation could possibly be. He was a mere connection to Abernathy. Daisy did not pose any threat to his position whatsoever, unlike Bess whose potential pregnancy could disinherit him. She felt her hackles rising and wondered why he would try to antagonize her.

"I find the marquis and his wife to be hospitable and generous hosts. It shall be a pleasure to remain as their guest for a couple more days, as I am sure you shall soon find out for yourself. I assume from your question that this is your first time to be visiting here." She kept a polite smile pinned to her face as she watched his reaction to her words. She was surprised to see amusement once more shining in his eyes.

"Actually, I have been here on a couple of occasions, most notably my uncle's marriage to Abernathy's daughter. But I can see why you made the assumption. I hope you find the rest of your stay here as enjoyable as you have so far."

"Thank you, my lord. I wish the same for you. I am certain it shall be an easy hope to fulfill." With as gracious a smile as she could muster, she turned away, directing her attention back to Lord Fulton. His sweet attentions toward his wife would be easier to stomach than Lord Hawkridge's snide questioning.

Daisy wondered what a debutante would ask an earl if she were seated across from him at dinner. "Have you heard any good speeches in the House of late, my lord?" That probably wasn't what a debutante would ask, but it was what interested Daisy, so it is what issued from her mouth. She accompanied the question with a winsome smile, hoping the earl would answer the question honestly rather than in a way that he would expect would be socially accepted by a young miss.

"As a matter of fact, Miss Pembroke, there have been several interesting discussions recently, thank you for asking. Are you interested in the politics of our land?"

"Not necessarily the politics, my lord, but the results should be of interest to us all, would you not agree? I understand a degree of negotiating and wrangling might be necessary to accomplish the most good for the highest number of people, but I do not think I would wish to be in your shoes. I do think it would be fascinating to witness a session, though."

"Why not do so, then? The gallery is open to visitors for most sessions, even ladies. My wife, on occasion, will come when she knows I am to speak." He said this with a note of quiet pride. Daisy again felt the nasty bite of envy but refused to give in to it. Lord Fulton continued, "In fact, I am sure she would be glad for your company. She has mentioned she feels decidedly outnumbered on the occasions that she visits."

His wife must have been listening to their conversation, though she was speaking with the person on her right, because at his words she glanced at Daisy momentarily with a welcoming smile on her lips before she turned her attention back to her companion.

A flush of pleasure suffused her body for a moment before Daisy remembered that she would never be able to accept Lady Fulton's invitation. When she returned to London, she would be returning to her real life as a governess. That is, if she could find a position; the thought rolled rather hysterically at the back of her mind. She shoved the thought back into the furthest corner, refusing to allow her concerns to disturb her pleasant evening.

Keeping her attention on the earl before her, she probed a little deeper. "That would be lovely, thank you, my lord. You mentioned earlier that there have been several sessions of note. Are they on a subject that you could share at the dinner table?"

It was obvious that the earl was surprised by her continued interest but gratified as well. He answered honestly. "I have met very few young women who are actually interested in what the government does, Miss Pembroke. To what would you attribute your interest?"

"Even though, as a woman, I do not necessarily have all the same rights as the male members of our Society, I do appreciate that it must be a difficult task to run the Nation. And whatever goes on in Parliament will undoubtedly eventually affect me." She offered a small shrug, unable to fully explain her interest. "I like to read the papers and be informed. I have rarely had the opportunity to speak with someone that actually witnesses firsthand the events that are discussed in the papers."

The earl gave a small nod as though he were accepting her explanation. "Well, Miss Pembroke, this may not affect you personally or directly, but one of the sessions of late that I found most interesting was with regard to the colonies. The discussion centered around whether or not they should be allowed a measure of autonomy. The representatives from the Canadas had some sound points, as did the opponents in the House. A decision has not yet been made, but it shall be interesting to see how it unfolds."

Daisy tilted her head, thinking about the earl's words. "Why would they want autonomy?"

"They do not consider the government here able to represent their needs and situation accurately, and therefore, they do not think our Parliament is in the best position to make decisions that would affect their future."

Daisy nodded and asked, "What do you think, my lord? Do you favor granting their request?"

"I can see their point about saying that a bunch of gentlemen living in a thriving metropolis like London cannot possibly know what it is to live in the New World, particularly if we have never even visited there. And if we do not grant them some concessions, I fear they shall become further disgruntled and demand complete independence as their neighbors to their south have. The war with the Americas was costly and could perhaps have been avoided."

Daisy was finding the earl's words fascinating. She wondered absently why such things were not discussed more openly. The constant conversation about weather or fashions was rather trying for her. She nodded encouragement, hoping the earl would continue.

"On the other hand, as some argued, if we grant them some concessions now, where will it end? Perhaps they will eventually want full independence too, but will just attain it without bothering with a war."

"That would be better for everyone, would it not?"

The earl smiled. "Well, yes, of course. No one wants another war, especially not to the west of us, as we have just managed to take care of the situation to the east. But you see, Miss Pembroke, the resources contained in the colonies are the full reason why we cannot allow them to distance themselves from us. The nearly constant war we have fought against Napoleon for the past eleven years has been dreadfully expensive. The taxes we receive from the Canadas are rather important to our national coffers at the moment and are one of the main sticking points for the representatives of the colonies. They want the taxes reduced. We cannot find it in our hearts to wish to agree."

Daisy smiled at his word choice but nodded somberly at his words. "Thank you so much for sharing this with me, my lord. You have filled me with relief that it is not my job to decide on such matters. And I have even greater respect for those who do take it upon themselves to deal with these necessary things. Do you find it particularly burdensome?"

"Not at all, my dear girl, but thank you for your concern. We shall manage to solve this dilemma without difficulty, have no fear."

Daisy found herself clenching her teeth in frustration as the promising conversation turned condescending without warning. She kept an agreeable smile upon her face with effort, nodding to him instead of replying as she had no idea how to answer graciously. Finally she turned to Jasper, surprised to see suppressed laughter dancing in his eyes.

"What have you found to amuse you so, my lord?" she asked primly.

"You, my dear," he replied, smiling at the ire that leapt to her eyes. "You have managed quite well to hold onto your temper despite both of your conversations thus far turning rather sideways on you."

"You are not supposed to be eavesdropping, my lord," Daisy said, her tone repressive, although amusement did begin to dance in her eyes. "It is not seemly in a viscount."

"Is it seemly in others?" Jasper asked, feigning intense interest.

"I do believe your father could get away with it," was Daisy's prim reply, much to the viscount's amusement.

"Be that as it may, my dear, I still think you have been handling yourself exceptionally well. Are you finding the experience to be daunting, or are you having a reasonably good time?"

"Oh no, my lord, I am having a grand time." She lowered her voice to not be overheard as she added, "Of course, there are a few moments where I have wished it would not cause a scene if I were to speak my mind, but for the most part I am being kept exceptionally well entertained."

"Perhaps you could share with me later what it is that you feel you could not express freely," Jasper offered.

Daisy was delighted with his offer. "Thank you, my lord, that would be wonderful."

Jasper was surprised at her acceptance. She so often held him at a distance and kept so much of herself a secret. He was learning to read her expressive face and knew quite well that the earl's conclusion to their conversation had earned her ire, but he looked forward to hearing what she had to say on the subject. He caught his mother's censorious eye upon him and realized he ought to be making a greater effort to converse with the people around him other than Daisy so, with a soft sigh, he applied himself to the task.

The rest of the dinner flew by, despite the many courses the marchioness had planned. Daisy was surprised by the variety and range produced by the Abernathy kitchen. Everything had been delicious, but it crossed her mind to wonder if she had perhaps eaten too much to be able to comfortably dance for the rest of the evening. When Lady Abernathy stood to signal the ladies to leave the gentlemen to their port, she confided in Miss Ecklestone as they left the room together.

"I fear I may have eaten a little too much," she whispered.

Miss Ecklestone giggled behind her hand. "Everything was delicious. I know exactly what you mean."

"I am worried I will cast up my accounts if I try to share in any of the more vigorous country dances," Daisy complained.

"Do not trouble yourself, my dear Miss Pembroke. It shall be several moments before the gentlemen join us and the orchestra strikes up the first number. Why do we not promenade about the room and allow our repast to settle itself comfortably."

"What a brilliant idea. And this will give us an opportunity to get to know one another a wee bit. I did not find it comfortable to speak with you on the angle as we were seated. I do hope you did not consider me terribly rude."

The young woman glowed with pleasure at Daisy's words, and Daisy congratulated herself on her developing social skills. "Thank you, Miss Pembroke, but no I did not at all consider you to be rude. I completely understood as I too felt it would be too difficult to be heard over the din if we had tried to speak. Now is as good a time as any." She smiled shyly, offering the opportunity for friendship.

With delight, Daisy seized upon the offer. "I gathered from our introduction that you have lived all your life around here. Did you know Lord Seaton and his sister well when you were children?"

Margaret laughed. "Oh no, not at all. For one thing, I am a number of years younger than them, and you know how it is with children, ten-year-old boys are beastly to five-year-old girls. And of course, we were not at all in the same sphere of social influence. The Abernathys did not spend a great deal of time here, as they have other estates as well as the need to be in London, whereas I have never left our little village."

Daisy sighed at her new friend's words. "But that in itself has its own beauty, though, does it not? Growing up in a village where you have known everyone your entire life is wonderfully comforting. And if you can remain there for the remainder of your days, you need never be lonely."

Margaret gazed at Daisy with shrewd eyes. "It seems to me as though you speak from experience, Miss Pembroke."

Daisy ignored her comment, instead imploring, "Oh please, do call me Daisy. My parents named me Margaret, which is another thing we have in common, but ever since then I have been called Daisy by my friends."

Margaret flushed with pleasure. "Very well, Daisy, and you must call me Margaret since no one has gone to the trouble of coming up with something else to call me."

The two girls shared a companionable laugh before they were interrupted by the arrival of the gentlemen. Daisy found that true to Margaret's prediction, she felt comfortably ready for the exertions of the ball.

As the small orchestra assembled at the side of the room struck up the first number, Jasper stopped beside Daisy with his hand held out to take hers. Bowing elegantly he asked, "May I?" and waited for her acceptance.

Daisy was shocked to find herself thrilled by his high handedness, but hesitated and cast Margaret a quick glance. Margaret accurately interpreted Daisy's look. "Go, enjoy." She shooed away her new friend with a happy smile, delighted that the other girl had given thought to her comfort.

Happy to oblige, Daisy tucked her hand in Jasper's and allowed him to sweep her onto the dance floor.

"I actually thought there for a moment that you were considering refusing my request," Jasper complained with a teasing tone.

"I did not wish to refuse, my lord, but I felt badly about leaving Margaret on her own," Daisy explained. "She is in much the same circumstances as me. I wanted to ensure that she would be comfortable on her own."

"That was kind of you to think of her," Jasper commented.

"It was kind of her to excuse me," Daisy countered with a sweet smile. "Thank you for asking me to dance, my lord. I am glad to practice for the first time with someone who knows how long it has been."

"No one would ever know, from the looks of you. You appear to be an expert in this as in all that you do."

"Now you must be trying to turn me up sweet for some reason with all this flattery." Daisy did not believe his words, but she enjoyed hearing them nonetheless. She stopped talking and threw herself into the enjoyment of the dance.

When the tune came to an end, Daisy was surprised to find Jasper's brother in law, the Earl of Welland, waiting to claim her hand for the next dance. She realized it was a cotillion and was excited to accept.

"You dance expertly, my dear," the earl complimented much to Daisy's delight.

"Why, thank you, my lord, it is very kind of you to say so."

The earl shrugged. "I have had the dubious privilege of dancing with some who would have done well to spend a little more time with a dancing instructor." He dismissed the topic by changing the subject. "Did you enjoy my nephew's company at dinner? He seems to be quite popular with young ladies. I thought you would enjoy being seated beside him."

Daisy struggled with how to answer the earl's question. While she would have enjoyed looking at the handsome Ethan Hawkridge throughout the entire meal, she had discovered he had taken more pains to be agreeable to Margaret than to her. Daisy was not sure what was behind the gentleman's strange conversation, but she didn't think it was the best idea to discuss it with his uncle.

She managed to come up with a diplomatic reply. "I can certainly see why he would be so popular, my lord. Are you very close with his lordship?"

"Oh yes, I practically raised the boy," came the surprising reply. "He was rather young when his parents died, and I became his guardian. Of course, he spent a lot of time at school and with his tutors, but I was all he had for family, really. We do not have much family other than each other, so we spent all of the big holidays together. Of course, now that I am married, I am hoping to be able to expand our family considerably. And the Abernathys have been gracious enough to include him whenever they invite Bess and me. And what about you, Miss Pembroke, are you from a large family?"

"I was an only child, and my parents have passed away, so I can relate to what your nephew must have gone through. Although I had the privilege of having my parents to myself until just last year."

"Oh, my dear, I am truly sorry. How very sad for you. So I guess that would explain why I have not seen you about Town for the Season, you have only recently left behind your mourning."

"In all reality, my lord, I feel that I shall be mourning my loss for the rest of my days. But yes, my official mourning period has not been over for very long. Do you usually spend a great deal of time in Town for the Season?"

"I have in times past. Since I inherited the earldom, I have taken my place in the House, of course, but while I spent most of my young manhood avoiding the Marriage Mart, I have always enjoyed attending at least a few of the *ton* events. You must realize the very best gossip is to be had at certain balls and routs."

"I can just imagine, my lord, but I must ask, of what use is the gossip to you? Surely as a Lord of the House, you must have better things to occupy your mind than gossip."

The earl laughed. "You would think so, would you not? But actually, some of the gossip is very useful. It is even better now that I am married. It is much less obvious when my wife is listening to the gossip and then she can pass on pertinent details to me as to who said what and about whom. You see, in politics, it always pays to be informed."

"Well, I suppose that makes sense to me. Might I ask you a similar question that I asked Lord Fulton over dinner?"

"Of course, my dear."

"Have you heard any speeches or lectures of particular interest in the House of late?"

"Of particular interest to me, do you mean?"

"That is a good question, my lord, yes, let us start with you."

"I hope this does not sound unbearably arrogant, but I have not heard any speeches that I found to be particularly noteworthy, due to the speakers' lack of ability. I have found myself struggling to pay attention many a time even when the subject is of note due to the dry nature of the speaker's address. But there have been several subjects that I have found interesting. You might agree with me."

His pause after those words caused Daisy to hastily prompt, "What were they, my lord?"

"One day was of particular note when one young lord brought up the works of Mary Wollstonecraft. Are you familiar with her, my dear?"

"I am, my lord." Daisy did not go into any detail. She was undecided how she felt about the outspoken woman striving for women's rights. She could tell her dubious feelings on the subject must have shown on her face, as she noted the earl's wry smile. He confirmed her thoughts with his next words.

"Yes, my dear, it is a questionable subject, but it is good to be informed."

"Of course, my lord." Daisy hoped she did not sound defensive. "I have read some of Miss Wollstonecraft's writings, and while I applaud her desire to elevate the situation that most women find themselves in, I cannot agree with some of her arguments."

"Quite right, my dear," the earl agreed with her assessment. "It did give rise to comical debate within the House, I can tell you. Many of the gentlemen present could not fathom why the subject would even be raised. A few felt quite passionately on the subject, but most were woefully uninformed. It was one of the most rousing debates I have witnessed in all the time since I took my seat in the House. It would almost seem that some of the gentlemen were afraid of the consequences if women are acknowledged as individuals separate from men. I am certain we have not seen the last of that debate. I just hope my fellow lords are more informed the next time the subject is raised. I am certain it will be much more productive if that is the case."

Daisy regarded the earl with scrutiny. "Might I be so bold as to ask you which side of the debate you were on?"

"Absolutely, I would expect nothing less, my dear. I am happy to inform you that I am quite convinced that my wife is an intelligent woman in her own right and would be absolutely able to decide her life for herself with or without a husband." He lowered his voice and leaned in closer to Daisy's ear. "You can be sure most of the gentlemen present felt the same way about their wives or daughters or sisters, which is exactly why they do not wish to agree to it. They do not want to become unimportant within their own families. Everyone knows the ladies already run the world — we just do not wish to acknowledge it. If we did, then where would we be?" He said this last bit with such a droll face that Daisy could not resist chuckling over his humor.

"Oh, my lord, your wit is delightful. Thank you for sharing your thoughts with me."

"I am always happy to share when a pretty lady asks for my thoughts," the earl replied with a rakish grin.

Daisy's gaze turned dubious. "It is a wonder you managed to remain single as long as you did, if that is the case, then, my lord."

"Not at all, my dear. You would be surprised how rare it is that anyone really cares to know what someone else's thoughts are. Have you not observed how often people just want to speak of their own concerns without paying any heed to what someone else might have to share on the subject?"

"Well, yes, my lord, I have observed that, but I was quite convinced it was only my limited experience. I fear you have near to broken my heart that even amongst the elevated circles in which you move the same can be said."

Now it was the earl's turn to chuckle at his companion's words. "Oh my dear, you are an original. You shall be all the rage when you have your Season, to be sure."

Daisy blinked at his words but kept a noncommittal smile pasted to her lips. She was relieved to hear the musicians winding down to the end of the song. She was saved from having to comment as the earl escorted her to the side of the room where his nephew was just bowing over Margaret's hand. Daisy smiled to see how her friend glowed with delight over whatever the young man was saying.

"Ethan, my boy, be so good as to introduce me to your friend. Mayhap she shall consent to accept my hand for the next number."

The two men exchanged a heated look, which Daisy could not interpret. Lord Hawkridge appeared reluctant, but politely performed the introduction as instructed. Margaret looked flustered over the attention but accepted the earl's hand prettily, her smile declaring her happiness with how her evening was progressing.

Lord Hawkridge turned his surly gaze to Daisy. "You appear to be without a partner, Miss Pembroke. We might as well join them on the dance floor."

It crossed Daisy's mind that she ought to take umbrage at his words, but she found them far too amusing. Her partner looked surprised to hear her tinkling laugh ring out.

"You are not the usual sort of debutante, are you, Miss Pembroke?"

"Not at all, my lord," she answered with a cheerful smile.

He eventually returned her smile with a genuine one of his own. "That is probably a very good thing," he finally replied.

They were separated by the steps of the dance for a moment and when they came back together, they maintained a companionable silence until they were separated and came together once more. Finally, Lord Hawkridge broke the silence.

"Are you enjoying yourself this evening, Miss Pembroke?"

Daisy could tell from the look on his face that he was finally showing a genuine interest in her as a person, and his interest had finally reached his eyes. "Thank you for asking, I am having a wonderful time. I have met many fascinating people today and I am enjoying the dancing. I do believe the marchioness will be able to count her ball a grand success."

The gentleman glanced over to where that lady was watching the swirling couples. "It would appear she agrees with your assessment, Miss Pembroke. She looks decidedly satisfied."

Unsure if he was being disparaging or not, Daisy decided her loyalties lay with the Abernathys even though Jasper's relationship with his family was precarious. "And well she should, would you not agree, my lord?"

Lord Hawkridge grinned at the young woman in his arms. "You are an interesting package, my dear Miss Pembroke, but I think rather too complicated for my taste."

With those words, he ended the dance with a flourish and escorted her to the side where Jasper was standing, watching them closely. Hawkridge bowed to Jasper and then to Daisy before taking his leave.

Jasper made every effort to ignore the jealousy that was roaring through him, refusing to acknowledge how misplaced it was. He mistrusted the bemused look upon Daisy's face.

"Did you enjoy your dance with Hawkridge, my dear?" He hoped his question sounded pleasant rather than accusatory.

"I am undecided, to be honest with you," Daisy said, blinking up at him with her eyes wide and innocent.

Jasper bit back the urge to pull her into his arms. He knew Daisy was oblivious to his thoughts, and for that he was grateful.

"What causes your indecision?" he asked.

Daisy offered a delicate shrug as she glanced over at the subject of their discussion. "I think he has conflicted feelings about your family, and I find myself firing up in defense of them, which is ridiculous since I have my own conflicted feelings about them. I fear he might be up to no good, but I think even he is undecided on the subject. That probably does not make any sense, does it?"

"It is an astoundingly astute observation, in fact, my dear. I have thought the very same thing the entire time I have known him. You see, as my brother in law's heir, the earl's marriage to my sister has threatened his position. But Hawkridge is a wealthy man in his own right and does not require the earl's blunt, nor even the title, to be able to lead a successful life. He and the earl have not been terribly close, although it seems my sister is trying to change that. It all combines to create a conundrum for the fellow. I think you are quite correct in your assessment — the man is certainly conflicted."

"Well, enough about him. We shall have the next couple of days to work on figuring out how we feel about Lord Hawkridge. What about you, are you having an enjoyable evening, my lord? I did not see you on the dance floor."

"I guess you could say that I too am conflicted. I am happy that I brought you here, and of course I am relieved that my parents are going to pony up the money I need, but it has been years since I have spent this amount of time under the same roof as them, and I am getting restless. I wish we had not said we would stay the entire week."

Daisy bit her lip in consternation at his words. "Do you wish to depart? Since I have received those messages from Charlotte we could say I have affairs to attend to at home."

"But you hate dissembling," Jasper pointed out.

"In this case, it is true, my lord. Remaining here, enjoying myself is only postponing the inevitable. Sooner or later I shall have to go home and face whatever the baron has in store for me."

"Well, I would very much rather it be later than sooner. In fact, I would like to arrange a way for you to never have to face the rotter."

"Thank you, my lord, I appreciate the sentiment, but you do realize I can handle the matter perfectly well on my own, do you not?"

"I know you are a strong, capable, independent young woman with all sorts of abilities that I am not even yet aware of. But the fact remains that you are a young woman with few protections surrounding you. If a man has evil intentions toward you, there might not be much you could do to protect yourself. Does that not trouble you?"

Jasper watched the blood drain from Daisy's expressive face and cursed himself for allowing her insistence upon independence to goad him into being too forceful in his speech. "Oh Daisy, I am so sorry, I should not have said all of that to you."

"No, no, my lord, it is perfectly fine. You are, of course, correct. I am a woman on my own. And as such, I do believe I would like to remain here just a couple more days to enjoy all the protections provided by all the fine gentlemen about." Daisy had her chin at a proud angle and refused to meet his gaze with her own. "Now if you will excuse me, I really ought to speak to someone." With that vague excuse, she left the viscount standing there gazing after her.

Chapter Thirteen

Daisy was fuming, but she was undecided if she was more upset with Jasper or with herself for allowing him to irritate her. She made her way to the ladies' withdrawing room, grateful to see that it was empty, and she took a moment to gather her composure.

Glancing in the mirror conveniently provided, Daisy was surprised to see how flushed her cheeks were. Her blue eyes were bright, and her whole face looked lit up from within. She had to laugh. It would seem that anger became her. Examining her face, her thoughts turned introspective. *Why did I get so angry with him?* she asked her reflection silently. *He was merely stating the facts. Mayhap the earl's discussion of Mary Wollstonecraft and her efforts for women's rights affected me more than I realized. I want Jasper to see me as a competent individual not some pet he needs to protect.* She paused for a moment, reflecting, and then realized she was not being entirely honest even with herself.

It does feel quite lovely when he is protecting me, though. It would be nice to have someone else do the worrying for a while. She sighed, shoving away the unattainable dream. She only had herself to rely upon. Charlotte was a dear, but Daisy did not wish to lay her burdens at her former governess' feet. She had not lied to Jasper. She only had herself to rely upon. It was nearly time for her to come up with some solutions. With a mischievous grin at her own reflection, Daisy resolved to worry about it when she had all the information. In the meantime, she would enjoy the last couple days of this alternate reality to the utmost before she had to return to her real life and the drudgery it was sure to become. Patting her hair to ensure all was in place and critically examining her reflection, Daisy nodded firmly and briskly left the room, resolved to wring every drop of enjoyment from the night.

"Daisy, my dear, I was wondering where you had gotten to," Bess hailed her as soon as she returned to the ballroom. "Are you having enough partners for the dance? Do you need me to introduce you to anyone, or is my brother keeping you well enough occupied?" She asked this last question with a teasing smile as she glanced around the room. "Where is he, by the way? I have not yet had the opportunity to dance with him."

"I have lost track of him," Daisy stated with a shrug. "He was being disagreeable, so I walked away."

Bess chortled. "That is wonderful, my dear. He usually has ladies falling over themselves to maintain his interest. It will do him good to have to work hard at a relationship for once."

Daisy blushed hotly as she remembered she was supposed to be playing the role of doting admirer in order for his family to believe they were about to make a match. She scrambled to try to resolve her verbal misstep but could not think of a thing. Her dilemma must have shown itself on her face, as Jasper's sister laughed at her.

"Oh Daisy, do not be a goose, it is perfectly normal to feel frustrated with a gentleman who is courting you. And with my brother, it would be strange if you did not, he can be an exasperating man. Do not let it bother you. He is usually fair and even tempered. He will come to his senses before long and come around." Bess linked arms with Daisy and steered her toward the table with the punch bowl. "Now come and join me in a glass of punch. All this dancing has made me thirsty."

Relieved, Daisy allowed herself to be towed along.

The rest of the night flew by. Daisy could hardly believe it when she glanced at the clock and saw that it was already the early hours of the morning. She realized this was probably normal for the aristocratic crowd, but she was amazed that she was not slumped over in a corner from exhaustion. No doubt it was the excitement keeping her going. Before she could protest, Jasper was before her, taking her hand and leading her to the dance floor.

"I have it on very good sources that this is to be the last dance, so please do me the honor of sharing it with me."

It was impossible to resist when he was being gallant and gracious. She placed her hand in his and followed him, unable to wipe the pleased smile from her face.

"Are you ready yet to forgive me for being a boor and an oaf?" he asked, his most winsome smile on display.

"You could never be accused of being a boor, my lord, and well you know it."

"Well, what I really am cannot be named in polite company, so I did the best I could."

Now Daisy giggled at his words, unable to hold onto even a shred of the anger she had felt. "Of course I have forgiven you, my lord," she began, casting down her eyelashes and feeling a slight warmth tingling her cheeks. "In fact, it is I who should be seeking your forgiveness. You were only trying to be kind, and I growled at you for your trouble. I am terribly sorry. I do not know what causes such ridiculous behavior."

Jasper's hand tightened on hers as he swirled her through the steps with a flourish. He smiled at her as she returned to his arms. "All is forgiven. I am fully aware that you have had to look after yourself for well over a year. You have quite forgotten how it feels to have someone else wanting to assist." He looked into her eyes for a moment, seriously intent, before he wiped all seriousness from his face and smiled cheerfully. "But never mind about our troubles for now. We are going to relish the last of this dance and the rest of this house party. I do not care a fig about my parents and their airs and attitudes. We shall make use of their hospitality and enjoy ourselves to the limit before we have to face any form of reality, is that not correct?"

Daisy laughed at his droll air and thrilled over how well his words matched with the resolve she herself had just made earlier. She inclined her head in an imperial acceptance, causing him to laugh.

They were both flushed and in high spirits as the last strains of the orchestra drifted into silence. After a slight hesitation as they looked deeply into one another's eyes, they joined in with the assembled guests as they applauded the marchioness on a successful evening of entertainment.

Daisy stood with the Abernathy household as they said goodnight to the guests who were not staying overnight and then helped to get the houseguests settled. Lady Abernathy finally looked at Daisy when it was only the marquis, his wife, Jasper, and Daisy left in the room.

"You are strangely competent for someone so young, my dear. Thank you for your support this evening. I do believe you were of more assistance than my own daughter."

Daisy laughed at the strange compliment. "Thank you, my lady. As an only child, I have a different set of experiences than Lady Bess. Besides, she has the added distractions of being the countess."

"Perhaps, but you could be forgiven for saying that you have the excuse that you are a guest and not a member of the family. You need not have been so helpful this evening, and no one would have thought less of you." The marchioness' shrewd gaze was searching Daisy's face, but Daisy was unsure what she was looking for and she was somewhat embarrassed over the lady's words.

"Excuse me, my lady, if I have overstepped in some way. I did not wish to impose myself on you, if that is what happened."

"Oh no, not at all, my dear, I apologize if I have made you uncomfortable. I just was not expecting Jasper to bring such an exceptional young lady as his guest. It is our pleasure to have you in our home."

Daisy glowed over the older woman's words, although she bristled once more over the marchioness' attitude toward her son. Sighing and resolving to see what she could do about it on the morrow, Daisy took her leave of her hostess and made her way to her own bed. It had been an eventful day and she was full of excitement to see what tomorrow had in store.

ꟾ

The two men on horseback stared at the grand house before them, struck silent in their awe.

"Are you certain we have the right place, milord?" Elton asked, his voice plaintive.

"Unfortunately I am, Elton," the baron replied, his tight tone not hiding his own apprehensions.

"It would've been much better if his nibs was here."

"I agree whole-heartedly. But he had other things to deal with and wasn't going to be able to manage the timing. Or so he said."

"Maybe he took one look at this place and turned lily-livered."

The baron didn't disagree but refused to admit as much. He was sarcastic as he asked, "What did you expect a marquis' home to look like? Come along. Dithering here is not going to make this task any easier."

"What are you going to say when we get to the front door? Are you going to tell them the truth?" Elton fidgeted and worried, momentarily unwilling to proceed as they had planned.

"It is not for you to trouble yourself," Lord Sadbury answered, becoming angry at his sidekick's fidgets. "You had best be at my side when we get there if you know what is good for you, you dolt."

This got through to Elton, and he quickly goaded his mount into motion. Within a couple minutes they were knocking on the front door of the large, imposing limestone house. Elton, a servant, was awed at the prospect of being ushered in through the front door rather than the servants' entrance.

Even the baron was a trifle overcome at the prospect of being in the large house. It crossed his mind to question the accuracy of what he had been told. How could his former governess be a guest in this mansion? It just was not done. He gave a mental shrug. If the girl was here, she would not be welcome for long.

"Can I help you, sir?" the butler asked politely as he took in the disheveled appearance of the two men on the door step.

"I am here to speak with Lord Abernathy."

"And who shall I tell him is calling?"

"Lord Sadbury, Baron of Clifton, is here on a matter of some urgency."

"Very well, my lord, if you will wait a few moments, I will see if he can see you. You must know he and his wife have many guests in residence, and he may not be available to see you."

"It is most important that he does."

"Wait a moment, and I will see." The butler would not commit for his master. He was dubious about the marquis' reception to the unruly looking fellow and his companion.

The butler found the marquis in his library. It was midafternoon, and he had left his wife to see to the guests' entertainment while he escaped to see to some necessary business. Lord Abernathy looked up from his correspondence at the butler's entrance.

"What is it, Hartley?"

"There is someone here to see you, my lord. He claims the matter is of an urgent nature." The butler was unable to hide his true feelings.

"Does this person have a name? I can tell from your tone you are not approving of this particular someone."

"Yes, my lord, it is Lord Sadbury, Baron of Clifton."

"I am unacquainted with this baron and have very little interest in finding out why he has called. But I have even less interest in returning to my wife's guests at the moment. Very well, show him in."

"He has another fellow with him. He looks to be a servant of some sort."

"Then show him to the servant's hall to await the pleasure of his master. I have sufficient servants — he does not need to accompany Sadbury."

"Very well, my lord." The butler bowed himself out of the marquis' presence and went to collect the baron.

"His lordship will see you briefly, sir, but he mentioned that your companion could await you in the kitchens."

Lord Sadbury blushed that it was so obvious that his companion was of a low order. He would have felt more confident if he could display some consequence in this interview. He mustered up the fear that was motivating him and ignored Elton's protests. This matter needed to be taken care of — he needed the girl and he needed it done quickly.

"Very well, I will see you shortly Elton." Sadbury dismissed him with a curt nod.

The walk to the marquis' library seemed long and narrow as Sadbury fought to overcome his ongoing attack of nerves. Under other circumstances, he would have been impressed by the dark wood that shined so brightly and the various hangings and artwork, which clearly declared the wealth of his unwitting host. He reminded himself once more what was at stake and why he needed to be brave. He forced his knees not to quake as he followed the dignified, elderly butler.

"Lord Sadbury to see you, my lord," Hartley announced as he opened the door and bowed himself away from the room. If the marquis wished to provide hospitality for the baron he would ring for it later.

The marquis did not bother to stand up to greet his uninvited guest. He was a very busy man, and he felt affronted to be imposed upon when he was already overrun with a houseful of company, and the running of the marquisate would not wait out the week.

"What can I do for you, Sadbury? As you can see I am quite busy and do not have time to waste on the pleasantries."

"That is perfectly all right, my lord. In fact, I can be very quick. I understand Miss Margaret Pembroke is here. I wish to speak with her."

Now the marquis was intrigued. What would this upstart want with his lovely guest? He raised his eyebrow into his most haughty expression.

"What business do you have with Miss Pembroke?"

"Up until recently, she was the governess to my young children. She chose to leave our employ, but the children are missing her gravely and I have come to ask her to return to us. I am sorry if this inconveniences you, my lord. I was not aware that you had small children, but I will be happy to buy out her contract from you."

Not by a single blink of his eyelashes did the marquis reveal the surprise he felt by the little man's words. He had been well aware there was something afoot with the young woman given the letters she had received, but considering the refinement she displayed, he would have never guessed that she was a governess. It crossed his mind to wonder if his son knew before he dismissed the thought. Obviously if she could fool him, his son would never have been informed.

"Why did she leave the position in your house? Perhaps she has no interest in returning to your employ. I am quite sure she is perfectly content where she is."

"The children have been crying for her, my lord. I cannot bear to see them so unhappy." The baron nearly choked on his words. He would barely recognize his own children if he ran into them on the street, but to his mind it seemed like a believable reason to be trying to get his governess back.

The marquis realized the man had no idea Miss Pembroke was not here as a governess, so he decided not to inform him of that. He could tell the man was a shady character, and although he was put out that Miss Pembroke had been less than truthful, he was not about to throw her to this man's mercies either.

"But what of my children? Do you not think they will be crying for her if I allow her to leave with you?" he asked rather slyly.

"Well… but…" he sputtered. "She could not have been here for very long. Surely your children could get over it very easily. She has been with my children for more than a year."

"Finding a good governess is hard to do. I am not at all convinced that I wish to commence the search anew. I believe it would be best if you are on your way and find yourself someone else. Children are adaptable — yours will grow attached to someone new given time."

Now Sadbury was getting desperate. "Please, my lord, if I could just speak with her for a few minutes. It would be best to allow the girl to make her own choice, would you not agree?"

Lord Abernathy could hardly disagree with that, despite his misgivings about the weasely baron. "Very well, if you will have a seat, I will see about having her summoned."

The marquis sighed, realizing he was not going to be able to get any work done until this matter was resolved. Whatever Miss Pembroke's background might be, he did not for a minute believe Sadbury was telling the full story. Perhaps she had been his children's governess, but no titled gentleman rode around the country seeking to bring her back after she had left his employ.

"Hartley, do you know where Seaton might be? And where might I find Miss Pembroke?"

"Most of the guests are assembled in the garden playing croquet, my lord. I do believe both the viscount and Miss Pembroke are there."

"Thank you. Could you please have them brought to the gallery? I require some private conversation with them both."

"Very good, my lord." Hartley went to see to his master's bidding at once while the marquis went to await them in the gallery. He began to pace as he waited, planning for all the possibilities.

By the time his son and his companion entered the gallery, the marquis had worked himself into a state of anger over the situation he faced. He could not hide it as he greeted them.

"Miss Pembroke, I am sorry to tear you away from the games. I hate to disturb your little vacation from your duties."

Daisy's nerves became alert at the marquis' tone and his word choice. A sense of foreboding crept over her, but she hid it well, maintaining a pleasant smile. "It is no imposition, my lord. I was told you wished to speak with me." She couldn't help the questioning tone, although she hated how weak it sounded. The look on his face, which was even colder than usual, made her nervous and defensive.

"Yes, I did ask that you be summoned. Someone has arrived who wishes to speak with you. Lord Sadbury is waiting for you in my library. He wishes to offer you your old position back. He said his children miss you."

All the blood drained from Daisy's head. She had the sensation that it must be pooling in her toes, as those appendages began to tingle. Relief filled her, and she managed to keep her knees from giving out as she felt Jasper's presence behind her. The warmth of his hand seeped through her senses from where he had placed it at the small of her back. She felt his protective concern and was deeply grateful for it, although she also worried how it would affect his already damaged relationship with his father. Jasper began speaking to her in a low, soothing voice.

"You do not have to speak with him, Daisy. We can have him removed from Abernathy quite easily." He paused for a moment, searching her averted gaze. He lowered his voice still further. "Are you all right? Do you want me to have Kate summoned?"

At this reminder of Daisy's appearance of consequence, the marquis' eyes narrowed. "What is going on here, Seaton? Do you know anything about this Sadbury fellow? Ought I to be throwing him out of my house?"

Soft-hearted Daisy could not stand for this. Blushing bright red she protested, "Oh no, my lord, I do not wish to cause any trouble."

"I have already been put out by this upstart having the temerity to show up while my wife is entertaining. It would actually afford me a degree of pleasure to throw him out the door."

Seeing the cold glint in his eyes, Daisy knew he was serious. Her smile was wan but genuine. The marquis' gaze turned colder.

"It would appear that neither of you are overly surprised at the announcement that Sadbury is here to see you, Miss Pembroke. Is this what your friend was writing to warn you of?"

Daisy began to feel like a mouse facing a hungry cat as the marquis' cold eyes raked her dispassionately. She felt like cowering but refused to do so. Lifting her chin in a proud gesture, Daisy met the marquis' eyes as she answered him. "That was private correspondence, my lord."

"Mayhap, but you have been a guest in this house, and your presence here has brought an unwarranted complication."

That, at least, was an indisputable fact, and Daisy could no longer meet his eye. She looked to Jasper, wondering how best to handle this embarrassing encounter. She was surprised to see that he was glaring at his father. This prompted the marquis' ire to turn on him next.

"Seaton, you do not seem at all surprised to hear Miss Pembroke spoken of as a governess. Why is that, might I ask?"

"I am not surprised, my lord. She was one, now she is not."

"Have you brought your *petite amie* to your mother's party?" The marquis' rage was a cold flame.

Daisy gasped, and her hand twitched with the urge to slap the smug look off the nobleman's face. She controlled it with an effort borne of good breeding. She would not stoop to his level. Jasper's anger was boiling beside her. Daisy reached out and gently placed her hand on his arm as a restraint.

Jasper glanced down at the small hand on his sleeve. The mist of anger dancing before his eyes cleared as he saw the concern etched on Daisy's face. He could not plant his father a facer with her here watching anxiously. He tried to smile reassuringly at her but worried it may have come across as more of a grimace. She returned his look with a small smile of her own. His heart swelled with a strange emotion. He felt deep pride in this small woman at his side. The aplomb with which she handled most situations was breathtaking to him. He placed his own hand over her cold little one where it rested upon his sleeve.

Inclining his head as politely as he could muster, Jasper managed to ignore his father's rude question, merely answering as calmly as possible. "Thank you for the information, my lord. We shall go and see what the baron wishes to say to Miss Pembroke."

Feeling the flutter of Daisy's hand under his, he squeezed it, hoping she would not protest. While he did not relish the thought of facing the baron, the fact that he had shown up needed to be dealt with. He also wished to avoid a further confrontation with his father in front of Daisy, so he needed to get her out of there.

Seeing the incredulous look upon his father's face almost made Jasper burst out laughing. Clearly the older man had no idea his son was capable of gallantry. Instead of laughing, Jasper gritted his teeth to hold back his anger that once again his father was underestimating him. He had to think about Daisy right now and worry about his broken relationship with his sire later.

Grateful that the marquis did not follow them, Jasper strode quickly from the room. It took him a couple of minutes to realize he was practically dragging Daisy down the hall. He was impressed that she had been able to keep up and did not protest, despite the fact that she had to hike up her skirt with her free hand in order not to trip.

Jasper ground to a halt. "I am so sorry, Daisy. I did not intend to make you chase after me. Are you all right?" As he was asking her, he glanced around to see where they could have a few moments of privacy. Just ahead, there was a small alcove; it would not be completely private, but that was just as well. The last thing either of them needed at this moment was to find themselves in a compromising situation. Jasper set off in that direction, at a more moderate pace.

Tucking her back to the wall and placing himself in front of her, so as to shield her from any prying eyes, Jasper searched Daisy's face for evidence of how she was taking this latest turn of events. "You have not answered my question, my dear, are you all right?" he asked as gently as he could manage.

He heard her shuddering breath, and his heart constricted. But then he saw a tremulous smile trembling onto her lips.

"You have become rather managing and autocratic all of a sudden, my lord. I am struggling to decide whether I hate it or if it is unbearably attractive."

Jasper kept his voice pitched low, but he could not restrain the laughter that bubbled to the surface. "You are a delightful baggage, Miss Daisy." He lowered his head as though to touch his lips to hers, but then he thought better of it and pulled back slightly.

He felt her innocence evident in her wide-eyed gaze as she searched his face. He could tell she knew something was going on but didn't fully understand it. He sighed softly and pulled back further. To distract them both from the impossible situation, he drew their attention back to the matter at hand.

"Are you prepared to face Sadbury, Daisy? You seem to me to be a little bit in a state of shock. You have barely spoken about it. What is going on inside your pretty head?"

As usual, Daisy rolled her eyes at the compliment but applied herself to the question. "I would not really say that I am shocked that he has shown up. If you will recall, it was my fear, and you assured me he would not have the temerity. It would appear that you were wrong, my lord." Her accusatory tone made Jasper smile.

"So it would seem, my dear," he drawled.

"Your father did not seem at all pleased with either of us," Daisy said, her tone revealing her worry as much as the sight of her teeth nibbling on her bottom lip. Jasper forced himself not to stare.

"It is not a new sensation for me, Miss Daisy. He has not been pleased with me since I was a toddler."

"Why is that, my lord? You have never really fully explained it. It must have made for a terribly uncomfortable childhood. And how could you bear your youth without your father's proud support? I do believe I ought to have a stern discussion with the marquis about his treatment of you."

Again Jasper's low laughter filled the alcove. It had been years since he had laughed as much as he had this past week in Daisy's presence. He would happily stand here all day, listening to the audacious things coming out of her mouth, but Jasper determined that they really ought to deal with the baron waiting for them in his father's library.

"Are you feeling prepared to deal with Sadbury now, Daisy? If you would prefer, I could still have him escorted from the grounds by some sturdy footmen."

"While I would happily watch such a display, it is not at all practical. It would be best to find out what he wants while I am in the protected environs of Abernathy. No matter how critical your father might be, I firmly believe he will not allow any harm to befall me while I am a guest in his home. Or even the hired help, for that matter. I think he would consider it a matter of honor." She said this last as though she were still contemplating the matter.

"You are quite correct — you are perfectly safe here, but I would prefer to protect you from Sadbury completely, so that you need never face him if you do not wish."

"That is a lovely sentiment, my lord, but not at all practical. How do you propose to do that? After we are finished here, we are both going to return to our lives. Yours does not include playing nursemaid to a silly governess who got herself into a deeper muddle than she realized. Mine will involve sorting out that muddle." She paused to soften her words with a warm smile. "I am just grateful that I have your support while I face him. Hopefully this can be dealt with and straightened out before luncheon."

Jasper cast such a dubious expression toward her that Daisy could not help but giggle. "Are you questioning the fact that it could get straightened out or whether we will be welcome to share the luncheon with our fellow guests once it becomes known that I have been a governess?"

"Neither, really. I just cannot fathom your cheerful attitude about it. Yesterday, you were worrying yourself into a lather about this very thing happening. Now that it has, you seem rather serene about it all. How do you reconcile these two seemingly contradictory situations?"

Daisy's shrug was uninformative, and she smiled uncertainly. "I cannot explain it. It was much worse as an unconfirmed worry that may or may not happen. Now that the situation has arrived, in reality, it just needs to be faced and dealt with. I am much more troubled about your father's terrible attitude about you."

"Never mind about that for now. Let us get Sadbury dealt with, and we can think about other things later."

Jasper smiled over Daisy's rather wretched sounding sigh, but she obediently tucked her hand into his proffered arm and they strode purposefully together toward the library.

ꕥ

Standing before the library door, Daisy felt a shiver make its way down her spine. She had dreaded this moment ever since she had received Charlotte's notes. She could not fathom what Sadbury could possibly want with her. Daisy did not believe for a moment that he would be so foolish as to think she would return to his employ. Foreboding circled her heart and made her head feel as though she needed a good nap.

Throwing back her shoulders and lifting her chin defiantly, Daisy glanced at Jasper, surprised to see him watching her carefully. She smiled as confidently as she could manage, grateful that he took the situation out of her hands by pushing the door open and stepping through with her safe by his side.

Sadbury looked nervous and twitchy, standing by the large desk that dominated the room. Daisy wondered if he had been searching through the marquis' papers but figured Lord Abernathy was a mature enough man to concern himself with his own matters. She pushed the thought away and occupied herself with the problem at hand.

"Lord Sadbury, what a surprise to see you here." She could not find it in herself to be rude to the unscrupulous little man, no matter the provocation, but she was not going to be overtly welcoming either.

Sadbury's attempt at a pleasant smile fell rather short of its objective, but Daisy found the tight grimace to be more amusing than terrifying, so she allowed her own lips to lift in a slight smile.

"Miss Pembroke, I am so happy to see you." His oily smile made Daisy uncomfortable, but she held her ground. "You have to help me out. The children have been crying for you ever since your departure, and my dear wife is beside herself with concern over them. We have not been able to find an acceptable replacement for you. I would be most grateful if you would accompany me directly home to take over the nursery and set things to rights."

Daisy blinked at the baron. She never would have thought the obtuse little man would be so slow-witted as to think she would even consider returning to his employ.

"I appreciate your confidence in my ability to comfort your children, but I cannot accept your generous offer of employment."

"Is it the money? I could pay you a bit more, if that is the problem."

"It is not the money, my lord."

"How about if I double your wages?" Now the baron sounded desperate, and Daisy became more suspicious.

"My lord, it is commendable that you are exhibiting such concern over the well-being of your children, but I will admit to you that it is a surprising turn of affairs. When I was living in your home, I never knew you to show any interest in them. To be perfectly frank, I wondered if you would even know their names if we were to encounter you unawares upon the grounds."

Daisy was not satisfied to see the dull flush that rose in the baron's cheeks. She did not intend to embarrass the man; she was just stating the facts as she saw them. She pressed on in her argument. "I am sorry to disappoint you, and I mean no disrespect, but I do not find your explanation to be believable."

Sadbury's flush of embarrassment turned to one of anger, and he glared at Daisy. He didn't have another story, so he needed to stick with this one. He had thought it would be a good one. The stupid chit had seemed devoted to the children when she had worked for him; he thought it would be easy to convince her. He glared at her again. "Don't you care about the children?"

"I think your children are lovely boys and girls, and if it was just them, I would happily return to being their governess. But surely, my lord, you must be quite daft if you think I would return after what happened with Lord Wright."

Sadbury blanched. "To what are you referring?" he hedged.

"To the fact that he accosted me in front of your children, and you refused to do anything about it," Daisy almost yelled.

Daisy could not fathom why the wretched little man looked relieved over her words. "Ah yes, that was an unfortunate incident, for which I offer you sincere apology."

Daisy narrowed her eyes at him. "It does not feel very sincere since it is a couple of weeks too late."

"Surely you realize how it is amongst noblemen, my dear Miss Pembroke. If I had realized you would take it so hard, you can be sure I would have apologized immediately."

"Lord Sadbury, it really is neither here nor there at this point. I am sorry to have to tell you that you have come all this way for nothing, but I will not be accepting your offer of employment. I am quite sure your wife is perfectly capable of hiring a governess who will suit your children. I suggest you take greater care of her in the future. But it will not be me filling the position." Daisy edged toward the door, holding it open. "Thank you for the offer. I would wish you a good day."

Sadbury made no move toward the door. "You are making a big mistake, girl."

He suddenly seemed to realize that the viscount was in the room with them. Jasper had stood silently watching the exchange between Daisy and Sadbury. Now the baron's weasel eyes turned colder. "You have made other arrangements for yourself, haven't you, you little piece of baggage."

Daisy held herself as still as humanly possible and looked down her straight little nose at the ridiculous baron. "I do not like what you are implying, my lord. It is time that you leave."

Jasper quivered with anger beside her, but she was grateful that he held silent, allowing her to handle the situation as she saw fit. Even though she was fully convinced she would have been able to handle the indelicate situation on her own, she was grateful for Jasper's fierce glare that he directed full force onto the hapless baron, making him squirm and finally head toward the door. It would have taken her much longer to accomplish that on her own, she was sure.

Jasper followed the baron to the front door, and Daisy trailed after them. She was undecided about the situation. It was at the back of her mind that they should try to find out what he had really been after. It was plain to see that he had not been telling the truth. She nibbled on her lip but kept silent.

Jasper spoke with the butler, and it was all taken care of quietly and easily. Within a couple minutes, Jasper had her arm in his warm hand and he was escorting her to the dining room. "It should be empty at this time of the day," he muttered softly in her ear when she looked at him questioningly.

When they were alone in the large silent room, Daisy gazed at Jasper, waiting to hear what he would say. He looked undecided. She began to nibble on her bottom lip once more.

Jasper's gaze fastened on the evidence of her nerves. He reached over and covered it with his thumb. "I beg of you, do not do that. I shall not be able to concentrate if you continue."

His words confused Daisy, and she did not understand the butterflies that fluttered in her stomach over his actions. Goosebumps rose all over her arms, distracting her. She stepped away from the viscount, rubbing her arms with her hands, trying to get warm. The encounter with the baron had discomfited her.

"What shall we do?" she finally asked Jasper when he did not speak.

"About what exactly?" he asked, which Daisy thought was rather ridiculous.

"About Lord Sadbury's arrival upon the doorstep, and the fact that your father now knows that I was a governess," she blurted out. "Everything is ruined," she wailed softly.

"Nothing is ruined," Jasper said gently, taking her hands into his warm ones and chafing them to restore warmth. "Sadbury is gone, and now we just have to go find my father and explain to him that Sadbury is a toad and we got rid of him."

"But I am even more afraid of Sadbury than I was before. He was most certainly lying about wanting me to come back to care for the children. The baron would not put himself out over his poor children. I doubt if he even knows their names."

"What exactly do you think might be behind his visit here, if not what he said it was?"

"I have no idea, which is what troubles me. My impression of Lord Sadbury is that he is a lazy, selfish man who only thinks of himself. For him to go to the effort of seeking me out here at Abernathy makes me feel that there must be a powerful reason that would move him to do so. And for him, I do not think his children would be a strong enough motivator."

Daisy could feel Jasper's gaze on her. His next words made her more sad than fearful. "I can fully understand that. I doubt if my father would travel very far for my benefit."

"Mine would have crawled from London to Bath if necessary in order to be of assistance to me. To me, that is part of the very definition of being a father."

"In theory I agree with you, but sadly I have not seen it applied in practice very often, if ever. I am happy for you that you have experienced it for yourself. Perhaps you could tell me about it one day. For now, we need to come up with some plausible reasons why he might have sought you out."

Daisy's hands, which had warmed up nicely from his attentions, again turned to ice as she contemplated the matter. "The trouble is that I have no idea. I am just a simple girl. I lead a very normal life until my parents died. Since then, my life has been rather dull and even more simple. I have been serving as a governess for goodness' sake. While I was a governess, I did naught but spend time with the children. There is no fathomable reason for which he could be seeking me, I am nearly certain."

They both fell into an uneasy silence as they contemplated their options. "I am doubtful if this is comforting, but we need not trouble ourselves overly at this time. You can be certain if the baron had a big enough reason to search you out, if he has not accomplished whatever his purpose was here today, he will be back at some point."

"You are right — that is not comforting." She heaved a sigh, which she followed up with her sweetest smile. "But I will do my best to put it from my mind for the moment. What would you suggest we should do now?"

"Let us go deal with the marquis. We can be sure he is fuming quite nicely right about now."

"How do you propose we do that?"

"Just follow my lead, my dear, and we shall be perfectly fine."

Daisy's smile wobbled about the edges, but she managed to hold onto it. She gave a firm nod and said, "Lead on then, my lord."

Chapter Fourteen

They found the marquis where they had left him, and Daisy found that fact distractingly curious. It niggled at the back of her mind that there might be something significant about this, but the concerns at the forefront of her mind prevented her from thinking on it at the moment. She hoped she would remember later.

"My lord, thank you for letting us know that the toad, Sadbury, was looking for us. We have had him escorted from the property. Hopefully we will not have any further trouble from him." Daisy was relieved that Jasper had kept it simple and did not bother the marquis with her concerns.

Her relief was short-lived as she noticed the marquis' cold gaze boring into the two of them as they stood before him.

"So, Seaton, do I understand this correctly? You were aware of your guest being a governess?"

Daisy felt Jasper stiffen next to her. He stepped closer to her and put his hand gently at the small of her back. She welcomed the comfort but worried what sort of message he was sending to his father. It would break her heart to be the cause of an even bigger rift between the two noblemen. She wondered if she should distance herself from the viscount for his own good, but she was unable to make herself do so.

"I am aware that she has been so in the past, yes, my lord." Jasper did not elaborate.

"So was this all a ruse? Have you brought her to our home as a lark?" The marquis' grey eyes smoldered despite the cold glare he was directing at them.

"There is no rule of etiquette that says a viscount cannot court a lady who has fallen upon hard times. Having to make her own way in the world by means of finding a position as a governess does not put Miss Pembroke beyond the pale. In fact, I think it displays incredible resourcefulness and demonstrates what a remarkable match she will be. She did not sit down and wring her hands crying over the hard lot life cast for her when her parents died. She made do, and for that I am incredibly proud of her."

Jasper had made this speech in a hard voice that brooked no argument from the marquis, but Daisy listened to it with her mouth slightly agape and tears gathering in her eyes. In her entire life, no one had ever come to her defence so spectacularly. Making an effort to maintain her composure and prevent the tears from escaping, Daisy tore her eyes away from Jasper and glanced at the marquis. She was surprised to see the unguarded look of shock upon his face. She almost laughed but managed to restrain herself.

The desire to laugh was quickly wiped away when the marquis turned his attention to her. It would seem he had accepted Jasper's explanation, but he now had other concerns. "So are you after my son's fortune, Miss Pembroke? Have you finagled your way into his heart with your sad story and beautiful face in order to get your greedy claws into his pockets? Will you break his heart?"

Daisy gasped at the ferocity of this unforeseen attack, and then she burst into giggles. "Oh my lord, you are a complete hand. As if anyone could finagle the viscount. Surely you realize what a knowing one he is. He could spot a scam a mile away, I am sure. And certainly there have been ladies far prettier than me throwing themselves at his head since he came of age. I can assure you, I have not the needed skills to entrap anyone, let alone one as sharp as Lord Seaton. But I do thank you for the compliment. A miss like me can never receive too many of those."

The marquis appeared nonplussed by her outburst. He gazed at the two before him as though undecided whether or not he believed a word coming from their mouths. For Daisy, it was easy to appear guileless as she firmly believed in what she had said. She was unsure if Jasper had said what he had for the benefit of their ploy or if he truly meant it, so she avoided looking at him. Instead, she kept her own gaze steady upon the marquis, waiting to see what he would say.

Lord Abernathy remained disconcertingly silent. Daisy found this quiet maddening. She longed to break the spell that held the three of them still, but she had promised Jasper she would follow his lead, and she was determined to keep to her word. It was painfully difficult to do, though. Finally, Jasper had had enough of the silent game and broke it.

Taking Daisy's hand in his, Jasper nodded respectfully to his father. "If you have nothing further for us at the moment, we should be rejoining the other guests. I am sure Miss Pembroke is ready for her luncheon after the rigours of this morning's sports. We shall bid you adieu for now, my lord."

Daisy quickly dipped into a brief curtsy as Jasper tugged her to follow him. She had to hurry to keep up with his long-legged stride.

When they were out of the marquis' earshot, Jasper quickly turned a corner, stopped short, and pulled Daisy into his arms. She felt as though she had run into a very warm wall as her cheek made contact with his chest. When his arms came up to encircle her, Daisy had the dizzying sensation that she had finally come home.

Her heartbeat picked up and began pounding in her chest and sounded loud in her ears. She could barely hear him as Jasper whispered, "You were magnificent," just before he dropped a light kiss on her forehead.

It was all over before it had even begun. Jasper allowed his arms to drop from around her and picked up her hand once again. This time, instead of holding it and pulling her along, he placed it very properly in the crook of his arm and escorted her at a decorous speed to where the rest of the guests were gathered drinking tea and eating some of the Abernathy cook's delicious pastries.

Daisy had the sensation that she was in a strange fog and wondered how she could possibly force herself to swallow anything after the upheaval of the past interlude. It felt as though hours had passed, but a quick glance at the clock on the mantle revealed it was less than an hour since they had left the games to answer the marquis' summons.

The marchioness glanced curiously at her as she and Jasper slipped into the room. She thought of refusing the cup Lady Abernathy was passing to her, but then her stomach let out a soft gurgle. Daisy was torn between wishing to die of embarrassment and relief that she would be able to eat some of the delicious looking treats. She glanced over at Jasper and caught his amused gaze. They shared a smile before going their separate ways to mingle with the other guests.

Daisy could have screamed with frustration as she heard Lord Ethan Hawkridge hailing her attention. Instead she managed to offer a pleasant smile, seating herself upon an empty settee. Lord Hawkridge quickly took the place beside her.

Suppressing the sigh that tried to escape her lips over his presence at her side, Daisy nodded at him but did not say anything. Instead she brought her cup of tea to her lips and took a delicate sip. The familiar comfort of a cup of tea allowed her to relax for the first time since the footman had told her that Lord Abernathy wanted to speak with her. The moment would have been much sweeter if Hawridge was not at her elbow, but Daisy did not allow that to prevent her from enjoying the moment.

Hawkridge must have expected her to strike up a conversation with him as soon as he sat down. He appeared nonplussed by her silence, which made Daisy feel like giggling. Thankfully he finally began to speak.

"Where did you disappear to earlier today, Miss Pembroke? You were missed. The game of croquet just was not the same without you."

"Thank you for your concern, my lord. A messenger had arrived for me with whom I needed to speak."

"Was it a matter of grave concern? Is there anything I can assist you with?"

Daisy was perplexed over the strange man's sudden interest in her. "Thank you again for your concern, my lord, but all is well. Lord Seaton was with me, and we dealt with the matter without incident."

"Perhaps you would care to stroll with me in the gardens after we have finished our nuncheon."

Daisy blinked rapidly in surprise at the young man's words. *Is he trying to court me?* she asked herself dubiously. From the look on his face, she discerned he was trying to appear innocent, but there was a hard gleam deep in his dark eyes. She knew he was scheming something, but she could not for the life of her imagine what or how it could possibly involve her. Daisy began to feel as though she were on a runaway carriage without a driver, out of control and sure to come to a bad end.

Unfortunately, there was really no other answer possible. "A walk in the garden would be lovely, thank you, my lord." She only hoped her smile looked as sincere as his had been.

Before long, everyone was finished with their tea and pastries and began to move about and make plans for their activities before it was time to dress for dinner. Hawkridge stood and extended his hand to Daisy. She knew her smile was tight, but she was relieved it was not a grimace.

Daisy accepted Hawkridge's hand and allowed him to escort her from the room. She felt Jasper's gaze upon her as they made slow progress through the milling guests. She wondered if she ought to invite others to join them but realized he would recognize that as a cowardly move. There was nothing inherently improper about them strolling in the garden together, even if there was no one else about. But she could not shake the feeling that something was afoot. She resolved to be on her guard, squaring her shoulders and trying not to worry overmuch.

The gardens of Abernathy were extensive and breathtaking. "It must require an army of grounds men to keep the gardens so spectacular, and yet I have never seen anyone working on them while I have been here. Do you know what is the marchioness' secret?" Daisy hoped she would be able to keep the conversation light and flowing while she got over her inconvenient feelings of awkwardness.

"Lady Abernathy is nothing if not organized. You would not know it to look at her, but she rules the estate with an iron fist. She no doubt had the grounds men and even many of the footmen working long hours to have it looking so perfect before the guests arrived. And it cannot fall apart too much in a week, so the workers must all be assigned elsewhere for the time of the party so that our enjoyment will not be marred by the presence of those of the more lowly orders."

The nobleman's snide tone caused Daisy's eyebrows to rise in surprise. "I think I do not grasp your meaning, my lord." Was the man insulting her or the marchioness? She could not tell.

"Everyone credits the marquis or the marchioness for the beauty of this estate. Even you asked what Lady Abernathy's secret was for the spectacular garden. Do you really think either of them have ever lifted a finger to work on these properties? The marquis inherited this house from his ancestors. While it is true that they are well aware of how to ensure their servants obey them, would you not agree it is probably the gardener's secret that has the roses blooming so bountifully?"

Daisy fervently hoped her jaw was not hanging open in her shock. "You sound practically plebeian in your opinions, my lord. I would not have expected it."

"Why not, Miss Pembroke? Because you have found me in such exalted company here at Abernathy? What about your presence here? You are clearly not as high on the social order as many of the others present. Do you not agree with me that it is ridiculous for all of this to belong to someone just by the coincidence of their birth?" He gestured wildly, but Daisy surmised his sweeping arm was meant to encompass all of Abernathy.

"Your words sound remarkably revolutionary for an Englishman, my lord. Considering the fact that the war with France has just ended, should you not choose your words more carefully?" His words rang a bell at the back of her mind, but she was unable to concentrate on why.

"Are you going to tell on me, Miss Pembroke?" he asked, his sneer matching his tone perfectly.

"Who would I tell, my lord? I do believe his grace, the Duke of Wellington, has better things to do than be bothered with the ramblings of a few bored guests at a house party." She tried to make it a jest, but the nobleman's gaze remained disconcertingly fierce. *So much for thinking that discussing the scenery would be a safe conversational gambit*, she thought with a roll of her eyes.

"Have I done something to offend you, my lord?" she finally asked when she could no longer stand his strange, strained silence.

"Not at all, Miss Pembroke, why do you ask?"

Daisy was surprised by his answer. "Because you have been glaring at me as though I have. We met for the first time last night, and you have been acting strangely toward me ever since. I would think it was my lack of nobility that offended you, if not for the fact that you seem to be offended by nobility. You are a conundrum to say the least, Lord Hawkridge."

The daft man threw back his head and laughed. "I like you, Miss Pembroke. You do not bother with flattering speeches or missish airs. I can see why the viscount seems so enthralled with you. Perhaps I ought to try to cut him out of your affections."

Daisy was beginning to wonder if the young man was touched in his upper works. But then she once again saw the speculative gleam shining in his eyes. She feigned a shrug of indifference. "You could always try, my lord, but your success would be in doubt."

Hawkridge laughed again but merely tucked her hand more firmly in his elbow, directing her toward the rose garden further along the walkway. "Tell me a little more about yourself, Miss Pembroke. You have been remarkably reticent about yourself. Most young ladies like nothing better than talking about themselves."

"Really, my lord? Is that not considered ill mannered?"

"Perhaps, but that does not seem to stop most of them."

Daisy could not help giggling over his words. She could not discount them. Over the past several days it was one of the things she had been finding most trying about being here at Abernathy. While most of the other young ladies present seemed pleasant enough, they did not seem to have much to talk about aside from gossip and fashions or their own questionable accomplishments. She had to wonder how playing an instrument or being able to paint beautifully would help them run a household if they did manage to catch themselves a noble husband in the Marriage Mart. The nobility certainly were a strange lot.

She was finally becoming a little more comfortable in Hawkridge's presence when they were surprised to hear Jasper's voice hailing them from the other side of the hedge.

"It would seem the two of you have lost track of the time," he said, his face expressionless. "All of the other ladies have returned to their chambers to ready themselves for dinner. I know how you hate to be late, so I thought I ought to remind you."

Despite having warmed up to the nobleman, Daisy was happy to be rescued from his company. "Thank you, my lord, for coming for me. You are quite correct, I would be highly uncomfortable if I was to show up late to the drawing room." Always polite, she turned and bade Hawkridge adieu. "Thank you for your escort, my lord, it has been an interesting afternoon."

Hawkridge bowed and allowed her to be escorted away from his presence by the viscount. Jasper, glancing back, was surprised to see how attentively Hawkridge was watching them as they headed back to the house. He was on the verge of ringing a peal over Daisy's head for spending so much time with the other man, but she forestalled his words.

"Thank you for rescuing me once more, my lord. It seems to be our destiny, does it not? For one who prides herself on not needing anyone's help, I seem to be looking to you for it rather frequently of late. Is that not divertingly odd?"

Jasper eyed her curiously. "Were you in need of rescuing?"

"Is that not why you turned up?" Daisy countered with a question of her own. "I find Lord Hawkridge to be a strange, mercurial individual. When he asked me to walk with him in the garden, I did not know how to politely decline the invitation without seeming to be a prude or rude or worse. At first he was very strange, but then he seemed to make an effort to be pleasing. I am definitely not sorry that you interrupted us when you did. Is it really very late?"

"Not terribly late, but many of the ladies have retired for a time. I suspect some wish to have a rest after last night and the rigours of the sports today. Perhaps a wee nap would do you good as well."

Daisy laughed. "Are you trying to get rid of me? When I could no longer bear the Sadbury children I always discovered it was time for their nap."

Jasper joined her in her laughter. "I would never try to get rid of you, especially not in such a churlish way. If I had not desired your company, I would have left you with Hawkridge."

"That is true. So did you wish to speak with me in particular or were you merely being gallant?"

Jasper's chest swelled at Daisy's good opinion of him. He realized it could be addictive. He was so unfamiliar with anyone thinking well of him. Even his friends enjoyed him for a lark, but no one ever looked at him the way Daisy did. He knew she was as surprised as he was by her placing her trust in him. He meant to never make her regret it.

"Actually, I did wish to make you a proposition." He knew his tone of voice alerted her to the serious nature of what he was about to say. The laughter drained from her face, and she watched him with attentive, serious eyes.

"Very well, my lord, I am all ears."

Her turn of phrase made him smile, but he did not allow himself to become distracted. "I do not wish to alarm you, but I have been thinking about your situation with Lord Sadbury. I cannot be comfortable with you returning to Bloomsbury on your own. I think we ought to investigate what he could possibly want with you." He paused to see how she was taking his words. So far, she seemed to be agreeable. "My sister has invited us to return to their home with them after the house party ends. She says she would like to get to know you better without the distraction of the other guests around. I think we should go."

Jasper had known she would be resistant, but he was disappointed by how vehemently she was shaking her head. "That will not do at all, my lord. We cannot involve your family in this mess. What if it is unsafe? I could not bear to bring danger to your dear sister. I hate the thought of you getting mixed up in all of this, too, but that cannot be helped as your involvement seems to be an extension of this crazy ruse we have entered into. But we cannot allow your family to be involved."

"Why not?" Jasper demanded baldly.

"For one thing, by extending our relationship beyond the agreed upon week, especially by spending more time with your family, we will only make it all the more messy. We will either compromise ourselves in some way so that you will feel duty bound as a gentleman to offer for me for real, or your family will find out it was all an act, and you will be disowned completely. Neither of those options is acceptable."

Jasper shook his head at her words. He could see she was adamant, but he was determined to make her see reason. "Those arguments are ludicrous. You said for one thing, what are your other arguments?"

"My arguments are not ludicrous, my lord, especially not this next one. If you are concerned for my safety, you cannot possibly wish to bring my dangerous presence into your sister's home."

"To be frank, I am more concerned about your safety than Bess'."

He had not meant to reveal so much, but it need not to have troubled him. Daisy did not accept his words how he had meant them. She turned upon him with a scold. "You really ought to make more of an effort with your family, Lord Seaton. Do you not realize how much I would give to have my family back? You should be grateful that you have them and try to get along with them better. I know your parents seem to be rather difficult to please, but your sister is a delight. You should be in alt about that. And you definitely should not be looking to bring a potentially dangerous situation to her doorstep."

"Do not presume to tell me what I should or should not do, you managing little baggage. I am trying to keep you safe!" Jasper surprised even himself with the vehemence of his tone.

Rather than being cowed by his attitude, Daisy flared up into a righteous indignation. "You do not own me, Lord Jasper Seaton. Just because we are friends does not give you the right to tell me what to do. I will be just fine on my own, in Bloomsbury, thank you very much."

Her flashing eyes, rosy cheeks, and pursed lips were enough to drive Jasper to distraction. For the second time that day, he hauled her into his arms and squeezed her tight against his chest. She felt so right curled into his arms, and he could have stood there holding her all day, but he felt her stiffen and did not want to make her any more uncomfortable than he already had.

"Daisy, my dear, please accept my abject apologies. I do not mean to make you angry. I am worried about you and this wretched situation with Sadbury. Do not fly up into the boughs about my highhanded behavior. Please, promise me you will at least think about accepting my sister's invitation."

Jasper carefully put her away from himself, holding her at arms' length and searching her eyes to ascertain her thoughts. He was happy to see that most of the ire had died out, and she was returning his gaze rather ruefully.

"I will think on it, my lord. I apologize, too. I should never have allowed my temper to get away from me like that. It is most unlike me. I do not know what came over me. It was both exhilarating and embarrassing."

Jasper had the urge to kiss her pert, wrinkled nose as she contemplated her strange behavior. He resisted, but it was difficult. She was concerned about them being compromised into making a real match of it. He was beginning to wonder if that would not be a wonderful thing, but he pushed the thought from his mind for the moment. Having gained her promise to think about going to his sister's house rather than back to Charlotte's, he allowed her to pull from his grasp and he escorted her back to the house, briskly and efficiently.

Another dinner flew by along with an evening of entertainment. Daisy was not sleeping well, so concerned was she about the situation she faced with Sadbury. She was tempted to take Jasper up on his offer of seeking refuge at his sister's house, but Daisy truly was concerned that she would be bringing danger to their doorstep.

It was the last night of the house party; once again the marchioness had planned a ball. This was less formal than the first one, with many of the surrounding gentry invited to join the wellborn guests. Daisy found herself in Jasper's arms, easily following his lead around the crowded dance floor.

Jasper persisted in seeking a commitment from her to travel on the morrow to his sister's home rather than back to London.

Daisy finally sighed. "Jasper, my lord, you are exasperating me. Very well, if you will tell his lordship about the potential danger, and he is all right with it, I will accompany you there. I do not mean to be difficult, my lord, you do realize that, do you not? I just do not wish to bring any more trouble to your family than I already have."

Jasper squeezed her a little closer than was decorous for the dance, making Daisy's heart skip a little beat. "Excellent decision, my dear." She basked in the warmth of his smile but regarded him severely.

"Promise me, my lord. Promise me you will tell him clearly that there is the potential of danger if I come to them."

"I promise, you little termagant. I will explain the situation as best I can although surely you realize that it is rather inexplicable."

"I do realize that, my lord, and I am not trying to be difficult, but that is the deal. If the earl is as fully informed as possible and still wants us to come, I will happily accompany you to your sister's house."

She wanted to giggle over his incredulous face. She truly did not wish to cause him aggravation, but this was her problem to deal with and she wished he would understand her reluctance to involve anyone else in it.

Chapter Fifteen

As the carriage lurched into motion, Jasper couldn't quite look Daisy in the eye. He was relieved that she seemed a little too bewildered by their departure to notice. He suspected she hadn't slept enough and the conclusion of the Abernathy visit had crept up on her. He hoped to avoid telling her about his most recent conversation with the marquis.

"Your little friend certainly brings trouble with her."

"Whatever do you mean?" Jasper stiffened in rejection of his father's words.

"There was another person asking for her this afternoon."

Despite his effort to conceal all feelings in Abernathy's presence, Jasper knew surprise was written on his face. "I was certain we had taken care of Sadbury."

"According to the butler, this one seemed like a messenger of some sort and was easily discouraged from dallying upon the property. Do not trouble yourself over it. Mr. Bloom is well able to sort out such matters."

Jasper stared at the marquis for a moment. "Is this why you have decided to accompany us to Welland?"

He was surprised to see a self-conscious look cross his father's usually impassive face before the marquis brushed it aside with a shrug. "Somebody has to keep an eye on the two of you."

Without another word Jasper had turned on his heel and left the conversation, but it now weighed on his conscience. He ought to tell Daisy, but he didn't want her to worry. He devoutly hoped they would soon have more answers than questions. Jasper hated to see the worry creasing her forehead. With relief, he noticed that she now only looked bemused rather than weighed down with concerns.

ꟾ

Daisy was unsure how it had been contrived, but before she fully realized, it the house party was over and she was once again shut into a carriage with Kate and the viscount, bowling along at a brisk pace, on the way to Welland. Even more surprising was the knowledge that Lord and Lady Abernathy would also be joining them at their daughter's home.

"Did you tell your father about our concerns regarding Sadbury?" Daisy asked quietly, breaking the comfortable silence they had all drifted into.

She was surprised to see a light blush staining Jasper's cheeks. She giggled despite her discomfort. "Oh, my lord, how could you not have told him?"

"You only made me promise to tell my brother-in-law — you said nothing about my father."

She fixed her glare upon him, delighted to see the colour deepen on his cheekbones. "Did you not understand the principle behind why I made you make such a promise? Had I known your parents would be accompanying us, do you not think I would have asked you to promise to tell them as well?"

"Why do you think I failed to mention my parents?" Jasper muttered, not quite meeting her eyes.

"You, my lord, are a devious sneak. I think you will be a perfect match for Sadbury." She sighed in resignation, unable to change the course of events at this stage. "Have you any idea how we are going to investigate Sadbury in order to figure out what he could possibly want with me?"

"I have already sent a few messages to London. I know a few experts in the field of investigation. Mayhap there will be information awaiting us upon our arrival at Welland."

"Why did you not tell me? You do realize I would appreciate that sort of information, do you not?"

Jasper turned his attention to gaze out the window. "You have been too busy with all your new friends to have any time to discuss the case with me." His dismissive tone did not deceive her for a minute.

"You could not possibly be jealous that I have made some friends, could you, my lord?" Daisy was shocked at the possibility, but the evidence before her told its own story. The only reply she got from the viscount was a dismissive sniff.

Daisy turned her head and caught Kate's amused gaze. She did not dignify his reaction with any further words. They continued in silence for a while longer, but then Daisy grew weary of sitting still. She wanted some conversation to break the monotony. Not wishing to spoil Kate's enjoyment of the passing scenery, she determined the viscount ought to entertain her.

"Is it very much further to Welland, do you suppose, my lord? Shall we be stopping anywhere along the way, or did you have the cook pack us a basket of goodies? I would certainly not refuse if you said there are some of your mother's cook's pastries somewhere about. That man certainly knows how to make a pastry. I can tell you, none of my baking efforts ever resulted in anything so scrumptious."

Jasper's gaze turned interested. "Do you cook, Miss Daisy?"

Daisy shrugged. "I am a decent cook but only a passable baker. If you had to rely on me, you would not starve, but there would be none of the enjoyment that there is at the Abernathy table."

"Well you will be happy to know that he did, in fact, send along a basket of goodies for us. And it is not too awfully far to Bess' house. We should be there within another hour, I would think."

"I am not sure if I am looking forward to arriving or dreading it. Do you have any idea why your parents have accompanied us? It would have been almost a lark to spend a few days with your sister and her husband, but having the marquis and marchioness along does bring it down to being almost a trial." Daisy's eyes flew to Jasper's with apology clear in their depths. "I am so sorry, my lord. It is terribly ill mannered of me to speak thusly about your parents?"

"I beg of you, do not let it trouble you. I could not agree more. Not that I am terribly close with Bess, but we rub along tolerably well. I did not realize until this morning that my parents would be joining us. I cannot fathom what would have prompted them to do so. I would have thought they would be happy to have a few days of quiet by themselves after all their guests had departed."

"Are you going to tell them?" Daisy could not keep the worry from her voice and frowned when she heard how nervous she sounded. The suspense was starting to get to her. She dearly wished she knew what to expect from Sadbury. She caught Jasper's eyes staring at her hands, which were fidgeting nervously in her lap. She stilled the telling action.

"Not unless it is necessary. I only told the earl because you made me promise to do so. I am quite sure we will receive word very soon after we arrive at Bess' house. Then we can deal with whatever it is and move on with our lives, hopefully without incident and without anyone else needing to be informed."

"That would be lovely," Daisy agreed. "But if the information is not so clear or easily acted upon, will you tell the marquis?" she persisted.

Jasper could see from her earnest gaze that it was important to her. "Daisy, I promise you, we are in this together. After we hear from my messengers, you and I will sit down together and discuss the entire situation and decide on the best course. If you still feel it is important to inform the marquis then we will do so. Does that plan meet with your satisfaction?"

Daisy's eyes filled with tears, and she nodded her agreement. "Thank you, my lord. I truly appreciate your consideration. Even your involvement! You really could have just washed your hands of the whole thing and sent me back to Bloomsbury, you know."

"Not really, my dear. I would not be able to live with myself if something happened to you and I did nothing to prevent it. Now never mind about that, we have at least another hour before we will be any the wiser. Let us put the matter from our minds for the time being and think of more pleasant things. What did you really think of your first house party?" He turned his head and nodded at Kate. "You too, Kate, I would be delighted to hear your impressions as well."

"Oh, my lord, it was the bestest time I ever did have," Kate enthused. "I'm not ashamed to say that at first I was mighty intimidated by the upper servants, like the butler and the marquis' valet, but once I settled in, everyone was real nice to me. And the food. Oh my, I've never had such food. Wouldn't my brothers have just liked to have some of those pastries."

Jasper laughed. "You girls certainly enjoyed the baked goods."

Daisy giggled. "They were one of the highlights, even you would have to agree, my lord." They shared an amused glance before Daisy proceeded to share her impressions of her first house party. "I will admit to you that I had a remarkably good time. I enjoyed making new acquaintances. I was surprised that despite how nobly born most were, very few were overly high in the instep, as I had feared. I was made to feel quite welcome. Of course, that has something to do with the fact that your father did not reveal my secret. I am not convinced that they would have been so welcoming if they had known." She anticipated Jasper's protest, so she forestalled his words by carrying on with her list of things she had enjoyed about the week. "I loved the games. As an only child, growing up I never got to play many of those games. And the dancing was so much better than I had anticipated. And of course, Abernathy is breathtakingly beautiful."

Jasper began to laugh as she enumerated all the things she had enjoyed. "All right, enough, we do not need to relive the entire week. I am relieved that you did not find it a dead bore."

"One would have to be a barbarian to find time spent at Abernathy boring, I should think, my lord. What about you? Did you enjoy your week?"

Jasper's face was suddenly an inscrutable mask. "It was reasonably passable, my dear. Abernathy is not one of my favorite destinations, I am sure you realize. But the company was enjoyable."

Daisy laughed and did not press him for more details. "Miss Ecklestone was a delightful girl to meet. I had thought Lord Hawkridge was interested in her, but then I was not so sure."

"Why were you not so sure? Because of his display of interest in you?" Jasper's question made Daisy blush.

She quickly replied, "No, I did not think he was taking any sort of interest in me. He strikes me as a trifle odd. Do you know if your sister gets along well with him?"

"He gave her trouble when she and her husband were newly married. Their courtship was quick, and they did not wait long to get married, so I think Hawkridge was surprised by it. He did not have a chance to cause trouble before it was too late. There is the very real probability that he will be disinherited if Bess has a son."

"It seemed to me as though he were wealthy enough in his own right that he would not be coveting his uncle's wealth," Daisy opined.

Jasper shrugged. "Most people would say 'you can never have too much money.'"

"So then why is he accompanying them to Welland, if they do not get along?"

"Perhaps to keep an eye on the competition?" Jasper asked with a wry grin before continuing. "Actually, they get on just fine now. Hawkridge expressed some concern about the age difference between Bess and her husband. And perhaps he did not take well to being replaced in his uncle's affections."

"I am sure his uncle feels quite differently about him than he does about his wife." Daisy's dry tone caused Jasper to smile.

"One would hope," Jasper replied. "Family matters can be complicated. I am having second thoughts about exposing you to mine, now that we have been discussing this. I do apologize, Daisy, this might not have been the best idea."

Daisy's laughter rang out in the small confines of the carriage, making the other two occupants smile despite being unsure what she was laughing about. "My lord, you are a complete hand. It is a trifle late to be having cold feet about this. I tried to tell you it was a bad idea."

Jasper interrupted. "That was for a completely different reason, which I still do not accept. I do not regret keeping you away from Bloomsbury until we have the Sadbury situation sorted. It is merely the necessity for prolonging the exposure to my family that I am concerned about."

Daisy tilted her head and regarded him curiously. "What do you fear might happen, my lord?"

"My main concern is that you will be hurt by my father's cold attitude."

"Bah," Daisy countered, "I have been exposed to worse. You should have seen some of the nasty little girls at Miss Tyler's school. Everyone thinks girls are such lovely little creatures, but let me tell you, they can be beasts, especially at a certain age. If I could survive that, I should have no trouble with the Marquis of Abernathy."

Jasper appeared unconvinced. "You have not seen him at his worst."

"Mayhap not, but I can imagine it after having seen the way he treats you. If you have turned out as well as you have despite extended exposure, I am certain a few days shall not harm me overmuch." Daisy paused, considering how concerned the viscount really appeared to be. "How about we agree to keep each other informed about how we are feeling? If either of us can no longer bear the chill, we shall come up with another plan. Or I could always head back to Charlotte's, if it becomes too difficult."

"No!" Jasper insisted with some force, making them all jump. "I apologize for my outburst, but that is not going to be an option for now. You agreed, Daisy."

"I know, I know, I was teasing." Daisy sighed and changed the subject. "What do you suppose we are going to do while at your sister's house, my lord?"

"Much the same as we did at Abernathy, I would imagine, but without the balls, most likely. I cannot imagine Bess will be able to organize anything on too large a scale at this late date, but perhaps there will be gatherings at the local assembly rooms. You might enjoy that. It would be a little like the Season, but on a more provincial level."

"I am sure it shall all be lovely. Your sister is a dear, and it was kind of her to invite us."

Jasper's smile did not quite make it to his eyes. Daisy regarded him as her own narrowed. "You are rather dreading this, are you not? Oh Jasper, I do wish you were not such a gentleman. Why did you have to take my troubles onto yourself? I am going to feel ghastly about this."

"Do not, I beg of you." Jasper reached across the carriage and clasped one of Daisy's hands in his own. "I promise you, while I do not cherish the thought of spending more time with my family, I am looking forward to spending it with you." Jasper's warm tone sent a shiver down Daisy's back. He must have felt it through her hand, as he let it go. His tone became more brisk. "Besides, we will be occupied with figuring out what Sadbury wants with you. Everything else will get straightened out as soon as we know what he is after."

Daisy leaned back and studied him carefully. Jasper averted his eyes, gazing out the window at the passing scenery. She sighed. The charming man would not let her into his private thoughts. She told herself that it did not matter. He was entitled to his privacy. And really, they had only known each other for a couple of weeks; she did not have the right to demand he tell her all his thoughts. But she did wish to know them. She, too, gazed out the window and allowed her mind to drift.

Daisy was staring out the window on a similar voyage. All was right in her world but she was bored. Her mother must have heard her sigh.

"Daisy, my darling, what ails you? Did you finish your book already?"

Turning to her mother with a smile, Daisy tucked her hand into her mother's larger but still dainty, warm one. "No, mama, I have not finished yet. I am just bored of this drive. Will we ever get there, do you suppose?"

Mama's rich, warm laughter rang out. "Yes, my darling daughter, we will get there eventually. In fact, from the view out your window, it would seem that we are very nearly there. You will enjoy playing with your cousins, will you not?"

"Absolutely!" Daisy's childish enthusiasm had brought a smile to both of her parents' faces.

Their remembered doting on her was such a source of comfort as she remembered the incident. Times had been so simple then. Her cousins had been such fun to play with. It would have been so lovely if they could have stayed close throughout their entire lives. She would not be here with the viscount, wondering why the baron was showing such interest in her, that is for certain. That thought triggered another memory. This one more recent.

"It's just the way that it is Sadbury. One decision always leads to another. You cannot go back. The path is laid. We are in this. You are not trying to tell me you have grown a conscience after all this time, are you?"

Daisy had not meant to eavesdrop, she had merely been on her way to the library to return the book she had been reading. It was so rare in this household for any of the books to get used, so she supposed no one had expected any visitors to the library at this hour.

Sadbury had looked up at her, and the look of surprised hostility on his face had made Daisy blink. She dipped into a curtsy. "I apologize for interrupting, my lord, I was returning a book."

"Be quick about it, girl, we have work to do."

"Yes, my lord."

Daisy hurried to shelve the book she had in her hand, wishing she had never come to the library. The presence of Lord Gerard Wright always made her uncomfortable. She feltl his hot stare boring into her back the entire time she was in the room. She made short work of returning the book and scurried back to her chamber.

As Daisy relived that moment, she was aware that there was something about it niggling at the back of her mind. She suspected she had heard more than she could remember, but all that stuck in her mind was how Lord Wright's expressions of one thing leading to the other tied in with her own thoughts about her family and Lord Seaton.

Lord Wright had always made her uncomfortable. She supposed it was an instinctive reaction. The first time she had met him was very soon after she had become a governess. The way that he had looked at her had made her feel as though she needed to bathe. She had been very careful to never find herself alone in his company. Of course, in the end, it had mattered little whether she was alone or not, which is why she no longer worked for the Sadburys.

With a slight shiver, Daisy hoped Lord Wright was not involved in why the baron was searching for her. She could not bear to see the rotter again.

The change of the motion of the carriage alerted the occupants to their new environment. Kate and Daisy pressed their noses to the windows to try to get the best view of this new destination.

"Ooh Miss, ain't it beautiful? I've never seen such a pretty place. I mean, Abernathy was grand, of course, but this is something else, isn't it?" Kate's enthusiasm could not be expressed in words.

"It certainly is, Kate. I agree. I have never seen such a lovely place. I have no doubt we shall enjoy our visit here."

Daisy's positive attitude always buoyed those around her. She caught Jasper's smile before he opened the door as the carriage came to a stop.

Stepping down briskly, Jasper turned and offered his hand to assist the female occupants of the carriage, ignoring the footman who was waiting to perform that duty. Kate emerged first, eager to look around with her youthful gaze and anxious step. Daisy was a trifle more inured to the prospect of staying in another nobleman's home.

"Thank you, my lord." She accepted his assistance graciously, her voice pitched low, making Jasper's palms begin to sweat. Jasper gritted his teeth against his reaction, praying fervently she would not notice.

Bess and her husband had left earlier than Jasper and his companions, so they were already on their doorstep waiting to welcome them.

"Daisy, my dear, I am so thrilled to have you here. Can you believe my brother has only been here once? I am so glad that your presence has finally moved him to visit once more."

Jasper tried to pretend he did not notice Daisy's incredulous gaze focused on his face. He stepped close to bow gallantly over his sister's hand. "Thank you for your kind invitation, my lady. We will be grateful for your hospitality."

Bess giggled. "I can see that Daisy's influence is working on you, Seaton. It is a pleasure to witness."

Jasper saw that Daisy was about to come to his defence. He found it heartwarming and charming, but he did not want her to make herself uncomfortable with his family for the coming week. He grasped her arm firmly in his hand, catching her eye as her gaze flew to his. He shook his head slightly. From the way her eyes flared he could tell that she had caught his meaning, but he was unsure if she was going to obey his silent directive. Finally, her eyes dropped, and he felt her acquiescence as her shoulders drooped slightly. Jasper wanted to hug her for feeling so dejected on his behalf. He knew he was going to have to talk it out with her sooner or later. It would be best to get it over with before she ended up in a fight with any of his relatives. Jasper grinned over that thought.

"You look happy," his sister observed. "It is a sight to behold. I cannot say if I have ever seen you looking thusly."

Now Jasper thought she was going a bit far. He turned the subject. "Have you been home long? Was your voyage as uneventful as ours?"

Bess answered as they neared the house, her husband had yet to say a word; although he smiled and shook hands, he had a worried air about him. "Oh yes, our ride was fine. Rather tedious, but it was nice to have a little while to visit together just the two of us after a week at Abernathy and now having you all arriving today." She must have realized that could have been taken as being less than delighted to have them visiting. "Not to say that we are not thrilled to have you here, of course, Miss Pembroke. It shall be our pleasure, to be sure. It was just nice to have a couple hours of quiet. We made good time and have been home for about an hour already."

They were now in the large entry way of the gracious country manor. It was on the newer side, unlike Abernathy, and had been constructed all together in one era. The architectural consistency was pleasing to the eye and had been enhanced with tasteful decorations and fresh tapestries and window dressings. Daisy wondered if Bess had redecorated as soon as she had taken up residence. It certainly looked as though there had been a recent update about the place.

She thought to refer to it or compliment Bess on their surroundings but then saw Lord Hawkridge nearby and thought better of it. It could be one of the contentious topics Jasper had referred to. Daisy wondered if she would have to watch her every word all through their visit. She hoped there was news from Jasper's messengers and the visit could be short.

Trying to keep her smile bright, Daisy managed to keep her thoughts to herself. Bess gave them an abbreviated tour of the main rooms on the first floor before escorting them to their assigned bedchambers.

"Daisy, we thought you and Kate would enjoy the Rose Room. It has a lovely view of the gardens and gets a lot of light during the day. I hope you will be comfortable here."

Daisy glanced into the room, unsurprised to see the walls covered in a floral paper. *It looks as though the garden has come inside,* she thought rather dazedly as she looked at the abundance of flower patterns displayed in the brightly lit room. "I am sure we will have a grand time here, thank you, Bess." She avoided Jasper's eyes as she knew quite well he would be amused by her diplomatic answer, and she was having a difficult enough time maintaining a straight face without his humor adding to it. It would seem Bess' renovations had not extended to the guest rooms.

Kate was already in the room shaking out Daisy's gowns and getting everything unpacked. Daisy was left in her tender care to freshen up, with the promise that they would meet in the receiving room shortly.

"Isn't it wonderful, Miss Daisy?" Kate cooed as she made quick work of the luggage. "This is just the sort of place I would like to be employed. Small enough that I won't get lost, but big enough that they need plenty of servants."

"Are you certain you wish to go into service, Kate? Your family will be quite lost without you, I am sure."

Kate looked at Daisy reproachfully as a tear came to her eye. "Well, of course, I will miss them something fierce, but if I could send them some money to help with things, I'm sure that would help them to be less lost without me. You aren't planning to renege on your promise to write me up a good recommendation so I can get a position once you're done with me, are you?"

"Kate," Daisy scolded, offering a reproachful look of her own. "How could you even think I would go back on my word to you?"

Kate ran to Daisy and threw her arms around her. "I know it ain't fitting for me to be so familiar, but I didn't mean no harm, Miss Daisy. I didn't mean you no insult neither."

Daisy returned her embrace and soothed her with her own words. "Of course not, no harm done, my dear. I did not mean to imply that you ought not take a position as housemaid or lady's maid. You have proven to be invaluable to me, so you shall do a fine job. I just wanted to ensure you have thought the matter through sufficiently to make a sound decision."

"Oh, miss, I have thought and thought. I am that excited about it. I know it won't always be parties and such, but it's ever so much better than looking after my pa's cottage in Bloomsbury with never a cent to my name."

"Very well, I will ensure Lord Seaton finds you a comfortable position when you are done with me."

"Maybe you're going to have to keep me on," Kate said, wiggling her eyebrows at Daisy. "I saw the way his lordship has been looking at you. I think he has a mind to make your little arrangement a reality."

The heat rose in her cheeks, but Daisy answered as repressively as she could. "Do not be entertaining such ideas, Kate, I beg of you. They shall only lead to disappointment for us both."

Kate showed no sign of following her order. She merely giggled and shrugged, saying, "I've got eyes in me head, Miss Daisy, and I know what I see. But never you mind, I won't tease you over it. Now did you want to have a little lay down before you go gather with the rest?"

Daisy rolled her eyes at her faithful maid and shook her head. "I do not think I would be able to even close my eyes, let alone get any sleep. I think I will just sit in this darling little alcove and gaze out the window for a few minutes."

"Very well, miss. I will bustle about and get all your things in order. Do you have in mind which gown you would like to wear for the evening?"

"I cannot find that I have a very strong opinion on the matter, Kate. Would you mind just preparing whatever you think is best?"

"That would be just fine with me, miss," Kate answered with a delighted grin, pleased that her temporary mistress trusted her so well.

Daisy sat in the window seat, carefully tucking her feet under herself, her attention caught by the beautifully maintained grounds outside her window. She sat there for several minutes enjoying the view and absorbing the calm. She rather thought Bess' husband must be a restful man if his family home had such a lovely effect on her. She looked forward to getting to know him better. He would no doubt be a calming influence upon the gathered family members. *Or at least I hope so,* she thought with a wry smile to herself.

After a few minutes and several restorative, deep breaths, Daisy felt ready to face the clan. By then Kate was getting bored and was glad to have something to do. Within a few minutes, Daisy was dressed in a lovely light green gown, one of the ones that had been deemed not too fancy but fancy enough. Daisy smiled as she remembered how they had debated over the classifications for each gown that she had packed.

Having her hair styled was such a relaxing experience for her, Daisy almost nodded off as Kate was brushing out her curls and arranging them in a deceptively simple style. It never ceased to amaze

Daisy what wonders Kate was able to accomplish with her hair. For her part, whenever she had to do for herself, the styles were utilitarian and simple, merely a way of keeping her long, blond hair out of her eyes and out of the way of children's small hands.

"Where did you learn such skills, Kate, my dear? You truly are a marvel. I could never do anything half so lovely on my own."

"Oh, Miss Daisy, that's right kind of you to say. I would practice all the time on my sisters and the neighbor girls. I always hoped for just such an opportunity. I wanted to be sure that I was ready if the chance ever came up for grabs. And here we are, so wasn't that lucky?"

"It was certainly very forward thinking of you, and I am benefiting greatly." Daisy paused for a moment, watching Kate's deft hands in the mirror. "Thank you for being willing to stick with me for longer and journeying heaven knows where."

"Are you jesting with me, Miss Daisy? Have you not been listening to me? I am thrilled to be here. I'm just glad you saw fit to appreciate my services enough to want me to come along. As long as you want me, I'll be here happily."

The two girls shared a smile in the mirror before Kate declared she was done. "You are as ready as I can make you, Miss Daisy. How are you feeling? Are you going to be all right without the crowds around to dilute the Abernathy presence?"

"Kate Simpson, do not speak so of our hosts."

Kate did not look at all repentant, although she made an attempt to lower her eyes bashfully and apologize. "But really, miss, you know I'm right."

"I will admit no such thing, and you ought to be trying to nurture a more deferential attitude toward the nobility. Not that I think it is of any value as a human need, but if you hope to cultivate a career as a lady's maid, it is, no doubt, a necessary skill."

Kate look much struck by Daisy's words. "That do make sense, miss. Thank you ever so much for pointing it out to me."

"Any time, my dear girl. We are in this together. I shall be happy to help in whatever way I can. Now I ought to be off. I hope it will not be a late night."

"Do not hope that on my account, miss. I shall be perfectly fine waiting up for you."

"Thank you," Daisy said with a grin. "But I was actually thinking of myself — I am getting tired." She left the room to the sound of her maid's giggles.

Chapter Sixteen

Daisy was mortified to find that she was the last to arrive in the withdrawing room. But she need not have wasted her emotional energy. So cold was the atmosphere when she entered the room, it seemed as though she had walked into a winter landscape. Jasper jumped to his feet immediately upon her arrival.

"Daisy, my dear," he greeted her, relief evident in his voice. "Were you able to have a rest after our arrival? You look well."

"Thank you, my lord, I feel quite refreshed. The room I am in is quite comfortable, and the view is lovely. I enjoyed sitting and looking at it for a few minutes. It was most restorative."

Bess' husband, like all the gentlemen in the room, had stood upon her entrance, and now stepped forward to speak to her. "I am pleased to hear you are enjoying the Rose Room. It has always been one of our favorite rooms."

"I am honored to have been offered the privilege of enjoying such a place." Daisy's answer was gracious and simple. She smiled to the room at large and took a seat next to the marchioness.

"How was your trip here?" Daisy asked solicitously, placing a gentle hand on the older lady's wrist.

"Good evening, Daisy, thank you for asking, it was uneventful and rather dull after the excitement of the last week, but we are delighted to be with our family. Do you know, it is has been at least five years since we have been together with just our family? We were all together for Bess' wedding, of course, but just like during the house party, there were constantly many others around. This shall be so lovely, do you not agree?"

Daisy looked closely at Lady Abernathy, wondering if she were perhaps jesting with her. While the noblewoman had always been pleasant during the house party, Daisy had not sensed any desire from her to deepen the relationship. Now she seemed so kind and approachable. She would give anyone the impression that she was looking forward to spending time with both her children. There was nothing else Daisy could do but reply, "I do hope you enjoy having your children to yourself for a few days." It was the truth and did not reveal how doubtful Daisy was that it would be anything resembling "lovely."

The butler arrived at that moment to announce dinner. Daisy hoped she did not bound to her feet too readily. She forced herself not to hurry but was actually quite hungry and wondered if she would be able to enjoy the meal or if the family tensions would interfere.

As the various courses were served, it seemed as though everyone was on their best behavior, merely exchanging amusing stories about the various gossip they had heard at Abernathy during the party.

"Did you hear that Lord Aylmer challenged Mr. Simmons to a duel?" Lord Welland asked.

"No!" exclaimed Bess.

"Yes, Aylmer says Simmons was encroaching on his fiancé."

Daisy had to blink over that particular little tidbit she overheard. She decided not to engage in the conversation. Not that she knew any of the parties anyway, but she felt sure there were all sorts of details being left out. It was no doubt heart breaking to Lord Aylmer's poor fiancé.

"Well she IS rumored to have a dowry of forty thousand pounds, so that would be well worth defending, if you ask me," Hawkridge interjected in an aside to Daisy.

Daisy hadn't asked and rather wished Lord Hawkridge would leave her well out of it. She offered him a wan smile and dredged up a far less objectionable tidbit of gossip she had gleaned from the house party. "Margaret told me that she was trying to raise funding for a charity house in the nearest village to her house. Do you think she will be successful?"

Hawkridge stared at her blankly for a moment before he broke into a grin. "I take it you don't wish to discuss duels?"

Daisy felt the flush rising in her cheeks but tried to shrug it off. "Why would you say that, my lord?"

He merely laughed and didn't bother to answer her, as the meal was drawing to an end.

When Bess stood up to signal the ladies would leave the gentlemen to their port, Daisy followed her and her mother to a charming room, different from the withdrawing room in which they had met before dinner. There were a couple of tables set up for card games as well as a pianoforte in the corner. Daisy wondered if they would be playing games or music. Or both were possible, she supposed. Either could be charming.

"You shall enjoy the scenery hereabouts, Daisy. I was thinking we should ride out to explore some of the ruins nearby. There is a great deal of history in this area."

"That sounds like it will be wonderful. I am sure we will enjoy it immensely. It was so kind of you to invite us for a few days."

"I was just so delighted that you and my brother were able to come." Bess smiled at Daisy, taking her hand in a friendly gesture. "I doubt if Seaton would have come if not for you, so I am grateful for whatever the reason that made you come."

Daisy had to struggle to keep her smile in place. Did the woman not realize how nervous she was about the situation with Sadbury? How could she be grateful for it? The marchioness, listening to their exchange, looked curious, but did not comment. Bess, seemingly unaware of Daisy's dilemma, continued on to another touchy subject.

"I hope my husband's nephew hasn't been making you uncomfortable."

Daisy blinked at her and struggled through an answer. "I haven't gotten to know him very well as yet," was her diplomatic response.

Bess laughed. "The poor boy hasn't decided what to do with himself. He hasn't had the easiest life, despite being of noble birth and with a comfortable fortune. He became my husband's ward when he was around twelve, but poor Welland didn't know what to do with him, so he was sent off to school for much of the year. They were only getting to know each other as adults when I came into the picture, so Hawksridge is still trying to work out if he is going to be a hero or a villain in his own personal story."

Daisy grinned at Bess' turn of phrase but had nothing to add to the narrative. Her own experiences in life had shown her that no one was forced into the way they coped with whatever life dealt them. She was once again relieved to see Jasper walking through the door when the gentlemen joined them.

"We thought of going to the billiards room but then decided that we ought to invite you ladies to join us," Jasper explained to her quietly. "Have you ever played billiards, my dear?"

"No, I have not, but I would be happy to watch." Daisy was eager to avoid any awkward conversations and hoped a simple game would do to pass the time that evening. She also needed an opportunity to speak with Jasper as privately as possible.

She found her opportunity not too much later.

"Have you heard anything of import, my lord, from the messengers you were hoping would meet us here?"

"I regret to have to tell you that they have not yet arrived. Perhaps tomorrow," he suggested by way of offering comfort.

Daisy just wanted to go to bed and pull the covers over her head. With a sigh, she applied herself to learning the incomprehensible game with the small balls and long sticks. The gentlemen enjoyed themselves immensely, and the atmosphere in the room was lighter than Daisy had ever witnessed amongst this particular group. She found herself relaxing slightly.

Relaxing made her all the more sleepy, and she was unable to suppress the yawn that bubbled to the surface. Daisy thought Jasper was completely occupied with his game, but as soon as she yawned, he turned and met her eye.

"Daisy, my dear girl, you ought to be seeking your bed. I hesitate to point out that you are not looking your very best, but you are beginning to wilt before us. Do not force yourself to stay up for our benefit. Seek your bed if you wish."

Once again, Daisy was reminded of what a kind gentleman he was. She smiled her gratitude and bade everyone a good night. It was not very late, but she was longing for her bed. Making her way up to her room, Daisy was glad she would not be keeping Kate up too late.

"Oh no, miss, was your evening dreadful? Why have you returned to your room so early?" Kate was aghast.

"No, no, Kate, it was actually rather fine. I am just weary and was excused. Jasper was kind enough to notice and send me to bed. I did not want to be the first to leave, but no one seemed to mind. The house party, followed by travelling here seems to have made everyone sleepy tonight. I promise, I shall be much more sociable tomorrow night and will keep you up waiting for me many more hours."

"Oh Miss Daisy you are joshing me, aren't you? I didn't mean to sound as though I was complaining that you have come back. I just want you to have a good time. I know you have your worries weighing on you."

Daisy offered a warm smile to her maid but did not bother to respond further. They made quick work of taking down her hair and getting her into her nightrail, and Daisy was asleep as soon as her head hit the pillow

"Ach, the poor dear lady was fair exhausted, weren't she then," Kate commented to herself as she bustled about straightening up her mistress' things and then made her way to her own trundle bed, ready enough herself to take her rest.

The next day dawned bright and clear, and Daisy felt much more prepared to face her concerns after being fortified with a good long rest. After Kate helped her to dress appropriately for the country pursuits Bess had spoken of the previous day, Daisy made her way down to the dining room where the morning's repast was spread on the sideboard, a veritable feast, much to Daisy's delight.

The only other occupant of the room was Jasper. Daisy felt as though her heart skipped a beat when she saw the viscount sprawled rather inelegantly, sipping his tea and staring out the window. When he caught sight of Daisy hovering in the doorway, he leapt to his feet with a feeble grin. Daisy remembered from previous days that the viscount was most definitely NOT a morning person. She tried to contain her amused smile so as not to offend him. He was trying to be gallant after all.

"Good morning, Miss Daisy, you look particularly fetching this morning."

"Why thank you, my lord, how very kind of you to say. Please have a seat. I will just be a moment. Everything smells delicious. I think your sister's cook was expecting rather more guests than there are — just look at the bounty she has spread."

Jasper was chuckling softly behind her, amused over her enthusiasm for the meal. She turned and pulled a face at him, which only served to make him laugh all the harder. Daisy could not understand why he found her enjoyment of the morning meal so amusing. She considered breaking her fast to be highly important. And just like Jasper could not function without his cup of tea first thing, she could be downright surly if she was not fed as soon after she rose as was practical.

Daisy filled her plate and sat down near him, ignoring his face full of laughter as he gazed in mock awe at the mound of food she had piled onto her plate.

"It amazes me that you have managed to remain so tiny with how much you are able to eat every morning."

"For one thing, my lord, surely you realize governesses do not eat like this on a regular basis. For another, I do not eat like this at all meals. The morning meal is of particular interest to me. I cannot help it. I am ravenous after a night of sleeping. It makes little sense, but it is a fact nonetheless. I would appreciate it if you would allow me to enjoy it without your mockery."

"I am not mocking you." Jasper huffed despite the grin still on his face. "It is charming to see a lady enjoying her food." He paused for a second as horror dawned on his face. "Wait a minute, did you say you would go hungry when you were working?"

"No, no," Daisy soothed. "I was always fed, of course. It was just that the Sadburys did not spread such a feast for their servants. I strongly doubt that anyone does."

"But could you not have gone to the kitchens and had the cook make you something if you were hungry?"

"I no doubt could have, but it would have been uncomfortable for everyone. A governess is in an awkward position. She is not a servant, but she is not of the same class as the master and mistress. It would have caused discomfort in the kitchens. Besides, I was kept rather busy with the children. I could not go wandering around the house looking for food." Daisy knew the viscount wished to argue the matter, but she cut him off. "Do not think that I went hungry. The kitchen always sent up plenty for the children's meals. I was well satisfied, I promise you."

Jasper looked unconvinced, but he allowed the matter to drop, resuming his examination of her as she forked up the delectable food. She began to feel embarrassed over his scrutiny. Finally, she put down her fork. She could feel the heat in her cheeks, and her mouth had gone dry. It was impossible to eat with him watching her like that. His gaze had turned from amused to interested, and she could not decide which was worse.

"Are you finished? Your plate is still half full."

Daisy could not believe Jasper actually had the nerve to look confused. She allowed a huff of annoyance to puff through her lips. "How could I possibly enjoy my meal with you sitting there watching me? I feel as though I am going to do something vulgar like chew with my mouth open, or you are going to see something stuck in my teeth. It is highly uncomfortable."

Jasper had to laugh. "Oh Daisy, I am so sorry! Please, do not allow me to stop you. Would it make you feel better if I was eating, too?" At her short nod he quickly got up from the table, went to the sideboard, and loaded up a plate for himself. When his back was turned she began to eat again, and they continued in companionable silence for a few minutes. Finally, Daisy had eaten enough and pushed back her plate with a contented sigh.

"That was quite lovely," she said, her smile happy and her face devoid of any ill will, but then a look of guilt flashed across her face. "Was I terribly grumpy, my lord? I fear I owe you an apology. I just cannot manage pleasantness until my fast has been broken."

"Pay it no mind, my dear. I will just be sure to keep that in mind for the future." Jasper paused for a moment, allowing his words to sink in, watching the emotions chase themselves across her face. "Are you ready to hear what the messenger had to say?"

Daisy's jaw dropped open slightly in her shock. "Merciful heavens, I actually forgot for a moment. Yes, please, right away, my lord. What have you found out?" Daisy leaned toward him, eager to hear every word despite the nerves that began to tremble in her belly. She wondered if knowing would be worse than not knowing but then dismissed that, as her ignorance was maddening.

She tried not to fidget as Jasper searched her eyes; she surmised he was looking to see if she really was prepared to hear what he knew. She gritted her teeth. "My lord, I beg of you, get on with it. You are not making it better by prolonging the suspense."

Jasper grinned at her words. "I apologize, my dear. I was just trying to prepare myself. I hope you will not be terribly disappointed. I cannot find any connection between him and you to explain directly why he would be endeavoring to regain control of you specifically. But I have been able to find out that he runs in the same circles as Lord Gerard Wright, which is bad news indeed." At Daisy's audible gasp Jasper paused, his eyebrows elevating in question. "Are you familiar with Lord Wright?"

The blood drained from Daisy's face as she wondered how much to tell him. With a sigh she finally admitted, "He is why I left the Sadburys. He made an effort to be overly familiar with me. Lord Sadbury did not defend me. I quit."

Daisy was surprised to find a smile forming on her lips when she saw the anger emanating from Jasper's face. She could tell he was trying very hard to contain it so as to not hurt her with it, but the clenching of his fists and the grinding of his teeth revealed to her that he would dearly like to hit something. He kept his voice low, but it trembled slightly as he asked, "Did the bounder hurt you? I will hunt him down and tear him limb from limb."

Daisy put her hand out, soothing one of his clenched fists. "I managed just fine, my lord, thank you. My father's grooms had been quite thorough in teaching me what to do if I was ever in a difficult position with a man with questionable intentions. Lord Wright was made most uncomfortable as payment for his unwelcome advances. It would have gone even worse for him if I had not been concerned about the children witnessing such violence."

"The children were there, and he still made advances?" Jasper was incredulous.

Daisy shrugged. "I had been successfully keeping him at bay by means of their presence. I guess he decided he no longer cared if they were there."

"And you said Sadbury did nothing? I am shocked that even if he did not have a care for the governess, I would think he would be angered that his children were subjected to such a display."

"His indifference toward his children is why we knew he could not be telling the truth when he sought me out at Abernathy claiming to wish to hire me back because the children were missing me," Daisy reminded gently.

Jasper's response was a growl. "I should have planted the bounder a facer when I had the chance."

Rather than finding his threat of violence unnerving, Daisy was amused by it. She felt protected and cared for, which was a sensation she had sorely missed since the death of her parents. She gazed speculatively at the viscount; she knew they had more to discuss about Sadbury, but she realized there was a pressing matter she wanted to ask him about.

"Jasper, the first day I met you, you appeared to be bosky. And yet, since we have been away from London I have not witnessed you overindulging at all. Which is the aberration?"

Daisy was surprised to see the colour high on his cheekbones, as Jasper sought to find an answer to her question. "Why would you ask me such a question at a time like this?" Jasper's incredulous, slightly belligerent tone caused Daisy to have to bite her lip to keep her amusement from showing.

She shrugged and did something she usually despised; she skirted the truth to get what she wanted. "I do not feel quite ready to discuss Lord Gerard Wright. I want to talk about something else for a minute, and this question popped into my head."

"Well it is a rather stupid question. Ask me something else."

"Well, now, I really want to know the answer. Why do you not want to talk about it? And why are you blushing like a school girl about it?" The heat in his cheeks increased with her words.

"I am not blushing," he insisted.

"If you are not, we perhaps ought to call a doctor because you might have a fever," Daisy retorted.

Jasper huffed. "I do not need a doctor." He paused and thought about her question, not meeting her eyes. "If you must know, I feel like I need to keep my wits about me. Being around my family makes me agitated. I would love to have a few drinks, or several, but I worry what will happen to you if I do."

"Why, Lord Seaton, that is the sweetest thing anyone has ever said to me."

"Stop it, Daisy, now I really am blushing."

Daisy laughed easily with him. Then she sobered. "Very well, my lord, I think I might be ready now. What else did you find out about Sadbury and Wright?"

"They arc involved in a conspiracy."

"Conspiracy, my lord? Are you perhaps being a touch melodramatic?"

Jasper grinned. "Perhaps a touch. But they are dangerous men to have gotten involved with. Well, Wright is, at any rate. From what I can tell, Sadbury is merely his weak-willed sidekick."

Daisy stared at him, wide-eyed, without anything to add, waiting for him to continue.

"Wright has managed to make himself the head of a smuggling operation along the majority of the coast of Kent. Which must be how he got Sadbury involved. His lands near Camber would be ideally located for his purposes."

Daisy was still watching attentively. "That is wicked, of course, but I still do not see how that could make them at all interested in me."

"Is it possible you heard some of their plans? Or perhaps they think you did?"

"Not that I am aware. Like I told you, I tried to have as little contact with Wright as possible, and Lord Sadbury paid very little attention to me or the children, even when he was in residence, which wasn't that often."

"Think back to what little contact you did have. Could they have been talking about brandy, or tobacco, or spices, maybe even silk or something else?"

Daisy pondered for a moment, doubting she could possibly know anything, but then she felt her eyes grow round. "Oh, good heavens! Is it possible to smuggle people? They were talking about lace of Lyon. I thought they were discussing fashions and servants. But perhaps not. I still don't understand why they would pursue me over this, though. Isn't smuggling a very common activity in those parts?"

"Common, yes, but very illegal. The penalty has increased to death, if it can be proven. Of course, as a peer, it is very unlikely he would face death, but if they think you are a threat to their empire, they would want to silence you."

"But I don't know anything!" Daisy almost wailed.

"Do not allow it to trouble you, my dearest. We will solve this problem now that we know what we're dealing with."

"I do not see how. If we try to reason with them that I don't know anything, they will be all the more convinced that I do."

Jasper had to laugh over her words. "I don't disagree with you, but you should be perfectly safe here. We'll spend the next couple of days thinking about what is best to be done. Welland might have some suggestions, too." He paused while searching her face. "Will you be able to enjoy yourself or should we just head to London and go straight to the Home Office?"

Daisy giggled. "Do not be absurd, my lord, I beg of you. I am perfectly willing to enjoy your sister's hospitality while we figure out our plans."

Chapter Seventeen

They were riding along the winding trail in companionable silence. Jasper's brother-in-law was in the lead, followed by Bess, then Hawkridge, Daisy, and Jasper was bringing up the rear. Lord and Lady Abernathy had decided to remain behind at Lord Welland's home. They had claimed to be tired from the journey, but Daisy suspected Lady Abernathy did not want to hold them back. Jasper had told her she did not ride, and Bess had explained that the particular place she wanted to visit was not accessible by carriage.

The scenery felt comfortingly familiar, very typical of this part of England. Daisy had grown up in very similar surroundings, and it brought a slight ache to her heart as she thought of her childhood home. She stifled her sigh. If only her father had thought to make provisions for her, her life would have turned out so much differently. But such thoughts were less than productive, so she shoved them from her mind. She was having a fine time with Jasper and his family. She ought not to pine for what might have been.

After a rather long ride for someone who had not been upon a horse in some time, they finally arrived at their destination. Bess had been right. It was a fascinating ruin of an old abbey. Bess' husband was rattling on about the history of the place and its surroundings. At first Daisy found it fascinating, but then she wanted to explore it for herself. She wandered away to examine a tumbled wall. Jasper had made himself comfortable, stretched out on a sunny patch of grass. Lord Hawkridge was talking about doing some hunting in the surrounding forest. As Daisy drifted away, Bess called out to her not to be gone too long, as they were going to spread the picnic their cook had packed shortly.

"I shall return momentarily — I just want to see what is over there." Daisy pointed off in the distance, but no one was paying her very much mind. She continued to amble along, fascinated with the ancient, abandoned architecture.

After several moments Daisy found herself quite alone, although she had the creeping sensation that someone was watching her. She glanced around, hearing Bess and her husband talking and giggling in the distance. Daisy tried to ignore the feeling, but the fine hairs on the back of her neck continued to shiver a warning to her.

Disgusted with herself, Daisy figured it was the talk she and Jasper had that morning that put suspicious thoughts in her head. But she could no longer enjoy her solitary explorations, so she turned to rejoin the others.

Out of nowhere, a pair of rough arms grabbed her from behind. She barely got out a gasp before a hand was clapped over her mouth. She struggled to free herself.

"I was not going to be so foolish as to approach you from the front this time, my pretty. I remembered how accurate your aim is." Daisy stiffened when she heard Lord Wright's oily observation in her ear. Her struggles began in earnest as he dragged her backwards, further away from her group.

Their movement was very awkward. Lord Wright was trying to get as far away from Daisy's companions as possible, but her twisting and turning while dragging her feet made it very difficult. Finally the hand covering her mouth slipped.

"Help, Jas—" Her shout was cut off as her assailant slammed his fist into the side of her head.

Jasper had been in a sound sleep, but he sat up abruptly, calling out to his sister. "Did you hear that, Bess?"

"Hear what?" she asked absently.

"I am not certain, but something woke me up just now. Where has Daisy wandered off to?"

"She was heading in that direction a few minutes ago." Bess indicated with a vague gesture. "I told her to be quick as we would be eating shortly."

Jasper stood, a sense of foreboding overwhelming him momentarily. "Something is not right. We have to find her."

"She just went to the other side to admire more of the old building. Most people are curious about it the first time they see it. I am actually surprised you did not wish to explore as well." Bess seemed offended that her brother was not more interested in the ruins she was displaying.

Jasper ignored her, setting off at a brisk pace, almost running when he did not see Daisy when he went around the wall Bess had indicated. He called out to his brother-in-law. "Welland, have you seen Daisy?"

His lordship shook his head, rising to his feet as he sensed his brother-in-law's agitation. He could just see his nephew off in the distance. Welland indicated to Jasper perhaps she had accompanied Hawkridge.

The earl set off to intercept his nephew while Jasper continued in the direction Bess had indicated. His worry made him hurry, and he was nearly tripping over the tumbled stones and debris. There was no sign of Daisy. His stomach turned over, and he was nearly consumed with worry. He began running, calling her name. He almost fell over as he came across the hat she had worn. She had declared it darling and loved it like only a lady could. He had thought it ridiculous and teased her about it. He knew she would not have dropped it heedlessly.

Grabbing it up, Jasper ran back to the others, yelling for their help.

Bess was pale as Jasper described what he suspected had happened. He was sure Daisy had been abducted. He suspected it was Sadbury and Wright but had no proof, nor any idea of where they would have taken her.

Catching up their horses' reins, all in the group quickly gathered their things and set off in pursuit. Fortunately, the groom who had accompanied them to help with the picnic was also experienced in leading the hunt. He would be able to help them find a trail, if there was one. Jasper had similar experience, but he was concerned that his distress would make it difficult to concentrate and observe.

Jasper was frantic as they searched. It took a while for the groom to find the trail, as they had all been wandering around and trampled some of it. Finally he was sure he had discovered the trail of two horses that had recently been through the area. They followed the trail as quickly as possible, but it was slow going. Jasper tried to keep a grip on his emotions, knowing it would do no good to become angry. The nervous young groom would be even more anxious if he realized the noblemen were becoming upset.

For the first time in his life, Jasper found himself praying. He knew he was on the verge of making a fool of himself, but he was beyond caring. He needed Daisy to be all right.

ꙮ

Daisy felt a dull throb in her temple and wondered why she was so very lethargic. She tried to put her hand to her head to see what the trouble was but found that she could not move it. With a start, she realized she was bound, and it all came rushing back to her. Lord Wright had grabbed her and struck her in the head when she had resisted his abduction. Fear seized her, and she felt momentarily paralyzed. But then an anger sharp and fierce, like she had never felt before, swept through her ,and she was mobilized.

Struggling with her bonds, she realized they must not have expected her to wake up so had not tied them tightly or well. She listened carefully but could hear nothing, not even anyone breathing, so she knew she was alone. Daisy quickly divested herself of the ropes around her arms and then reached for the cloth covering her eyes. For a moment, Daisy wondered if she wanted to know where she was and hesitated before pulling it off. Chastising herself for being such a ninny, Daisy quickly grabbed it from her face.

Looking around, it appeared to Daisy as though she had been tossed in a woodshed. She was confused about her location but realized her captors did not care overmuch for her comfort. She still had no idea why they had taken her, but Daisy knew she had to get away. Fighting the urge to start screaming for help, Daisy forced herself to take deep breaths and stood gingerly. Realizing that she was fully intact, and aside from the throb in her head she was fine, Daisy determined to extricate herself from this bizarre situation.

Exploring the room carefully in the dark, Daisy tried not to get splinters as she felt around trying to determine the environment she was in. There was so much chopped wood, she figured it must be the storehouse for some crofter's cottage. Her panic was beginning to rise despite her best efforts until she came across what she was pretty certain was a door. She felt around some more, and sure enough, she came across the latch. Easing it open slowly, she was relieved to see light but no people. She was rather shocked that they had just taken her and then dumped her here, but she was not about to waste the opportunity.

Furtively, she crept around the cottage, nibbling on her lip, wondering which direction she ought to go. She was pretty sure she would be able to figure out which way was north, east, south, and west, but that did her very little good since she had no idea which direction Welland was. But the instinctive drive to be away from here moved her to pick a direction and strike out. She decided to head east, figuring if worse came to worst she would end up in London. She smiled at her own small joke and worried that the knock on her head might have done some damage.

She was unsure how long she had been gone from Jasper and the others, but the sun was still fairly high in the sky, so it could not have been too awfully long. She was relieved that she had several hours before dark. It offered her more time to find help or shelter. Daisy contemplated what to do if she suspected her assailants were pursuing her. Glancing down at herself, she was glad that her riding habit was green. Hopefully it would help conceal her if she had to hide herself in the woods.

Daisy had been keeping her ears strained to hear any sound of pursuit. Her nerves were beginning to fray because every sound in the underbrush was making her jump. But finally she heard the sound she had been dreading — hoofbeats. She hurried to get off the trail, concealing herself under a low hanging elder bush that had grown rather wildly.

She did not dare to even peek, but when the ground around her vibrated, she suspected there were more than two horses passing her. Should she take a chance and look? What if it was Jasper looking for her? She could not bear the thought of being captured again, but if she could be rescued, was it a chance she ought to take?

Taking a deep, steadying breath, she parted the leaves slightly, hoping to remain concealed and still see what was around her. To her profound relief, she saw Bess' bright plum riding habit.

Daisy lost her breath momentarily, and her first try came out as a whisper, "Bess!" and then with much more force, "Jasper! I am here."

She almost stumbled over her skirts as she crawled out of her hiding place and ran after the search party. Jasper was the first to get off his horse and make it to her side. He swept her up into his arms and crushed her to him. A sense of well-being and homecoming filled her and she wrapped her arms around him with the intention of never letting go.

It didn't take long before sense returned to Daisy. She remembered there was an audience, and she pushed herself back from Jasper. It took a bit of effort. He did not seem prepared to follow her lead.

Speaking in a low tone, Daisy said, "Jasper, everything is fine now. I am perfectly all right, you got to me in time, all is well." She stroked his back as she spoke, and slowly he let her go. As she stepped away from him, she saw Bess, her husband, and his nephew all surrounding them, staring at her in varying degrees of horror. Daisy became afraid at the expressions on their face.

"What is wrong? Have I been disfigured?" she asked, looking at Bess nervously.

"No, no, you are just a wee bit filthy," Bess soothed. "What happened to you, my dear? We have been rather frightened for you."

"Well, I have been frightened, too." Daisy looked around, fear returning to her. "In fact, if none of you would mind, I would much rather have this conversation somewhere else. I just had a terrible time, and I would hate to run into Lord Gerard Wright again."

"I, on the other hand, would very much like to run into him." The murderous glare shining on Jasper's face made Daisy gulp. She fervently hoped they would be able to leave before violence was required.

"Please, my lord, I want to get out of here. I am dirty and cold and need a bath and a cup of tea."

Jasper looked at her fully for the first time, and Daisy watched his anger come under control. He was not able to quell it completely, but he was able to manage it. "You are quite correct, my dear. Let us get you back to Welland, and everything else can be sorted out later."

When Jasper saw that Daisy had begun to shiver, he grabbed a blanket the groom had brought for the picnic and wrapped her up in it. Once he had her situated, he realized she would be unable to ride like that, so he gathered her up in his arms and rode with her in front of him, grateful that he had chosen to ride his brother-in-law's largest gelding. The horse would be just fine with the two of them. *Daisy barely weighs more than a feather anyway*, he thought with a frown.

The group was nearly silent as they made quick work of returning to Bess' manor. The earl sent a groom to fetch the doctor as soon as they rode up the long lane to the house. Pandemonium briefly burst out when they entered the house. The butler, usually stoic, was unprepared to have one of the guests brought back to the house in the viscount's arms. Kate was called, and she shrieked at the sight of her injured mistress. By this time, Daisy had insisted that Jasper put her down. She was so embarrassed by all the fuss that her colour was high, and she suspected she could not possibly look all that ill. But then she remembered the dirt, and most likely the blood, and allowed that she was not fit to be seen. She trailed obediently after Kate as she took her up to her room for a bath. Jasper promised to have a pot of tea sent up for her as soon as she was ready for it. Her wan smile did little to comfort him.

The marquis and marchioness had shown up when they heard the commotion but had remained uncharacteristically silent until Daisy had been led away and the rest of the group were seated in the withdrawing room. Bess had ordered tea to be served, but most agreed they needed something a bit more potent. Jasper especially was in need of fortification.

"We really ought to ride back there and search for the bounders," Jasper was saying. "They cannot be allowed to get away with this."

"Really, Seaton, what do you think can truly be done? Wright is a peer and Sadbury, a baron. What do you really know about Miss Pembroke? Perhaps they had good reason for carrying her off."

Bess gasped over her father's words but grabbed her brother's arm to prevent him from physically expressing his wrath.

"How dare you?" he demanded, his glare enough to quell the marquis slightly. "Are you trying to say that perhaps she brought it upon herself to be knocked in the head and carried off as though she were a sack of potatoes? No one, least of all a gently bred female, deserves to be treated thusly. And they deserve retribution for their very existence before ever they sought to involve Miss Pembroke in their schemes. I know not why they are after her, but I can assure you I will not stand by and allow her to be accosted."

"Why not, Seaton? What is she to you, really?" the marquis' voice dripped with sarcasm, and Jasper had had enough.

"If you cannot speak well of my future wife, you may leave our presence," he stated simply. "I will not ask her to travel after the ordeal she has been through, so the onus is on you to remove yourself." His own words shocked him momentarily, but he was soothed by the deep sense of satisfaction that filled him. It may have taken him overlong to realize his own feelings, but he saw in that moment that they had been there from the beginning. Jasper didn't have long to dwell on his thoughts. His mother was beaming at him.

"Oh Jasper, are you really going to marry her?" the marchioness breathed. "How very delightful."

Jasper wondered momentarily if his mother had lost her mind. He ignored the double standards of his parents' mercurial moods, instead turning to his brother-in-law. "How long do you think it will take for the doctor to get here? I want that injury on her head attended to as quickly as possible."

"It should be soon, as long as he can be found. If he is out visiting someone the groom will have to track him down, but it could be a little while. Have a drink, Jasper, you are looking a little wild."

"Thank you, Welland, but I cannot avail myself of your kind offer. I need to have my wits about me in order to protect Daisy from the marquis." Jasper's tone was kept polite, but the look he directed at his father was as hard as granite.

"Oh, Jasper, do not be so quarrelsome," his mother chided, but Jasper paid her little mind.

Bess made an effort to be conciliatory. "Jasper, I am sure our father did not mean to be insulting. Try to understand. Calm down and have a seat — working yourself up into a fury is not going to help Miss Pembroke."

"Your sister is quite correct, Jasper. I had no intention of being insulting to your little friend. There is just nothing we know about her except that she has trouble following her."

"I know everything I need to know about her, and I have every intention of keeping her safe. She will be the perfect bride for me."

Daisy had just entered the doorway when she heard Jasper's declaration. She could not suppress the gasp that burst from her lips, revealing her shock as well as her presence.

"But what about the fact that I am a governess?" she blurted, ignoring the uncomfortable glances of everyone in the room who were clearly embarrassed to be caught discussing her.

Jasper ignored their audience as well, scoffing, "Why would that matter to me? You are going to be a viscountess."

Daisy searched Jasper's eyes, looking for his true feelings. Her own delight threatened to turn her head and prevent her from being rational on the subject. Jasper must have sensed her concerns because he quickly overcame the objections she was trying to raise.

"Do not get yourself worked up over this at the moment, my dear. I know I have done it all backwards. I have not even asked you if you will be so kind as to have me. Never mind about all this right now. We have to deal with the little problem of Sadbury and Wright. Then we will have all the time in the world to work out our situation."

Daisy saw him glance at his father as he said that last part. She nibbled on her lip in indecision. She knew Jasper was right; nothing could get worked out until the baron and earl were dealt with. She sighed and nodded.

Again the marquis stepped in. "I still do not see what you think you are going to be able to do, Seaton, Wright is an earl."

"That is true, but you are a marquis, my lord, and are you not also the magistrate for your area? And Welland here is also an earl. Surely between the three of us we can exert enough pressure to ensure there are some consequences for these dastards."

At first, Abernathy looked uncomfortable but then Daisy saw him look around the room. Whatever he observed caused a change to take place. The marquis stood straighter and declared, "You are quite right, Seaton. Let us be about establishing some justice." Turning to his wife he continued. "My dear, you should stay here and wait with Miss Daisy for the doctor to see to her wounds. We should have this little mess taken care of momentarily."

It seemed to Daisy as though the shortest five minutes of her life passed by. Before she could barely blink, the four gentlemen were hurrying from the room, summoning footmen and grooms as they went.

Daisy's mouth was agape as she saw Jasper nearing the door. "Wait, wait, wait," she exclaimed. "Do you actually mean to leave me here?" Her incredulous tone indicated just how she felt about this idea.

Jasper's shocked blinking would have amused Daisy if she were not so incensed. He tried to explain. "But you have been through an ordeal. Surely you do not think to accompany us, do you? There is a very strong possibility that there will be violence. I did not think your sensibilities would be up to witnessing that."

Daisy could not believe the viscount was being so obtuse. "Of course, I wish to accompany you. This is my problem to deal with. While I certainly appreciate your assistance, I cannot allow you to deal with it without me." She paused for a moment. Seeing his resistance, she switched tactics. Her tone became wheedling, "Do you not realize that I am likely to have nightmares for the rest of my life after this ordeal, as you called it? I am inclined to think that if I see it through to the conclusion of Sadbury and Wright meeting a just end I shall feel much more settled over the entire matter."

Seeing Jasper wavering in his resistance, she pressed her advantage. "Surely you realize I am not the squeamish sort of female that will cause you problems. My lord, I promise you I shall be perfectly fine, even if you are required to visit some violence upon Sadbury and Wright. I will admit to you that I may even enjoy witnessing such an occurrence."

This seemed to amuse Jasper, and he could obviously not argue with her logic. With a sigh he acquiesced. "Very well, my dear, but only if you swear to me that you will do exactly what I tell you, and you will stay behind me at all times. I do not want to have to be worried about your safety. You will be there to witness what transpires, not participate."

Daisy was nodding vigorously, about to reassure him that she would behave, when the marchioness interrupted. "You cannot be serious, Seaton. Daisy cannot accompany you." She turned to Daisy. "You must allow the men to take care of this, my dear girl. You sit down. The housekeeper will bring us a nice hot pot of tea, and we will start making plans for your wedding."

Bess chose this moment to add her thoughts. She laughed outright at her mother's foolish notion. "My dear lady, you must realize poor Daisy will not be of a mind to sit and discuss anything to do with the wedding at a time like this. For one thing, Jasper hasn't even asked her properly, and for another, she cannot be settled in her mind until these villains are properly disposed of. No, Daisy is quite right, she must accompany Jasper. In fact, I would love to go, too, but I'm afraid I will just be an impediment. But Daisy will not be in the way, and she really must go." Bess took Lady Abernathy's arm. "Come along, Mother. We shall have that tea and discuss the wedding ourselves. I think Daisy would much prefer that anyway."

She was perfectly correct and Daisy was delighted by her words. While she still could barely believe that Jasper's proposal was anything but gallantry on his part, if there was to be a wedding, she shuddered at the thought of planning it.

Chapter Eighteen

The grooms hastily saddled another horse when they saw Jasper striding toward the stables with Daisy in tow. The earl raised his eyebrows with a touch of skepticism, but Daisy was gratified to see that the marquis looked almost as though he approved when he saw her in Jasper's wake. Daisy shook her head, dismissing the thought as wishful thinking on her part.

She had to grit her teeth to staunch their chattering when Jasper searched her eyes carefully before he threw her up into the saddle. Daisy knew he wasn't completely convinced it was a good idea for her to accompany them, so she was determined to hide her own trepidation. He would leave her behind for sure if he knew she was having doubts. Despite her fear, there was no conceivable way she could allow them to go on this particular errand without her. She was absolutely convinced her emotional well-being depended on seeing this thing to its conclusion.

Plastering as believable a smile as she could muster onto her cold lips, Daisy kept her word and stayed behind Jasper, keeping her horse close to his as the group set out on their grim errand. She could feel Jasper's watchful eye upon her from time to time as the group retraced their steps in the hopes of catching Lords Sadbury and Wright where Daisy had been found. Gone were all traces of the indolent gentleman the viscount usually showed observers. He was sharp-eyed and alert as they set off in pursuit of Daisy's captors.

Glancing around, Daisy noticed that all the gentlemen were looking rather grim. A shiver of dread ran down her spine as her mind raced with all the possible outcomes of this particular expedition. None of them were very good. She should have asked more questions before making Jasper bring her, she realized rather late. But in all actuality, no matter the outcome, she felt she needed to be there when it happened, whatever it was.

Her mind was scrambling, having trouble focusing on any one thing. She could hardly believe it when they arrived at the place where Jasper and the others had found her. She had apparently lost all sense of time. There had been very little discussion amongst the group as they rode, but now the earl gestured for complete silence. Daisy glanced around nervously as she realized that all of the gentlemen and most of the grooms were armed. They rode forward a short distance and then they all halted. They would go on foot from there. All the better to make a silent approach.

Jasper leaned in close and whispered in her ear. "Are you perfectly sure you want to go through with accompanying us?"

Daisy was shocked by the question even while his hot breath in her ear caused a hitch in her own breathing. "At this point, I will admit to you that I am terrified, but there is absolutely no way you are leaving me behind. I think I would faint from fear if you left me on my own."

Jasper had the temerity to grin, much to Daisy's disgust. "Of course, I clearly did not think through my question. Forgive me. And remember your promise to stick close."

"That will not be difficult to keep," she assured him fervently as she clasped his hand tightly. She could barely believe that even at a moment like this, she felt the pull of attraction to the handsome man before her. If it were possible, the danger seemed to heighten the sensation. Daisy made an effort to shove the sensation to the furthest recesses of her mind. Now was most certainly not the time to be entertaining such distracting thoughts.

Stepping back from Jasper, Daisy gave her head an emphatic shake. "Very well, my lord, lead on."

Daisy could not decipher the look on his face, but Jasper didn't say anything as he grabbed her hand once again and followed the earl's lead as the gentlemen quietly made their way toward the wooden structure. She held on tight and followed him, trying to keep her skirts from impeding their rapid progress.

She must have been preoccupied with her own thoughts and missed the plans being made, as everyone except her seemed to know what was going on. Daisy just shrugged and made an effort to keep up. It wasn't as though Jasper would allow her to participate anyway.

The closer they got to the ramshackle place the louder the voices became. They heard Lords Sadbury and Wright yelling at each other. It would seem that Daisy's disappearance had been discovered by her captors.

"You fool. I told you to make sure her bonds were tight enough," Wright was bellowing at Sadbury. "Could you not do even this small task correctly? Why do I bother putting up with you?"

"You had hit her so hard, it didn't seem likely she would be moving until tomorrow," Sadbury whined before seeming to grow a backbone. "And you put up with me because you need my cooperation, my lord. The question should really be, why I bother with you."

There was a heavy silence before the group heard the shattering of glass. It would seem the two gentlemen were growing impatient.

"Breaking things is going to do you no good, Sadbury. We need to get that girl back. This is all your fault — figure it out," Wright screamed, no longer his calm, urbane self. A shiver started to wriggle down Daisy's spine at the hysteria she heard in the man's voice. She feared what he would do in this state. She tightened her hold on Jasper's hand.

࿇

Jasper felt Daisy's fear rising the closer they got to the shed she had been held in. He wanted to reassure her, but his anger kept rising at the thought of her being tied up in that low place. Everything inside him was straining toward the desire to pummel the cretins who had done this to her. Knowing they were here was comforting and yet frustrating. He was quite sure Daisy would not allow the violence he wished to visit upon them. The girl was far too soft hearted for her own good.

The earl gestured for some of the men to go around back. Seeing that there were three horses tied up, it was obvious that there was at least one more than the two they could hear. No doubt, the servant who had accompanied Sadbury was about somewhere.

With the sound of the two yelling at each other, Jasper felt Daisy's hold tightening on his hand. He didn't want to leave her, but he had to take a hand in their capture. He gestured for one of the grooms to join him. Hurrying Daisy over to stand behind a tree, he uttered his commands in a low voice.

"Tom, I see you are well armed. Stay here and guard Miss Pembroke." Seeing the man's willing agreement, Jasper turned his attention to Daisy. "Stay here with Tom, my dear. I do not want you in the thick of things. There may be bullets flying around shortly. Duck down behind this tree and stay uninjured."

It was clear that Daisy did not want to obey. Her lovely blue eyes had turned mutinous. "You promised, remember?" he reminded her.

"You promised to let me tag along," she persisted.

"You have tagged along. You can watch from here. But you will only be an encumbrance to us all if we have to worry about you getting hurt. Stay here and behave." Jasper didn't wait for her to agree. He placed a firm, quick kiss upon her shocked lips and hurried after the rest of the men, confident that she would obey him, even if she was stewing about it. She had given her word.

ཛྷ

Daisy huffed her annoyance but obeyed Jasper's imperative command. "The nerve of that man, ordering me about," her fierce whisper was directed at Tom.

"Sorry, miss, but it is for the best, you know. The gents would be right worried about you if you was to get any closer. It's best if you jest waits here for the dust to settle, so to speak." Tom was matter of fact in his refusal to offer sympathy.

Daisy hated to admit it, but she was a little bit relieved to be put on the side. The thought of re-entering that dark shed sent shivers of dread rippling through her flesh. It might be cowardly, but she was rather happy to watch from here.

"I apologize that you are missing out on the action, Tom. No doubt you would have loved to be with the rest of the men."

Tom gave a negligent shrug. "Lord Seaton trusted me with a responsible task. Guarding you is the most important thing for all of us, so I'm satisfied, miss, don't worry about me."

Daisy appreciated his kindness. She was sure it would be difficult for a man to stay away from the action. But she was even more relieved that he was faithfully staying by her side. The thought of being left alone so close to her enemies scared her into silence.

The action was swift and over before she even realized it. It would seem that Lord Sadbury's servant had put up no resistance when faced with a couple of grooms with guns. Sadbury and Wright had been so busy yelling at each other that they had been oblivious to the approaching men and only resisted once it was far too late. They had been caught unawares, so they were taken into custody without one shot being fired.

However, there had been sufficient roughness to satisfy the bloodlust Jasper had obviously been feeling, a fact his wide grin attested to as he approached her not too many minutes later. "All is well, and the way is clear if you would like to join us as we determine what to do with these lowlifes. Do not fuss over me," he implored her when she saw the scrapes on his knuckles and the bruise forming on his cheek. "Wright didn't go down without a bit of a struggle, but it is merely superficial, I assure you."

Daisy would never understand the manly need to release pent up feelings with a show of violence, but she knew enough not to fuss too much. She assured herself she could let him know what she thought of his enjoyment later. There were other, more pressing, issues at hand.

"Are you sure they are sufficiently restrained, my lord?"

"Quite." His brief reply was accompanied by another wide grin. Daisy merely shook her head.

"What are you going to do with them now that you have apprehended them?" Daisy had to hurry to keep up with Jasper, as he was returning to where all the men were assembled.

"That is being worked out now."

ꟿ

Jasper was astonished to be relieved that his father was along. The marquis had taken over once the two dastards were restrained. He had dispatched a groom to fetch the local magistrate while he lent an air of calm to the assembled group.

Lord Wright was not taking his treatment in stride, though. "How dare you tie me up? I am a peer of the realm," he sputtered, much to Jasper's amusement.

"You should have acted like one," the marquis' replied calmly.

"This is ridiculous, Abernathy, what is the meaning of this?" Despite being dirty and tied up, the earl was not willing to concede defeat.

"This is what happens when you abduct my future daughter-in-law."

Jasper was surprised by his father's choice of words. He felt Daisy's shock vibrating from her, but he was glad she managed to keep her thoughts to herself for the time being. Lord Wright did not take well to the marquis' words.

"Future daughter-in-law," he sputtered. "Do you seriously expect me to believe you are bothering with the governess?"

"I do not care what you believe, Wright, but you really should not have accosted a member of my party. It was really poorly thought out on your part."

"Everything has been poorly thought out since I took up with Sadbury," the earl exclaimed.

"Now you are just being childish, my lord," the marquis chided. "It is obvious that Sadbury is not the mastermind of any of these efforts. Do not try to shift the blame. It will do you no good."

Now Jasper was grinning again. He found it vastly entertaining to see the marquis' cold disdain directed upon someone else for a change.

Wright refrained from any further comment, instead glaring silently at all around him. Sadbury was still sniveling but had nothing to add as silence fell upon the group.

Relief filled everyone except the trussed up men when the groom returned, followed by the magistrate. Mr. Samuel Jackson looked to be a trifle awed by the company he found himself in, but he managed to keep himself well in hand and deal with the grave situation.

"Abducted the young lady, you say?" Mr. Jackson repeated what he had been told. "Because of smuggling?" The magistrate was appalled. "Did the gents not know how very illegal smuggling is?" The little man grinned over his own question before looking seriously at the marquis who was clearly in charge.

"What did you have in mind, my lord?"

"I think some time spent in the colonies might help these scoundrels see the wisdom in keeping themselves on the right side of the law."

"You cannot be serious!" exclaimed Lord Wright, while Sadbury snivelled, "But I cannot leave my family behind."

"You should have been thinking about your family before you embarked upon this venture," the marquis replied coldly. Turning back to the magistrate, he said, "I do not see that it would do any of us any good to send them to trial. I think this would be the simplest, most expedient means of dealing with these two."

Jasper saw that the magistrate was in agreement, but he had one more point to make. "You do realize, though, my lord, that they will, no doubt, return."

"I have no doubt that they will, but by then, Miss Pembroke will no longer be in any danger from them, and their smuggling enterprise will be out of business. I will keep my eye on them, have no fear, sir."

Mr. Jackson shrugged indicating his lack of concern. "Very well, I will make a record of these events, my lord, if you would like to see to the arrangements."

"It will be my pleasure." The marquis' silky reply caused Sadbury to start snivelling again, and even the earl looked cowed by the future awaiting him.

"You'll be sorry for this, Abernathy." Lord Wright tried to brazen through his misgivings.

"No, my lord, it is you who will be sorry if you ever even think of involving yourself with anyone in my family again."

Within minutes, they had the three bound men mounted, and the group retraced their steps back to Welland. Jasper felt deflated after the intensity of the chase. It was in silence that the group rode into the stable yard. He realized that Daisy, too, was withering after all the excitement, so he helped her to dismount and sent her to the house while the rest of the arrangements were finalized for getting the three onto a ship bound for the colonies. The only argument was which destination would be the least savory for the likes of them.

Chapter Nineteen

Daisy couldn't remember ever feeling so tired in all her life. Not even during her days as a governess. This day felt as though it were, in fact, three. She longed fervently for her bed. But when they returned to the house, Lady Abernathy insisted that everyone needed to eat a proper meal. After the day they had experienced, Daisy doubted that anyone would be hungry, but she was soon proven wrong. The gentlemen, it would appear, were ravenous.

She had very mixed feelings when Jasper noticed that she was wilting. "Daisy, my dear, you look done in. I do believe it is time for you to seek your bed," he declared when everyone had been fed.

Bristling half-heartedly, Daisy tried to object to his words. "Has no one ever told you that you really ought not to make any reference to a lady not looking her best?"

Jasper didn't appear to be put out by her words; his indulgent smile made Daisy want to slap it off his face. This thought brought her up short. "But it would seem you are quite correct, my lord. I am not myself at the moment, and it would be best if I take to my bed."

"My dear Miss Pembroke, it is nothing short of miraculous that you are still standing at this moment after the day you have had. Please know that no one present will take the least offence if you retire for the evening." The marquis actually sounded almost kind as he spoke to her.

Daisy blinked owlishly at the marquis' words. "Th-thank you, my lord." Her words coming out in an incoherent stammer brought heat to her cheeks. She hurried to bob a curtsy to the room at large and fled to the sanctuary of her room.

Kate was there waiting to fuss over her. Daisy was too tired to protest but was grateful that within a few short minutes she was tucked up in the warm bed. She succumbed to oblivion before her head was even settled on the pillow.

ᘓᘐ

Jasper turned to his father, hoping he didn't look as shocked as he felt over the marquis' words. "That was kind of you, my lord."

Warm colour splashed across Abernathy's cheeks, bringing an amused smile to Jasper's face. The marquis blustered. "It was certainly better than what you were doing, Seaton. The girl was right. You should have thought of a more tactful way of sending her off to her bed."

"But it was clear she was dead on her feet," Jasper protested even though he knew his father was right.

"Despite all she has been through today, there is no doubt in my mind that Daisy would have preferred it if you complimented her instead of telling her she looked ragged," Bess chided her brother.

"I did not tell her she looked ragged," the viscount protested, even as he saw that no one was taking his side. He stopped defending himself. "I will make it up to her tomorrow. Now that we have all been fed, I would like to thank everyone for all that you did to help today, both in finding Daisy when she was missing and then later in tracking down Sadbury and Wright."

"Of course, my son. We quite like Miss Pembroke and were glad to be of service to her," Jasper's mother reminded him, while his father was much less effusive in his comments. "We could never leave a young woman defenceless."

Jasper wondered absently if he would ever understand his father. He gave up on the effort needed to maintain his façade as a gentleman. "I will bid you all a good night. I find that the rigours of the day are catching up with me as well."

"Good night," everyone chimed in as Jasper headed for the door. He was chagrined to find his father joining him as he left the room.

Holding on to his composure by a thread, Jasper raised questioning eyebrows at the marquis. "Was there something you wished to discuss, my lord?"

Jasper was surprised to catch a glimpse of discomfort crossing the marquis' face before he continued to look his usual haughty self. "We will need to discuss your Miss Pembroke tomorrow, Seaton."

"I highly doubt I will wish to discuss her with you, my lord." Jasper's cold drawl made it clear he would accept no criticism of his chosen lady.

"Do not fly up into the boughs now, Seaton, I mean no disrespect to Miss Pembroke. But if you are intent on marrying the chit, we shall have to make every effort to ensure that no hint of a scandal touches on her. This business with Sadbury and Wright will need to be sorted properly if you do not want in hanging over you for years to come."

Jasper fervently hoped that his jaw was not hanging open exhibiting his shock over the marquis' words. "Yes, of course, mayhap once we have all rested we shall have more thoughts on the matter." Jasper doubted he was making much sense, but he was relieved when his father merely nodded and headed for the library.

"Sleep well, Seaton," were the marquis' parting words.

Jasper shook his head in wonder as he watched his father walk away. It had been a remarkable day.

ꕤ

Daisy swam to the surface of consciousness with reluctance the next morning, grateful that her maid had left the curtains closed so she could sleep later than usual. Feeling somewhat disoriented, she wondered how long she had been asleep. Hearing quiet rustling across the room, she raised her head.

"Good morning," she called out in a soft voice.

"Oh, miss, I sure hope I didn't disturb you!" Kate was aghast at the thought.

"No, no, Kate, do not trouble yourself. I do believe I have slept quite long enough. Surely the day is well advanced." Daisy could not see the clock from where she lay on the bed, despite straining toward the mantle.

"While it is a little later than usual for you, it really isn't all that late. Perhaps you should try to sleep a little longer."

Daisy threw back the covers and swung her legs over the side of the bed. "I was too tired to eat much last night, and now I am ravenous. Besides, now that Lords Sadbury and Wright have been apprehended there is no need for us to be dithering here. I need to get up and see what Lord Seaton has in mind."

"But surely his lordship won't be asking you to travel any time soon after the ordeal you have been through."

Daisy laughed at her maid. "I am perfectly fine, Kate, I promise. It is not so very far to London. If his lordship wishes to go, I can be ready." She paused at the dubious look on Kate's face. "Of course, there would be the packing to see to, and the day has advanced, so tomorrow might be a better option, but I would still very much like to get up and see what he has in mind."

"His lordship is a good man — I'm sure he would rather you rested some more." Kate's tone was wheedling, making Daisy laugh.

"Your opinion of him sure has changed."

"He has been good to me," was all Kate offered.

"You are quite correct — he is a good man. But I am done with sleeping for now. I will need to get dressed so I can go see if breakfast is still being served."

"Oh, but miss, I could surely send to the kitchens to order you a tray," Kate continued to protest despite the fact that her mistress had strode across the room and was now peering into the wardrobe.

Ignoring her maid's protests, Daisy pondered which gown would best disguise the pallor she was certain still covered her cheeks. "I think the green muslin with the sawtooth trim will do the trick quite nicely."

Kate adandoned her protests, seeing that her mistress was quite determined. Within a short time, Daisy was dressed and coifed and on her way to the breakfast room. Despite her hunger, she was nervous and took a moment before entering the room to take a deep breath and calm her nerves.

"Good morning," she greeted as cheerfully as she could muster. The occupants of the room had been subdued before she entered, but the gentlemen quickly rose to their feet while Bess and Lady Abernathy exclaimed over her presence.

Bess hurried to Daisy's side, ready to be the hostess. "We thought you would sleep a bit longer. How are you faring today? Did you sleep well enough? Are you hungry?"

Daisy laughed over the string of questions, oddly feeling at ease by the countess' chatter. "I slept like a baby, thank you. And yes, now I am quite ready to break my fast."

"Well come along to the sideboard. The dishes are all still here." Realizing that the gentlemen were still standing, Bess quickly urged them to their seats. "She will be at least another minute, so you might as well sit back down. There is no need to stand on ceremony anyway as we are practically family."

At Bess' words, Daisy's stomach plummeted, and she wondered if she would be able to eat after all. She swept a nervous glance toward Jasper, but he seemed unperturbed by his sister's words as he refilled his coffee cup and took a sip. She released the breath she hadn't realized she had been holding. Relieved to see her hands weren't shaking despite her nerves, Daisy put a little bit more food on her plate and then took her place at the table.

Daisy tried not to glare at him when Jasper looked her plate over and declared, "You must not be feeling yourself, as I have never seen you eat so little in the morning."

ജ്ജ

Jasper watched the battle taking place in her mind as he searched her expressive eyes. She kept a polite smile pinned to her lips, but her eyes gave her away. She was torn between her desire to keep the peace and her exasperation with him. She was obviously a little jumpy still from the events of the day before. Jasper just hoped she would see her way clear to confiding in him as soon as he could figure out a way to have some privacy with her.

He was disappointed on a certain level when she lowered her eyes to her plate but relieved to see her grab her fork and apply herself to the food before her. Jasper looked around the table, glad that the marquis wasn't present. Even though he had seemed to be thawing toward his only son, Jasper didn't think Daisy was ready to face the marquis just yet. The rest of the companions at the table must have sensed Daisy's need for calm since quiet conversations began around the table as though everything were normal.

As soon as he saw Daisy put her fork down on her empty plate, Jasper stood up, drawing all eyes to him. "I think my fiancé and I have much to discuss, so if you will excuse us, we shall adjourn to the drawing room."

Ignoring the look of panic on Daisy's face, Jasper rounded the table, grabbed her hand, and strode from the room, bemused to see the varying looks of approval and amusement on the faces of his family.

"Jasper, my lord, this is not seemly," Daisy hissed, as soon as they were out of earshot of the breakfast room.

"It is perfectly acceptable for an engaged couple to be afforded a degree of privacy. There is nothing unseemly about it."

"But you should not continue this farce about us being engaged. It is not fair to your family." Jasper's lack of concern over his family's feelings on the matter must have been obvious to Daisy, so she continued in a much lower voice, "And it isn't fair to me."

This drew him up short. He stopped abruptly and turned her to face him. "What do you mean by that, Daisy? Am I so abhorrent to you that you will not even consider the possibility of marriage to me?"

He wanted to cut out his own tongue when he saw tears well up in her eyes. She had been so brave after the death of her parents and in the face of her captors, but now his blunt words brought her close to crying. Jasper condemned himself as a brute.

"Please don't cry, Daisy, I beg of you. I didn't mean to bully you. Come along to the drawing room and let us discuss this like civilized people."

Gratified to see that she wasn't going to burst into tears, Jasper retained his hold on her hand, but proceeded at a more sedate pace. After settling her on the settee, Jasper sat down on a stool facing her, managing to gather both of her hands into his own.

"Are you perfectly sure you have no further injuries after your adventures yesterday?"

Jasper was mollified by her gurgle of laughter. "Oh Jasper, thank you for your concern, but please stop coddling me. I am perfectly fine. You have no idea how comforting it was to wake up this morning and not have to worry about Sadbury and why he was looking for me. While I will acquiesce that yesterday was a trifle harrowing, the fact that it was all over in one day feels like a deliverance."

"Well that is wonderful news, so now we can safely discuss our future together. I beg of you, Daisy, consent to be my wife."

ᘎᘏ

Daisy's breath froze in her lungs at Jasper's words. He sounded so sincere, and she felt her traitorous heart tremble with the temptation. Impatiently, she dashed a hand across her eyes as tears once again threatened to fall.

"Jasper, I cannot marry you. I will bring nothing but tribulations to you. Look at all the trouble I have caused you in just the past two weeks."

"You didn't cause these problems — it was that ne'er-do-well Wright who was the source of trouble," Jasper insisted, tightening his grip on Daisy's hand. "I can assure you, even if you do bring troubles or trials, it will be my honour to help you with them. You see, my dear, I find that I really cannot face a future without you in it. I didn't even know I was looking for exactly you to change my life completely. Say yes, and the only children you shall have to see to in the future shall be ours."

Daisy couldn't prevent another gurgle of laughter from escaping her lips at his words. She was so tempted to accept his offer, but she had one more thing she had to make clear to him.

"There's one more thing you ought to know about me, my lord. If you take me about in Society, the Earl and Countess of Worth might make trouble for you."

"The Earl of Worth? Jack's grandfather? Whatever for?"

Daisy took a deep breath and plunged into explanation. "You see, they are my grandparents. They disowned my mother when she married my father. They told her they could never countenance her match, and she had better not come crawling back for forgiveness when she found herself starving in the gutter with her lowborn brats in tow. My mother never saw them again. While we did visit her siblings a couple times when I was very young, my father would never forgive them for their treatment of my mother and wouldn't allow her to reach out to them after time passed and tempers cooled. I do believe he would roll over in his grave if he knew I was considering marriage with a nobleman."

"Is that why you were so anxious to know who my mother had invited to the house party?"

She nodded. "Besides Sadbury, running into any relatives was my biggest concern."

"You're the Earl of Worth's granddaughter?" Jasper repeated in awe before he burst into laughter much to Daisy's surprise. "I should have put all the pieces of the puzzle together when you told me about your parents' death. You have the Worth nose, as well. And while you kept your poise remarkably, I could tell you were uncomfortable when I introduced you to Jack and Susan."

"What puzzle pieces are you talking about, my lord?" Daisy was bewildered by his words.

"The Earl and Countess of Worth have been searching for you ever since your parents died. It is well-known amongst the *ton,* but I had never heard it mentioned what the granddaughter's name was. The *on dit* is that they kept themselves informed of your parents' whereabouts throughout your life. They tried to make peace with your mother at various times, but apparently she rejected every effort they made. The rumor mongers have been speculating upon the size of the dowry your grandparents wish to settle upon you." Jasper laughed again. "No wonder you don't want to accept my suit. You could hold out for an earl or even a duke." He paused for a moment as another thought crossed his mind. "That must have been who the messenger was who came to Abernathy just before we left."

Daisy didn't seem to hear his last statement because she was filled with a sense of wonder. "Do you really mean it? I have family that wants me?"

"You have a rather large family waiting for you. It is an accepted fact amongst the *ton* that the Worths have deeply regretted their words and actions in connection with your mother. They have been pining for the day that they could welcome you into their family." Daisy felt his searching eyes examining her face. "But I would even more deeply like to make a family with you myself. Will you be able to get over your aversion to my title and put me out of my dejected misery and promise to be my viscountess?"

Daisy laughed with joy and threw herself into his arms. "I do believe my father would be able to see the delicious irony of this situation. It would be my greatest pleasure."

And they sealed their bargain with a ravishing kiss.

The End

Have you read the Mayfair Mayhem series

Enjoy this three book series set in Regency era England, written by Wendy May Andrews. Be swept away on this sweet, romantic suspense adventure as three friends find the happiness they never thought possible.

Book 1

Available NOW on Amazon

The Duke Conspiracy

Anything is possible with a spying debutante, a duke, and a conspiracy.

Miss Rosamund Smythe is finding the Marriage Mart a dead bore. She'd much rather continue working for her father as a spy than endure another minute of the Season. But things take an interesting turn when she overhears details of a plot against her childhood friend and first love. A family feud drove them apart years ago, but he still holds a special place in her heart, and she won't let anyone hurt him—not now, not ever.

Alexander Milton, the new Duke of Wrentham, has always longed for a simple life. His tumultuous childhood taught him to appreciate peace and quiet above all else. Rose is the antithesis of everything he wants in a proper wife, but her beauty, intelligence, and loyalty call to him. And spending time with her to unravel the plot against him makes him wonder if the simple life he craves might be entirely overrated. Maybe he really does need a little adventure in his life.

But it soon becomes clear that a nefarious conspiracy is afoot—one that puts not only Alex's freedom in danger, but Rose's life. Can they overcome all that stands between them? Or will their second chance at love be snuffed out before it can even truly begin?

Also by Wendy May Andrews: Travel to 1855 Midwestern America in the Orphan Train Series

ᴕᴥᴕ

Book 1

Sophie

She'd happily give him her heart … but it might cost her the only home she's known

Sophie Brooks thought she had everything she could want in life. Friends, loved ones at the orphanage where she was raised, a job that gives her purpose, and a chance to help children every day … what more could she need? But a chance encounter with a handsome stranger has her wondering if a life—and love—outside the orphanage might be exactly what she never knew she needed.

Renton Robert Rexford III has never wanted for anything. Until he meets Sophie. The charming, intelligent beauty draws him like no other. But, thanks to a disapproving benefactor who threatens to pull the orphanage's funding, his pursuit of her could cost Sophie everything she holds dear. She's all he wants in the world, but how can he ask her to give up so much when all she'd get in return is his heart?

It's not long before Sophie is forced to weigh her loyalty to the only home she's ever known against the needs of her heart. Can love prevail—or is the cost simply too high?

About the Author

Wendy May Andrews has been in love with the written word since she learned to read at the age of five. She has been writing for almost as long but it took her some time before she was willing to share her stories with anyone other than her mother.

Wendy can be found with her nose in a book in a cozy corner of downtown Toronto. She is happily married to her own real-life hero, who is also her best friend and favourite travel companion. Being a firm believer that every life experience contributes to the writing process, Wendy is off planning her next trip.

She loves to hear from her readers and can be found at her website, on twitter, Instagram or Facebook.

Website & Blog: http://www.wendymayandrews.com

Twitter: https://twitter.com/WendyMayAndrews

Facebook: https://www.facebook.com/WendyMayAndrews

Instagram: https://www.instagram.com/WendyMayAndrews

Made in the USA
Middletown, DE
17 January 2023

22371754R00125